Rescuing Bryn

Rescuing Bryn

Delta Force Heroes

Book 6

By Susan Stoker

Table of Contents

Acknowledgements

Tracy, thank you very much for letting me use your city, your children, your husband, your husband's job, and your prepper house in my story. I might make fun of you for buying a "prepper property," but it truly is beautiful. When am I invited out again?

Prologue

"LOOK AT ME," a harsh voice demanded.

Tearing his gaze away from where his arm disappeared under the metal of the Army vehicle, Dane Munroe brought his gaze up to the man kneeling at his side. He was huge and menacing looking, but it was his piercing brown eyes, surprisingly filled with compassion, that made Dane relax a fraction.

"Don't look away from my face again. That's an order. Understand?"

"Yes, Sir," Dane croaked. He knew his body was going into shock, but the order gave him something to concentrate on other than the excruciating amount of pain he was in. He kept his eyes on the other man's face as he knelt over him.

He knew his teammates were gone. When he'd first came to and looked around, he'd seen body parts everywhere. To his right was Quiz, half his head missing. To his left was Bear, his legs simply gone. His friends. The men he'd have gladly given his life for. They were gone in an instant.

Everything had happened so quickly. One moment he'd been sitting in the Humvee, on the lookout for hidden explosives, and the next he was lying on the desert floor, one arm trapped beneath the tangled mess of metal that used to be the vehicle he'd been riding in. Dane had no idea how he'd survived when carnage was all around him.

More importantly, *why*.

The man at his side and his comrades had appeared out of nowhere. The air had been silent and Dane's ears were ringing from the explosion, and suddenly the other men were there. They weren't wearing uniforms, instead dressed in black from head to toe. Their hair was longer than was acceptable in the Army and they all had beards that partially hid their facial features. Dane would've been worried he was about to be kidnapped by ISIS again, except for the fact the man kneeling over him had a distinct American accent. He knew as soon as the man spoke, they were like him. Delta Force. The good guys.

"Fletch, Hollywood, get on this side. Blade and Coach, the other. I need you to lift slow and easy, no sudden moves. Beatle and Ghost, once the truck is off, pull him out fast, but controlled. Got it?"

All six murmured their agreement and got into place. The man who'd taken charge leaned over Dane and looked him square in the eyes. Dane briefly noticed the big-ass scar on the man's face, but he was in too much pain and shock for it to really register. "Here's what's going to happen. I think you know we're sitting ducks here, so we need to change venues. We can't do that with you takin' a nap under the truck though." He grinned, as if they were shooting the shit in a bar back in the States. "So we'll get this Humvee off, then package you up and get the fuck outta dodge. I'm not gonna lie. It's gonna hurt. Like a motherfucker."

"What can I do to help?" Dane asked, gritting his teeth.

"Honestly? The only thing you need to do is keep quiet. Me and my team will take care of everything else."

Dane swallowed hard and nodded once. He didn't like it, but at the moment he was useless. There was no way he was getting out of there without them. He didn't know where they'd come from, but in his line of work, you never looked a gift horse in the mouth.

"What's your name?" Dane croaked out.

"Truck."

Dane couldn't help the wry grin that spread over his face. "Appropriate."

The right side of Truck's lips quirked up in a lopsided grin. The man had a full beard like his teammates, but the large, gnarly scar along the left side of his face was still clearly visible. Facial hair wasn't growing over the scar, and it left a large swath of skin showing through the beard. "Yours?"

"Fish," Dane told him through gritted teeth.

"Well, Fish, you think you're gonna be able to stay quiet? I've got some morphine and can knock you out if you don't think you can do it. It's your call."

"I won't make a sound, but a bit to take the edge off wouldn't be a bad idea," Dane said. He'd never been in as much pain as he was right now. Not even when he'd spent a few days as a guest of ISIS. They'd beaten the shit out of him and his teammates, but that had been a walk in the park compared to this. As much as he wouldn't mind being drugged to the gills so he wouldn't have to deal with everything, he'd much rather know what the hell was going on around him. If these were going to be his last moments on Earth, he wanted to be awake and aware. Probably a stupid move, but he'd never claimed to be the smartest man around.

Truck didn't waste any time or question him more, he simply nodded and turned to one of the others and gave him a chin lift. A dose of morphine was quickly injected into Dane's body and the team moved themselves into their assigned positions to lift the Humvee.

Instead of looking around at what the other men were doing, Dane kept his eyes on Truck's face, as ordered.

"Ready?" the large man asked quietly.

Dane nodded, pressing his lips together, preparing

for the pain he knew was to come as soon as the vehicle was lifted off his arm.

It took every ounce of will Dane had to keep from screaming in the next few moments. He'd never felt such extreme pain in his entire life.

The men lifted the truck as if it was made out of plywood instead of metal, and hands closed around his ankles and quickly slid his body away from the wreckage at the same time that Truck grabbed hold of his arm and clamped down—hard. Dane's back arched at the immediate, excruciating waves of agony that radiated from the man's grip on what was left of his mangled arm.

Words swam around him, but Dane didn't understand any of them. Concentrating on the scar on Truck's face that twisted and moved as the man spoke to his teammates, and clenching his teeth together, Dane refused to pass out. If something went wrong, and the terrorists moved in, he wanted—no, needed—to be able to protect himself. Something he couldn't do if he was unconscious.

Eventually, Dane realized they were on the move. He was slung over the shoulder of one of the men, and Truck walked next to him, his large hand still clutching his mangled arm with a firm grip.

"Am I gonna lose it?" Dane asked, keeping his eyes on Truck.

The other man didn't sugarcoat the situation and knew Dane was talking about his extremity. "Probably. You right- or left-handed?"

"Left."

"Bummer," Truck commended dryly without a hint of pity.

"Why haven't you bandaged it up? Wouldn't it be easier and leave less of a trail if you wrapped it?" Dane put out of his mind the fact he might lose part, or all, of his arm. He concentrated on Truck's eyes as ordered, not caring at the moment where they were going. Asking questions kept his mind off the pain...somewhat.

Truck shrugged. "Can't. I've got your radial artery between my thumb and forefinger."

"Shit."

"Hey, it's all good. No worries. I got this."

Dane snorted, then pressed his lips together, shutting off the sound almost as soon as it escaped. He knew the radial and ulnar arteries were connected to the brachial. And if the brachial artery was busted, he'd bleed to death in minutes. The large man so calmly walking next to him was literally holding his life between his large fingers.

Remembering the other soldiers from his platoon, including the man who'd been added to their group as a top-secret last-minute addition, Dane asked, "The

6

others?

Truck gave a quick shake of his head in response.

Dane closed his eyes and said a short prayer for the soldiers who apparently hadn't survived the IED.

"Where are we going?" Dane asked quietly.

"Over a couple hills, about two clicks, there's a small town. We know some villagers who will take you to the American base nearby. You'll be safe."

"Will it compromise you?" Dane wasn't an idiot. Regular soldiers wouldn't be hanging out in small villages, helping injured Americans who were hurt in the line of fire. The last thing he wanted was for them to get in trouble or to have their position or mission compromised because they'd helped him.

"No." Truck's answer was short and succinct.

Dane struggled to keep his eyes open. The pain radiating down his arm was increasing with every step they made. His head hurt from being upside down and he was on high alert as they prowled through the desert. There was a lot he didn't like about the situation he was in, but he had to trust Truck and his team to get him out alive. He literally had no other choice at this point.

As they trudged on, Truck's fingers didn't budge. Even slippery with blood, they kept a firm hold on the artery inside the ripped flesh and bone that used to be his arm, keeping his lifeblood from draining out onto the desert floor beneath them.

After what seemed like hours, but was probably only thirty minutes or so, they entered a village, keeping to the shadows. The seven men moved as one, in complete tandem. If Dane hadn't been in the middle of them, he knew he wouldn't even have known they were there.

They entered a small hut and Dane felt himself being lowered to the ground. Truck's grip never faltered as he kneeled on the floor next to him. The others were constantly on the move, and while Dane heard them speaking in the background, his eyes stayed glued on Truck.

"You doing okay?" Truck asked in a low voice.

Dane nodded.

"You're going to be fine. You've done the hard part."

"What's that? Letting you guys do all the work?"

"Living," Truck returned immediately.

Dane shrugged with his good shoulder. "Not sure that's looking all that good at this point."

Truck's jaw got tight and he narrowed his eyes. He leaned into Dane and growled, sounding pissed off, "Don't do that. Don't *fucking* do that. I haven't spent the last forty minutes holding your damn life in my hands for you to go and give up now. You better get your shit together and fight. I couldn't save your platoon, but I sure as shit will save you. I swear to Christ, I'll reverse haunt your ass if you even *think* about dying on me. I'll do séances and get out the Ouija board and call your spirit back to earth and harass you for the rest of eternity if you die. Got it?"

Dane knew he had a choice to make, and it started right here. In the middle of the desert, enemies all around, this stranger's fingers keeping him alive. He wasn't happy about anything that had happened, and knew what lie ahead would be harder than anything he'd ever done in his life.

He closed his eyes for the first time since Truck had ordered him to look at his face. He took a deep breath then opened them again.

Looking up at the serious countenance of the man who'd saved his life, Dane nodded. "Got it."

Truck nodded. "Good. Here's what's gonna happen now. We're gonna knock your ass out, I'll tie off this pesky artery enough so it'll last until you can get into surgery, then you'll most likely be delivered to the American base in Germany. They'll patch ya up and do what needs to be done and by the time you wake up, you'll be well on your way to recovery and home to the US."

"Will I hear from you again?"

"What's your name?"

"Dane Munroe."

Truck nodded once. "You'll hear from me again, Fish. In fact, you'll probably get tired of me. I saved your life, and I don't take that lightly. There are too many soldiers I *haven't* been able to. So yeah, you'll hear from me again. Remember this conversation, 'cause I'll be pissed if you don't take my call."

"I'll take your call."

"Good. Ghost? He's ready."

Dane's eyes moved from Truck to his right side, seeing one of the other men kneeling next to him, holding a syringe. "You ready?" the man who was obviously Ghost asked, wanting to hear confirmation from Dane's lips.

"Yeah."

Ghost nodded, then leaned over and injected something into the vein in his uninjured arm. Then he put his hand on Dane's shoulder. "I'm not gonna lie, the next few months are gonna suck. Hard. But you've made it this far; there are good things waiting for you back home. I know it. Don't let Truck down."

The last thing Dane remembered was turning back to Truck and seeing the gnarly scar on his face as the world faded away.

Chapter One

D ANE GLARED DOWN at his cell phone as it rang. He considered ignoring it, but dismissed the thought as soon as it formed. He knew Truck would just keep trying until he finally picked up. There'd only been a few times he'd ignored his calls in the last few months…and Truck had let him know in no uncertain terms that if he did it again, he'd find not only Truck, but his entire team on his doorstep. Not knowing whether to believe the man or not, Dane decided to err on the side of caution; he wouldn't put it past the man to do just that. He sighed, clicking the phone on.

"Dane."

"Hey, Dane. It's Truck."

Dane rolled his eyes. "I know. What's up?"

"Whatcha doin'? Am I interrupting anything?"

"I'm shopping."

"It's oh-one-thirty."

"And?"

There was a brief moment of silence before Truck commented, "You still fighting that demon, huh?"

"It's better." Dane hadn't talked about what was going on in his head with many people. But Truck was one of the very few who knew that what happened in the Middle East was still affecting him.

The man hadn't shied away from talking about it. Truck called all the time. Labeled it "forced therapy" or some such shit. Dane had other friends, but none like Truck. None who understood exactly what it was like. None who had literally saved his life.

He'd had them at one time, his teammates, and he'd thought he'd lost that forever. But spending time recuperating in Austin, and getting to know Truck and his team of Delta Force operatives, had gone a long way toward healing him. But it hadn't made his PTSD go away.

Being in crowds, around people, was tough. Intellectually, Dane knew it was highly unlikely someone would ambush him from behind. Or that there would be a bomb hidden in a parking lot full of cars. But emotionally, it was a different story. He could handle fireworks, gunshots, blood...even the phantom pains from his hand that wasn't there any longer didn't faze him. But being around people, and the occasional thunderstorm, was something he was still fighting to overcome. It had gotten worse ever since Kassie, his friend Hollywood's woman, had been kidnapped a few months ago.

He'd moved to Idaho hoping to finally find some

peace, but his paranoia was getting worse, not better. It was much easier to get any errands done in the middle of the night, when there were less people around.

"You haven't started drinking blood or anything, have you?" Truck teased.

"Not yet," Dane drawled. "You call to ask if I've turned into a vampire?"

"Pretty much."

"Shit," Dane drawled. "I don't need a babysitter."

"Good, 'cause you're too fucking old for one." Truck never missed a beat.

Movement to his left caught Dane's eye. He turned his head and saw one of the employees of the store stocking shelves. He narrowed his eyes in irritation. This wasn't the first time he'd seen this particular woman. Every time he shopped, she seemed to be following him around the store. She never really looked straight at him, but stayed at the end of whatever aisle he was in, pretending to straighten the shelves. He was working on overcoming his paranoia, but knew he wasn't imagining her following him.

Dane didn't turn his back on the woman, but sidled up against the shelves and side-stepped away from her. "Look, something's come up. I gotta deal with it."

Truck's voice lost its easygoing, teasing tone. "Sitrep," he demanded.

"Don't lose your shit," Dane warned in a low voice,

knowing he needed to calm Truck down before he called in reinforcements. He didn't know where the other man was at the moment, but knew without a doubt that he'd be able to get assistance to him all the way out to bumfuck Idaho in fifteen minutes or less if the need arose. It was the bone-deep knowledge that the man, and his team, had his back that helped Dane keep himself together. "It's a chick who has been following me."

There was silence on the other end of the line for a beat. Then Truck asked incredulously, "A chick?"

"Yeah."

"Fuck me. That's awesome." Truck's voice lightened and even sounded excited. "Don't scare her away, Dane."

"It's not like that. She's been stalking me."

Truck's voice had warmed again, and didn't lose any of that warmth with Dane's pronouncement. "If she's interested, you need to go for it. Break that dry spell you've been on."

"Did you not hear me, you prick? She's stalking me."

"What's she look like?"

Dane sighed in exasperation. Truck wasn't going to let it drop. "Not that it matters, but she's about a foot shorter than me, ugly as sin, and creepy...since she's been *following* me around the store every time I've been here."

"Sounds like she'll fit against you perfectly. Trust me, there's just something about having a woman against you who's smaller that makes you feel as if you're the only thing standing between her and the world."

"Fuckin' A, Truck. She's goddamned *stalking* me." Dane knew the man had a thing for the best friend of one of the other men's women, but trying to get him hooked up with someone who was stalking him was ridiculous.

"Maybe. Maybe not."

"This conversation is over."

"Call me tomorrow and let me know how it goes," Truck ordered Dane.

"Prick," Dane murmured and clicked off the phone. As much as he liked the other man, he could really be a pain in the ass sometimes.

Thinking over the last few weeks, Dane realized exactly how often he'd seen the grocery clerk...without actually seeing her. It shouldn't have been too surprising, considering how little he'd changed his routine since moving to the small town of Rathdrum, Idaho. It was a tiny community outside of Coeur d'Alene. Small enough that he didn't panic when he had to get out and do business, but not as large as the nearby city. He could still get lost, but not feel as if he had to watch his back every second of every day.

But he didn't like the feeling crawling up his spine now. The slip of a woman had managed to fly under his radar. Was she the reason his senses had been in overdrive? Even as he pretended to look at the shelf in front of him, he saw the clerk turn her head to look down the aisle at him. She had a serious look on her face, one filled with compassion.

Fuck that. He didn't need pity from anyone. Never mind someone as nondescript as her.

Dane hadn't lied to Truck. She was a tiny thing, at least compared to him. Her hair was brown and pulled back into a long, low ponytail on the back of her head. She was wearing a pair of jeans and the sneakers on her feet had seen better days. A brown apron with the store's logo on the front was wrapped around her waist and tied in the back, the strings hanging down to almost touch the floor. She had on a long-sleeve navy-blue T-shirt. Dane couldn't tell what kind of body she had, as the apron hid any curves she might have.

He was a ways from her, but if he had to guess, he'd say she was probably at least a foot shorter than his six-one.

He probably shouldn't be as weirded out as he was, it wasn't as if she was an actual threat to him at her size, but she made him feel uncomfortable, and the sudden realization that she'd been lurking around every time he'd been shopping brought back all the times while deployed that he'd felt watched...and hunted.

Making a decision, he clenched his teeth and turned toward her, walking quickly down the aisle. He'd nip this in the bud right here, right now. No one stalked Dane Munroe. Not anymore. Not ever again.

BRYN HARTWELL STRAIGHTENED the boxes of pancake mix as if her job depended on it. She'd learned over the last few weeks that if she looked busy, the man wouldn't notice her. The first time she'd seen him was about a month ago. She'd just started at the store, needing something to keep her busy at night, and he'd strode through the automatic doors at the front of the building as if the hounds of hell were behind him.

He'd wasted no time wandering up and down the aisles, grabbing typical bachelor-type food with his right hand. He kept a basket hooked over his left elbow. She probably wouldn't even have taken a second glance at him if it wasn't for the haunted look in his eyes. They never stopped moving, checking out the area around him. Whenever he saw another shopper, he'd skip that aisle and come back when it was empty. If there were too many people in the store, he'd simply turn around and leave, preferring to return when it was nearly empty.

Something about him drew her. She didn't know his story, but she had no doubt he had one. It wasn't until a later visit, when she'd seen the prosthetic on his left arm, that she'd connected the dots. He was a well-built, handsome, broken soldier. Or former soldier. He'd fumbled with the basket on more than one occasion and only reached for his groceries with his right arm. He only filled it with what he needed in the short term, which was why she saw him so much.

Bryn had memorized what he liked to eat after only three visits, then she'd spent the next two days rearranging everything he usually bought so those items were on the middle shelves, and not the top or bottom. She'd noticed with satisfaction that he no longer had to stretch to reach anything, nor squat on the ground either.

Also, he didn't like to be around other shoppers, Bryn had done her best to divert the few patrons that shopped late at night away from the aisles he happened to be in. It wasn't easy, and she knew the others thought she was insane, but so far it'd worked. The soldier looked more at ease when he could get in and out of the store without having to be around anyone else.

She got it. She didn't do too well with others herself. She couldn't relate well with most people, and the feeling was obviously mutual.

She'd spent her entire life in special classes. Those that were supposed to nurture her and help her grow into a productive member of society. Someone who would go on to do great things...cure cancer, find lost planets, discover new species. But the only thing Bryn had ever wanted to find was a friend. Someone who wouldn't look at her as if she was a specimen under a microscope. Who she could laugh with. Shop with. And simply sit on a couch and watch a silly movie with.

But being able to multiply three-digit numbers in her head when she was four had made that goal unattainable. Her parents didn't understand her. Her teachers had been uncomfortable around her, simply shoving worksheets at her and telling her how smart she was...then passing her on to the next grade.

She'd been evaluated by a clinical psychologist when she was around eight, and her parents were told that she tested on a genius level with borderline Asperger's tendencies. It meant nothing to Bryn, but they'd been upset by the report. Ultimately, there were some facets of Asperger's that were one hundred percent Bryn, like being the last to understand the punchline of a joke, or getting completely absorbed in one thing and losing sight of everything else. But there were also a lot of things that most children with Asperger's felt and did that didn't apply to her, like noticing small sounds others didn't, being fascinated by dates or numbers.

The psychologist had told her parents she was extremely smart, but had a hard time using common sense. Basically, it was explained that Bryn had a brain that was wired differently than most people's.

She had no idea if that was true or not, but she tended to get lost often and sometimes forgot to fill her car with gas when it was near empty. By the time she was sixteen, she had two undergraduate degrees, her graduate degree in physics, and had started on her PhD.

The day she turned eighteen, Bryn left her parents' house in Baltimore, Maryland. She'd moved around the country living in one small town after another and finally ended up in Idaho. Her parents had told her she couldn't live on her own, that she needed a caretaker, but she'd been determined to prove them wrong. She didn't want or need someone hovering over her all the time. She might be different, but she was perfectly able to live on her own.

Bryn actually didn't know her folks that well, since she'd spent most of her life away from them at special schools. She'd only moved back in with them while she'd been working on her PhD. Then she'd left Maryland and everyone who knew her. To start her life anew. But it hadn't been easy.

She was still odd.

She didn't fit into society.

At all.

And everyone knew it.

Most of the time it didn't bother her, but there were

moments when she longed to fit in with others. To blend into the woodwork.

She had a feeling the amazing man felt the same. Something inside her wanted to protect him from what was making him uncomfortable. She didn't know why. Only that she needed to do it.

It was crazy, really. The man was tall and built. It wasn't as if he couldn't protect himself. He had short dark hair, a five o'clock shadow, wore black boots and jeans. It was spring and still a bit chilly, and she'd never seen him in anything but the black leather jacket he was currently wearing. If Bryn met him anywhere but here, she would've been scared out of her mind, he was that intimidating. But watching him shop for things like SpaghettiOs, canned chili, and toilet paper—he preferred the strong and soft expensive mega rolls over the cheaper single rolls—she saw him as a person.

Bryn had been lost in her thoughts, and had moved to absently straightening the syrup so the bottles were facing out and were all at the edge of the shelf, when she glanced down the aisle where she'd last seen the man. He'd been on the phone and had been scowling at whoever was on the other end.

But he was now taking large strides down the aisle toward her. *Directly* toward her. In fact, he was staring at her—and he looked pissed.

Bryn gasped and took a step away from the shelf.

He'd never looked right at her before. Not once. She'd been pleased that she'd been able to slip under his radar, but obviously he'd caught her. Damn.

He began speaking even before he reached her. "Why are you following me?"

Bryn opened her mouth, but nothing came out. She'd only seen this man from afar, but up close? She could only stare.

He was beautiful.

When he stopped right in front of her, she slowly reached out and poked him in the chest before she thought about what she was doing.

She wanted to see if he was real. To make sure she wasn't dreaming.

At her touch, he gasped, and his right hand came up and grabbed her finger in a steely grip. He didn't say anything, but continued to glare at her.

Bryn couldn't do anything but stare up at his steel-gray eyes. His hand was warm around her finger and if asked, she would've sworn that she could feel the heat from his hand working its way down her hand and arm into her chest. Yup. Not a dream.

They stayed that way for a heartbeat, her finger enclosed in his palm, before he broke the spell, thrusting her hand at her and taking a step back. "What the fuck?"

"S-sorry," Bryn stuttered. "I—"

"Why are you following me?" he repeated, narrowing his eyes.

Bryn did what she always did. She told him exactly what she was thinking. She'd never been a good liar, couldn't really understand why people did that.

"Because you're uncomfortable around people. I saw it and wanted to help. I try to keep others away from the aisles you're in as you shop. It seemed to help. You've been calmer recently. Although you don't look calm now. Does your arm hurt? You don't have as much in your basket tonight as you usually do. Does your prosthetic go all the way up to your shoulder? I can't tell, although it's obvious that it's still relatively new to you. I'm sorry, by the way. Do you need assistance with anything? I moved the things you usually buy to the shelves in the middle. I was hoping that would help."

He stared at her, his brow furrowed, so she kept talking. Explaining. Trying to clear up the questions so clear on his face.

"I'm Bryn. I work here. I don't sleep much, so I took this job a month or so ago. I saw you shopping and realized how uncomfortable you were. So I fixed it. You really should eat better. You buy too much pasta. Experts say you should consume the majority of your carbs in the morning, and after you work out. You should stick with protein late at night though. You really need more veggies in your diet. I know they go bad quicker, but you're here at least three times a week anyway, so it wouldn't matter. I could give you some recommendations if you needed them."

If anything, the man looked even more confused, so Bryn continued, trying to ease his mind. "I don't know what happened to you, but this really is a safe place. You don't have to be worried about shopping here. I've got your back, so you can come earlier if you want. I start work around eleven and go home around three. It's only a part-time job for me, but—"

"Stop following me."

His words were low and hard.

"Oh, but I—"

"I mean it. The last thing I need is a freak like you following me around, stalking me, commenting on the food I buy. I don't care how much sleep you need or what you think of my eating habits. I *do* care that you're harassing me and making me uncomfortable."

Bryn took a step back, for some reason not expecting the hostility emanating from the man. "I don't mean to...I—"

He cut her off once more. "If I see you again, I'm calling the cops. This will obviously be the last time I shop here, but if I see you lurking around me anywhere else, I'll press charges for harassment and stalking. Got it?"

Bryn looked up into the eyes of the man in front of

her and her heart sank. She'd done it again. Freak. She *was* a freak. Weirdo. Psycho. Head case. Nerd. Dork. Reject. All the names she'd been called over the years swam in her head.

"Got it?" the man repeated in a harder voice.

Bryn nodded quickly. She'd forgotten he was there. She did that all the time. Got lost in her head. Biting her lip, she watched as the man edged around her, leaving plenty of room between them, as if her weirdness was contagious, and walked backwards, not turning his back on her until he'd rounded the end of the aisle and disappeared.

Bryn turned blindly back to her work, not even thinking about her task as her hands automatically continued what they'd been doing before, straightening the shelves.

She'd only been trying to help. He'd almost seemed at ease lately when he'd shopped. But she'd ruined it. Now he'd have to drive down to Post Falls to shop. It was bigger than Rathdrum, but not as large as Coeur D'Alene, and it would take him a lot longer to get to the city and back than it would to just shop here.

That was unacceptable. This was her fault, she had to fix it.

Bryn waited until the man was at the checkout counter. A teenager named Willy was manning the register, and the night manager, a forty-something woman named Monica, was chatting with another employee near the front of the store. Bryn walked up to her, removed her apron and held it out.

"I quit." She said the words loudly, making sure the man at the conveyor belt could hear her.

"What?" Monica asked, obviously confused. "You just started last month."

"And today I'm quitting." Bryn moved her eyes to the man who'd made her hope for the first time in years, then crushed that hope beneath his big black boots. "I won't be back." She prayed he understood her.

"Oh, but…well. Okay. Can't you work the rest of the shift? We just got a huge delivery in the back."

Bryn so wanted to ask the woman why, if there was a huge delivery, she was standing there shooting the shit with another employee, but bit her lip and refrained, barely. "No. I'm going. Thank you for the opportunity to work here, but I…I'm leaving now."

She didn't look at the man again. She'd done what she'd needed to do. He was now free to continue his grocery shopping in Rathdrum. He belonged there. She didn't. She didn't really belong anywhere.

Freak. The word echoed in Bryn's mind.

Monica took the apron from her outstretched hand, and Bryn turned to the doors. She walked across the parking lot and dug the key to her nineteen-ninety Toyota Corolla out of her pocket. She never carried a purse, because as smart as she was, she always forgot where she set it down. Bryn held her breath as she turned the key, praying it'd start. It did, thank God, and she pulled out of the lot toward her small apartment, the man's scathing tone slicing through her once more.

Freak. She was. It was all she'd ever be. Her shoulders slumped as she drove home.

DANE HANDED HIS credit card to the teenager, but kept his eyes on the strange woman who'd just walked out. He half figured she'd wait and confront him when he left the store, but he watched as she crossed the dark parking lot to a piece-of-shit white car and drove off. His mind was whirling as the middle-aged manager came up to talk to the boy who was bagging his groceries, now that he'd run his card.

"I can't believe she just quit like that."

The boy merely shrugged.

"I mean, she's been a good worker. A bit strange, but she was always on time and didn't mess around. Other than insisting people not go down certain aisles sometimes, that is."

Dane didn't even hide that he was eavesdropping.

The manager caught his eye and, happy she had someone's attention, since the teenager was ignoring her, continued, "I mean, seriously, she wasn't ever impolite about it, but she'd tell a customer that he or she had to wait because she'd just mopped an aisle, or she'd ask them what was on their list and steer them to a different aisle as she helped them shop. Damn weird if you ask me. But I had no idea she'd just up and quit. It's impossible to find good help these days."

The teenager cleared his throat as he held out the plastic bags to Dane.

"Oh, sorry. I didn't mean you, Willy," the woman tried to backpedal.

"Have a nice night," the teenager told Dane in a bored tone.

"Thanks." Dane clenched his hand around the bags and headed toward the same door the strange woman had gone out of. He stopped just outside and looked around. Nothing. She wasn't there, her car was gone. She really *had* just quit and driven away.

For the first time, Dane started to feel guilty. "Fuck," he swore under his breath. She'd quit because of him. And not because he'd threatened to call the cops. Somehow he knew that wasn't it. She'd done it so he wouldn't have to shop anywhere else. She obviously knew as well as he did that this was the only large grocery store in Rathdrum. He'd told her he wouldn't be back, and she'd quit so he could shop there without worrying about her being around.

He hadn't really understood exactly what she'd been doing for him until the manager had spoken. She truly *had* kept people away from him while he'd shopped. He hadn't noticed. And if he hadn't confronted her, she probably would've kept on doing it.

Bryn. Even her name was unusual.

Dane clicked the locks on his pickup and put the two grocery sacks in the back, then climbed into the driver's seat and closed the door. He rubbed his palm over his face. Why he felt guilty was beyond him. *She* was the one who was stalking *him*. He hadn't done anything wrong. Nothing. So why did he feel so bad?

Maybe it was because Bryn had seen him. Truly seen him. She'd seen his prosthetic arm and the difficulties he sometimes had grasping the items on the higher and lower shelves. He thought for a moment, and realized that a lot of the food he bought *had* been moved to more accessible shelves. It wasn't necessary, but she'd done it because she'd thought she was helping him.

And he couldn't deny that keeping others away from him while he was shopping had reduced the stress he'd felt. He never liked when his back was to people. The fact that it'd taken him four weeks to notice her meant she'd been good at what she'd done.

Dane turned the key in the ignition, happy that it started so easily. It was the first thing he'd done after moving to Idaho, bought a new, reliable truck. As he pulled out of the parking lot and turned in the opposite direction Bryn had, he remembered her lecturing him about eating too many carbs...and smiled.

The second his lips quirked up, he froze. When was the last time he'd smiled? Truly smiled? He couldn't remember. Fuck.

Chapter Two

BRYN TRIED TO concentrate on the crossword puzzle in front of her. She was trying to use it as a distraction. Something was bothering her. It was right there at the back of her brain, but she couldn't put her finger on what it was. She thought that maybe if she did one of her beloved crosswords it would magically come to her.

The distraction wasn't working very well though, because it wasn't as if the words on the puzzle were all that hard to come up with. Everyone knew that silver was argentum, and when the clue was "done in a careless manner," the answer was perfunctory.

She thought about her life and wondered what the hell she was doing. She was twenty-seven and could probably work for any company or corporation she wanted, but instead was in nowhere Idaho, working at a library, restocking books. Bryn wasn't being conceited, only factual. She was smart. Beyond smart. Had been her entire life. But she found that she'd gotten bored working with some of the greatest minds in the world. She wanted to live. To get out into the world and experience it. Not sit behind a microscope or computer and talk shop with other geniuses her entire life.

Was it really living? Maybe. Maybe not.

She kept her mind busy with the crosswords she loved.

She occasionally called one of the scientists she used to work with to see what he was working on and to exchange ideas.

And she downloaded the newest dissertations from Yale and Harvard, for fun.

She might be keeping her mind busy, but she was lonely.

Bryn knew she simply wasn't good with people. She tended to say what she was thinking, no matter if it was appropriate or not. And she knew way too many useless facts, which she spouted off whenever she was reminded of them.

Moving from one small town to the next had been fun at first, seeing the world and all that, but each move just pointed out once again how much she didn't fit in with everyone around her.

She sighed and put her chin in her hand. *Maybe I should move to Seattle or LA. Somewhere big. There have to be loners like me in a big city. Maybe I wouldn't stand out so much if there were more people around.*

She immediately dismissed the thought. She didn't like cities. Too many people, too many buildings, and too many dangerous criminals looking for their next mark. And she knew she was an extremely easy mark. She took people at face value and had a hard time figuring out when someone was lying to her.

And besides, Bryn hated how many homeless people there were in the city. They were her weakness. It just didn't seem right for her to have a safe, warm place to live when there were men, women, children, and pets who had to sleep on the streets. She always gave them money. Every time. When she'd lived in Chicago, she'd begun to think they were gossiping about her and letting each other know what a softie she was, because every day it seemed as if there were more and more homeless on her route to and from the corner grocery store where she worked.

It finally got so ridiculous that she was taking the bus the four blocks to work, so she didn't pass so many and didn't have to give out as much money as she had been.

Bryn wished, not for the first time, that she had a brother or sister to talk to. To have her back. But she didn't. She had no one. She shook off the depressing thought. It was useless to wish for something that wasn't possible.

Blinking, she looked over at the clock. One forty-five in the morning.

Her thoughts went to the man she'd been helping in

the grocery store. How he'd looked as if he wouldn't let anyone take advantage of him, how tall and strong he was, and she wondered if he had anyone watching after him. Probably not, since he'd reacted like she'd stabbed him in the chest when *she'd* done it. Thinking about how he'd confronted her about her assistance the week before made her wonder if he was grocery shopping right now. She worried people would be bothering him. That he'd get that trapped look in his eyes, as he had before she'd started running interference for him.

Bryn closed her eyes and gave herself a pep talk.

He didn't appreciate anything you did for him, stupid. He's a grown man and can deal with his issues on his own. You're a freak. You know it, he knows it, and he doesn't want to see you again. He said he'd call the cops. Remember?

Bryn's eyes popped open as she finally realized what was bothering her. The storm.

Earlier that evening there had been a doozy of a spring thunderstorm. They usually didn't bother her, but tonight she'd been restless and had flinched every time there was a loud boom and the lightning lit up her little apartment.

What if the thunder reminds him of being at war? What if he had a flashback and he's worse than before?

She had no idea where he lived, but she suddenly had an intense urge to see him. To make sure he was all right.

Before she'd even thought about what she was doing, she was on the move.

Even knowing the man would be pissed if he saw
her, Bryn didn't slow down. Ignoring the voice in the
back of her mind that said if he was having issues
dealing with the storm, he wouldn't be shopping, but
would be holed up wherever he lived, trying to drown
out the sound of the thunder, she quietly shut her door
behind her, careful not to wake the mean older man
who lived in the apartment across the hall.

The air smelled like pine and wet leaves...a smell
that usually made Bryn smile, but tonight she barely
noticed it as she climbed into her little car. She'd bought
it used for a steal a couple years ago, but the Corolla was
on its last leg. It took three tries, but finally started.
Bryn checked the gas gauge...a quarter tank. Good. She
sometimes forgot to fill it, but luckily was good to go for
tonight at least.

As she drove toward the grocery store, she argued
with herself.

*I'm not going to go inside. I'll just see if his truck is in
the lot. If it is, I'll turn around and head home.*

He's not going to want to see you.

I know, that's why he'll never know I'm there.

What if he's not there?

I'll just drive around a bit to see if I can find his truck.

No, that isn't stalkerish at all.

Bryn wrinkled her nose and sighed. She'd gotten

good at having conversations with herself, especially since she really didn't have too many other people to talk to. She knew she wasn't being rational, but something wouldn't allow her to stay home and let it drop.

Pulling into the grocery store lot, Bryn saw immediately that he wasn't there. There were only a few vehicles in the lot, and none were a truck. Keeping her car running, not wanting to take a chance that it wouldn't start again, Bryn tapped her fingers on the wheel. Making up her mind, she turned left out of the lot.

The night was quiet. There weren't many cars on the street and Bryn scanned around her for any sign of the man's vehicle. At the other end of town, opposite from where she lived, she finally saw it. She knew the vehicle was his. Brand new. Dark green. Army sticker on the back window. She almost couldn't believe she'd been so lucky. Pulling into the gravel lot in front of a rundown bar called Smokey's, she parked as far away from the truck as she could so he wouldn't spot her.

Rathdrum was small, but it was two in the morning and this wasn't the best side of town. She would've left, satisfied that he wasn't holed up wherever he lived having flashbacks, but just then the door opened and a man came out with his arm around a woman. He was wearing dark jeans and a T-shirt covered by a leather vest. He had a long beard, which looked like it badly needed a trim, and the hair on his head was greasy and hung down around his face. The woman had on four-inch heels, a black leather skirt that barely covered her womanly parts, and a white tank top pulled down so low, Bryn could almost see her nipples peeking over it.

The weather was losing its winter chill, but it was in no way warm enough for the woman to be wearing the clothes she was. The man had one arm around her waist and, as Bryn watched, he spun the woman into his chest and lowered his head. Instead of kissing her, he bypassed her lips and buried his face into her ample cleavage.

The woman shrieked with laugher and thrust the fingers of one hand into the hair at the back of his head, and Bryn watched in shock as her other hand zeroed in on the man's crotch.

Bryn blushed and turned her head away from the couple and their erotic clench. She'd had sex before, but it hadn't been like that. Not even close. The three times she'd been in bed with a man, it had been clinical, and she hadn't been able to turn her brain off. Asking too many questions about what he was doing and what he wanted her to do, as usual, and with each encounter, as soon as the man she was with had climaxed, he'd rolled off, thanked her, and left. Leaving her confused as to why women actually wanted to have sex in the first place.

But seeing the passion between the two just outside the door, Bryn supposed there had to be more to it. She risked another glance and saw that the man was now on a motorcycle and the woman had climbed on behind him. She was wearing his leather jacket, plastered to his back, her arms around him, caressing his belly, thighs, and crotch, and Bryn could see her rubbing herself against him as they pulled out of the lot and headed back toward town.

Swallowing hard, Bryn decided that she'd just take a quick peek inside the seedy bar to make sure the man she came to find was all right. If this was a biker bar, he had to be out of his element. Not that it was *her* kind of establishment either—no bar was—but something wouldn't let her simply drive away.

He was probably with a woman, and while the thought hurt, it didn't deter her. The man affected her, had from the moment she'd first seen him, and she wanted—no, *needed*—to make sure the storm hadn't adversely affected him.

Pocketing her keys, Bryn walked toward the door. Taking one last look up at the blinking sign, which now she could see said Smokey's Bar, the last word not visible from the road in the dark because the bulbs were burnt out, she pulled the door open and stepped inside.

The first thing she noticed was that it was almost deserted. There might have been several cars in the lot, but the only people she saw were a bartender, two waitresses picking up empty bottles and sweeping the floor, and the man she'd set out to find.

He was slumped against his arm at the end of the bar, his back to the wall. The smoke in the hole-in-the-wall place was still thick in the air, and Bryn coughed at the pungent smell of the cigarette smoke and spilled beer.

"We're closed," the bartender barked.

Bryn nodded and took a step backwards toward the door. The man was here and obviously fine. It was time to leave before he noticed her and called the cops as he'd threatened.

As if the bartender's words had woken him, he picked his head up, looked at the other man and slurred, "Another."

"No. Last call was thirty minutes ago and you're fucking trashed. Time to go."

"I need another beer," he insisted.

"And I said no," the bartender repeated. "Look around you, man. You're the last one here. Bar's closed. Time to pay your tab and get gone."

"Fuck." The man swore then reached around with his right hand to try to grab his wallet...which was in his left pocket. It was a feat not a lot of sober men could do, and the fact he was completely shit-faced only made the job that much harder.

Bryn's feet were moving before her brain could tell them to stop. She reached his side, brushed his hand away from his ass, dug into his pocket and retrieved his wallet. She held it out to the bartender—then froze, realizing what she'd done.

Expecting the man to rail at her and do as he'd threatened if he saw her again, she was surprised when she felt him brush her hair over her shoulder, lean into her, and take a deep breath.

"Fuck, you smell good," he drawled drunkenly. He picked up a lock of her hair and brought it to his face, once again inhaling deeply. "Coco-cocomut...fuck. Beach. You smell like the beach."

Bryn brought wide eyes back to the bartender, who was holding out his hand. "Thank fuck you're here to take him home. We're already fifteen minutes late in closing and I didn't think I'd be able to get a fucking cab out here to pick his ass up. Give me his card and I'll close him out, and you get him the fuck outta my bar."

"He's drunk," Bryn told the bartender.

"No shit, Sherlock," he responded tartly, turning away once she'd handed him a credit card from the man's wallet.

"I'm still conscious," the man slurred, "so I'm not drunk enough."

"Here, sign." A credit card slip was thrust into the drunk man's face and he blinked at the bartender, clearly not understanding.

Bryn took the paper and pen from the irritated employee and flattened it on the bar top. She glanced at the credit card when it was slapped down next to the slip. Dane Munroe. She liked his name. It was strong. Like him.

"Dane? You need to sign this. Here." She took his right hand into her own and placed the pen between his fingers. "Take this and sign right here." She placed the tip down above the signature line and waited.

"I'm left-handed," Dane said sadly, staring blankly down at the hand holding the pen.

"Can you sign with your prosthetic?" Bryn asked, realizing she knew next to nothing about how they worked, and vowing to get on her computer the second she got home to learn everything she could about arm and hand prosthetics.

At her question, Dane dropped the pen and sat up straighter on the barstool. He brought his left arm up from where it had been resting in his lap and pulled the long sleeve of his T-shirt up, exposing a stump just below his elbow where his arm used to be. He wasn't wearing his prosthetic. He smirked at her, obviously expecting her to be shocked or disgusted.

"Okay then, that's a no. Fine. You'll have to sign with your right hand. Go on now." Bryn held his gaze, waiting patiently.

"You didn't even blink. Seen a lot of these, Smalls?"

"Smalls?"

He grinned. "Yup."

"What's that?"

"You."

"Me?" she asked dumbly.

"Uh huh," Dane nodded vigorously, too enthusiastically, and Bryn had to throw an arm around his waist to keep him from toppling off the chair. "You're small. Tiny. Teeny. Little. Cute. Smalls."

"The average height of an American woman is five-five. I'm only a few inches below that. I'm not *that* small," Bryn protested.

"Yeah, you are," the bartender interjected. "Now, can you have him sign the damn slip so you can get him the fuck out of here?"

"I can sign," Dane sighed. "Give me the pen."

"It's right in front of you," Bryn told him.

"Oh, yeah." With that, Dane grabbed the pen he'd dropped earlier, bent over the paper, holding it still with the stump on his left arm, and painstakingly signed the credit card slip with his right hand with a childlike scrawl. He wasn't kidding, he definitely had been a lefty. He looked up at Bryn when he was finished. "Can't see to add a tip. And can't write worth a damn with my right hand anyway. Can you do it?"

Bryn knew Dane was drunk. Knew he had no clue who she was, otherwise he wouldn't be so nice to her, but it felt good that he was trusting her to add a tip onto his bill. She could be in cahoots with the bartender and add an exorbitant amount and he'd never know until it was too late. Memorizing the feeling in her chest, pleasure that Dane was trusting her, she merely nodded and took the pen from him, adding a twenty percent tip, figuring the bartender probably deserved it. She slid it over to the impatient employee.

He glanced at the amount she'd written in and nodded his thanks, probably thinking he'd be screwed by the extremely drunk man and the unknown woman who'd come to pick him up.

"You need help getting him to your car?"

Bryn picked up Dane's credit card and slid it back into the slot in his wallet. She glanced at the address on his driver's license, relieved to see it wasn't too far away and that she recognized the street name. It wasn't in the city of Rathdrum, but was only a few miles away. She closed the wallet and eased it back into Dane's back pocket.

"Careful, Smalls, I might think you're hittin' on me."

Ignoring Dane for the moment, she turned to the bartender. "Yes, please."

"Give me five."

Bryn nodded and turned back to Dane and held out her hand. "Keys."

He narrowed his eyes at her. "Do I know you?"

Bryn's heart rate sped up. God, he couldn't recognize her now. He'd never get home. She shook her head and lied. "No."

"You look familiar, Smalls."

Bryn smiled at his continued use of the nickname he'd christened her with.

"You don't know me." Bryn wasn't lying. He'd seen her, but he didn't *know* her. No one did, really.

Raising his hand, Dane grabbed another handful of her long hair and brought it back up to his nose and inhaled again. "God. You smell so good."

"It's my shampoo. And I hate to say it, but anything would smell better than this dump."

Dane's eyes twinkled as they looked at her. Their heads were close, even with him sitting and her standing. "Truer words have never been spoken."

"You ready to go home?" Bryn whispered, feeling off-kilter at the tender look in his gray eyes. The last time she'd seen them, they'd been shooting daggers at her. She much preferred his current look than the one of hatred he'd aimed her way at the grocery store.

"Yeah, let's go home." His voice was low and seductive.

Bryn shivered. "Keys." She was still whispering.

"They're in my pocket, Smalls. My *front* pocket." He grinned shamelessly and leaned back in the chair.

Bryn looked down at his lap and gasped. The bulge

in his jeans was huge. She whipped her eyes back up to his.

"Like what you see, Smalls?"

Straightening her spine, Bryn teased, "Wow, that's a big key ring you have there, soldier."

He laughed. The sound echoing around the now empty room. Shifting in the seat, he reached into his pocket and drew out the key ring. "Killin' me, Smalls. Killin' me."

He held out the key ring, which consisted of two keys…one obviously to the shiny new truck in the lot, and the other looked like it would fit a house lock. "What you saw is allll me. And when we get home, I'll show it to you up close and personal."

Bryn grabbed the keys and blushed at the heat radiating off them, warmth from his body, his cock.

"Let's go. I got shit to do." The bartender's voice was harsh and cut through whatever flirting they'd been doing, bringing Bryn back to earth with a thump. Dane wasn't flirting with *her*, it was only because he was drunk as a skunk, couldn't even see straight, and she was female. Men didn't flirt with *her*. Ever.

"Thanks. It's the big green truck in the lot."

The bartender nodded and hauled Dane upright, putting his arm around his waist as he stumbled. They shuffled toward the exit, and Bryn hurried ahead to open the door. They made their way into the crisp night air and toward Dane's truck. The bartender held on to his arm as Dane all but crawled into the cab of the truck. He slammed the door impatiently behind Dane and stalked back toward the bar without a word.

"Thanks," Bryn called out.

The bartender waved his hand in recognition of her words, but didn't turn around or slow his trek back to the bar.

Bryn didn't watch him disappear through the wooden door, but walked around the truck to the driver's side. She looked over at her car on the other side of the parking lot and shrugged. She'd have to walk back to pick it up when she got Dane settled inside his house, but that was fine with her. She'd just make sure Dane got home all right then come back. Not a big deal.

Climbing up into the seat, she grunted in dissatisfaction. Her feet didn't come anywhere near the pedals and she could barely see over the dashboard.

Dane roared in laughter, holding his sides in mirth as he doubled over.

Bryn glared at him with her arms crossed, waiting for him to breathe normally again.

"Told ya you were small."

Bryn wanted to be pissed, but she'd never seen anything so hot in all her life as Dane Munroe laughing as if he didn't have a care in the world. Somehow, she knew it wasn't normal. Not for him. "You done?" she asked, trying to sound stern, but knowing she'd failed.

"Yeah." Then he chuckled again. "Okay, no. Seriously, I'm not sure you're gonna be able to drive Mish May."

"Miss May?"

"My truck."

Bryn rolled her eyes. She had no clue why men named their vehicles. It wasn't logical. She reached down to the side of the seat and smiled as she found the knob that would move it forward. She tilted the bottom of the seat down to bring her feet closer to the pedals and sighed in relief when they comfortably reached. Looking around, she spied a jacket in the backseat.

"Can I use your coat?"

"You cold, Smalls? I can keep you warm."

Bryn shivered. His seductive voice reached deep within her and curled around her heart. She couldn't remember anyone ever speaking to her like that. Not once. Without breaking eye contact, she said in a low voice, "I need to put it behind my back."

"I can support you," Dane began, reaching his arm out. He stopped abruptly and scowled at where his arm used to be. "Fuck. I forgot. Yes, you can use my coat," he finished, and sat back in the seat with his arms crossed over his wide chest.

Hating to see his good mood vanish, Bryn reached behind the seat for his jacket and said what she was thinking, as usual. "Thanks. This'll work for the most part, but if you support my back as well, that'd help more. You can scoot over to the middle if you think you can't reach. I don't mind if *you* don't."

Dane looked at her with glazed eyes and held up his left arm. "I only have half an arm."

"So?"

"So?" He looked confused.

"Yeah, so?" Bryn reached out and grasped his biceps and squeezed. "You feel strong enough to hold me. You said I was small. So what's the problem?"

Dane narrowed his eyes at her. "It doesn't bother you?"

"No." Bryn didn't pretend to not know what he was talking about. "And it shouldn't bother you either. Dane, you're extremely good-looking. You're strong and buff. And even though you're drunk off your ass, you're still a gentleman. I don't care if you touch me with your stump. It's not like it's contagious or anything. And besides, I'd like us to get to your home in one piece, and you helping support my back as I'm driving Miss May would be appreciated."

He looked confused, and Bryn almost felt sorry for him. Almost.

"I'm left-handed."

"Good. That means that arm is stronger then."

"Yeah."

"Yeah. Okay then, I'm starting the truck."

"You can drive a stick shift?"

Bryn laughed. "Now's a fine time to ask me that. Yes, I can drive a standard transmission. I wouldn't think *you* would want to with your missing hand, but I suppose since you still have your elbow, it's easy enough to steer while you're shifting with your right hand. Now, buckle up." She turned to stuff his jacket behind her and sat up straight. She could've used something to sit on to make it easier to see over the huge hood of the truck, but she didn't have too far to go. Besides, if she sat on the jacket, her feet wouldn't reach the pedals. She'd make do.

Putting the truck in reverse, Bryn looked behind her to make sure no one was there, and jerked when Dane's arm touched her upper back. She glanced at him. He moved over to the middle seat and put one leg on either side of the gear shift.

Bryn swallowed hard. He wasn't smiling, his serious and piercing gray eyes fixed on her face. "I might be missing my hand, but I'm still all man. And real men drive stick shifts." He paused, then continued. "You're sure we haven't met? I feel like I remember you."

"I'm sure." She reached out and grabbed his knee, then blushed and moved her hand to the gearshift, which was what she'd been aiming for. "Sorry. I was trying to shift."

They both looked down, and just like that, drunk, flirty Dane was back. "Gotta say, Smalls, I've wanted your hand between my legs since you walked into the bar...but this isn't exactly what I had in mind."

Bryn shifted into first gear and brought her hand back to the steering wheel. "Hang on, Dane. I'll have you home in no time."

He didn't say anything, but Bryn knew he hadn't passed out. She felt the hard length of his biceps against her back and the stump of his arm, just below his elbow, was pressed against her left side. If he leaned over just a couple inches more, he'd be touching her breast with what remained of his arm. As she turned or shifted gears, Dane pressed his arm into her, supporting her and helping her stay upright. The warmth from his skin, even through his shirt, seeped into her very being. Not having experienced much body contact in the past, Bryn tried to memorize the moment as she drove Dane home.

She didn't think he'd remember anything about the night, but knew it was an experience she'd never, ever forget. Not even if she lived to be one hundred. How could you forget the moment you were treated as a normal, desirable female for the first time ever?

Chapter Three

DANE WAS STILL conscious when she pulled up to his house, thank goodness. He pressed the opener, and she pulled into his spacious garage. She couldn't see his house very well in the dark, but it was surrounded by a couple acres of land, if the long driveway was anything to go by, and looked to be a one-story house.

She jumped out of the truck and went around to the passenger side. Dane practically fell out of the cab and laughed like a maniac as they stumbled inside.

"Where's your room?"

"Down the hall. First door on the left. I can't wait to see your tits."

Bryn almost dropped him at his words, but managed to steer him in the right direction. She helped him to his bed and winced as he fell forward onto it face first.

"Get up onto the mattress, Dane," she begged, knowing she wouldn't be able to lift him into position if he passed out with his legs hanging off the bed as he was.

It took some work, but eventually she got him rolled over onto his back and more or less lying properly on the mattress.

"You comin'?"

"I don't think so. You gonna be all right?"

Dane pouted. "I don't even get a peek at your tits? It seems only fair."

"I don't understand what looking at my breasts has anything to do with me helping you home, and making sure you didn't drive drunk and kill yourself—or anyone else."

Dane looked stunned for a moment, then laughed once again. Throwing his head back and guffawing as if she'd said the funniest thing he'd ever heard in his life. When he finally had control over himself, he moved his hand to the button of his jeans and fumbled, attempting to undo them.

After watching him struggle for a moment, she ordered, "Move. I'll do it." She wasn't happy with how much difficulty he was having, trying to undo the stubborn button with only one hand. It was just one more thing she hadn't ever thought about, but seeing firsthand how hard it was made her suddenly more aware of how tough doing simple everyday things must be for Dane.

She made quick work of the button and pulled down the zipper. "There. You gonna be able to get those off by yourself?"

"No," he retorted immediately. "I need your help, Smalls."

Taking him at his word, Bryn immediately went to his feet. She unlaced his boots and pulled them off. She peeled his socks off, then ordered, "Lift your ass and I'll tug."

"Aw man…that's not what I meant."

"Up, Dane."

He lifted his butt off the bed, and Bryn pulled his jeans down his legs and laid them on the floor. "There. Now your shirt."

He merely stared at her. All humor off his face now.

"Dane?"

"I don't take my shirt off to sleep."

"What? Why not? It's a scientific fact, supported by a dissertation by Milton Grumball, who graduated Magna Cum Laude from Harvard in nineteen eighty-four, that men sleep better naked."

He blinked at her, then the right side of his mouth twitched. "Was that a joke or a fact?"

She grinned for a moment, but said, "It's a fact. Arms up." Her voice was no-nonsense, and she moved to the head of the bed and waited for him to comply.

For the first time in her life, Bryn felt tall as she hovered over Dane on the bed. She looked into his eyes and saw hesitation and uncertainty. "What? What's wrong?"

"I don't want you to see me."

"But you wanted to see *me*."

A spark of interest blossomed in his eyes, chasing away the insecurity that had lingered. "True. How about a trade?"

Bryn thought about it for a moment before clarifying, "You'll take off your shirt if I show you my breasts?"

"Yes."

"Deal. You first. Arms up," Bryn repeated.

Dane lifted his arms as if in a trance, not taking his eyes off her face. Bryn felt herself blushing, but helped lift his shirt up over his chest and off his arms.

She got a good look at his left arm for the first time. It actually looked a lot less…injured…than Bryn expected. She'd only gotten a quick glimpse in the bar, and wasn't sure what she *thought* it would be like, but it really did appear as if his arm just ended halfway between his elbow and where his hand should be. The skin over the stump was healed and, other than a few raised pink scars, was smooth. She had no idea what had happened to him, but she figured he was probably lucky he hadn't lost the arm above his elbow. The range of tasks he could still perform would've been more restricted if he didn't have his elbow, in her limited opinion.

Thoughts of how a prosthetic fit onto his arm and

how it worked swam in her mind. Tilting her head, she wondered what the stump felt like, how much feeling he had in it, if he experienced phantom pains...and a million other things.

Bryn reached for his arm without thought.

He jerked it away from her. "Don't."

"I want to touch it," Bryn insisted, her desire for knowledge overcoming the unwritten societal rules that said you weren't supposed to touch people's pregnant bellies or scars.

"Why?"

"It's amazing. I'm fascinated."

"It's hid-hidemous...ugly," Dane got out.

"It is *not*," she exclaimed harshly. "Don't say that, Dane. It's a miracle. I can't imagine what happened to you, but I'm impressed at the doctors who worked on you. They did a great job."

As if her words were hypnotizing, Dane didn't move away when she reached toward him a second time.

Running her hand over the stump on his arm, Bryn whispered, sitting on the mattress next to his hip, "It's smooth. Does it hurt?"

"Not really. Not anymore," Dane said in a low tone.

Bryn examined his arm, lost in scientific facts and images in her mind. She even bent down at one point to run her cheek over the skin, amazed at how soft it was. She wasn't sure how long she'd been running her hands over his stump and examining it when Dane finally slurred, "Your turn, Smalls. I showed you mine—show me yours."

She looked up into Dane's face and his gray eyes pierced into her soul. She couldn't decipher the look, but a deal was a deal. And he'd more than kept his end of the bargain.

Grabbing the edge of her T-shirt, she pulled it up to her chin without hesitation, showing Dane the plain white cotton bra she'd put on hours earlier.

He didn't say a word, instead bringing his right hand up to her chest and running his index finger along the edge of the cup, not touching her skin but making goosebumps rise on her arms nevertheless.

When he continued to run his finger up and down the edge of her bra, making her more than nervous, Bryn told him, "They aren't big. They're only B cups. Forty-four percent of American women are this size, and less than one percent are larger than a D. Men seem to think every woman should have huge breasts, but really, we don't have a choice in the matter, it's all genetics. Except of course if someone has breast augmentation."

Without taking his eyes off her chest, Dane said, "They're perfect for your size, Smalls. Any bigger and you'd be top-heavy. You've got enough for a man to be able to squeeze and plump, and that's what's important. I bet they're sensitive." His finger followed the edge of the cup to the hollow between her breasts and he moved it a scant few millimeters, until it rested on her skin rather than the cotton material.

Bryn shivered at the feel of his touch on her sensitive bare skin. She'd had men suck and squeeze her breasts, but all it took was one brief touch of Dane's finger along her bra to make her nipples pucker and push against the cotton.

"Uh, thanks. I didn't mean to imply that I wanted large breasts, but some men seem to be attracted only to women who are more healthily endowed than I am."

When Dane licked his lips and leaned closer, obviously seeing the effect his touch had on her and wanting to do more than look, Bryn abruptly stood and moved away from the bed, letting her shirt cover her once more.

As much as Dane fascinated her, and as strongly as she suddenly wanted to feel his hands on her skin, she couldn't do it when he was intoxicated and had no idea who she was. It wasn't right or fair. He'd hate himself if he remembered it was *her* that he'd touched.

His eyes moved up to hers again and he held out his hand. "Join me?"

"You're drunk. Too drunk to have sex."

He chuckled. "Unfortunately, I know. Just talk."

Bryn eyed him sideways, then nodded. She could no sooner walk away from this man and the feelings he aroused in her than she could pass by a homeless person begging on the street. She walked around to the other side of the bed and eased down on top of the covers next to him. "What do you want to talk about?"

"What's your name?"

"Bryn Hartwell."

"Pretty."

Bryn shrugged. "It's just a name."

"I'm thirty. How old are you?"

"Twenty-seven."

Dane brought his hand up to her face and smoothed her hair off her cheek and behind her ear. "Where did you come from?"

As usual, Bryn took his question literally. "My parents met when they were in their late twenties and fell in love. I was born not too long after their wedding."

His lips quirked up, but he didn't say anything else.

"You were hurt in the Army?" she asked, breaking the slightly awkward silence.

Dane nodded, but didn't elaborate.

They were both quiet for a long moment. Finally, he murmured, "The room is spinning. I'm gonna pass out. But thank you for bringing me home. And for showing me your tits. You're beautiful. Much too pretty for the likes of me."

"You're welcome," Bryn whispered, wanting to protest the last part, but sucking in a breath when his hand came toward her again.

Dane took hold of a length of her hair and brought it to his face, inhaling deeply. "Smells so good."

It was the last thing he said to her before the alcohol did its thing. Bryn watched as Dane's eyes closed and his hand went lax, her hair falling out of his grip.

She lay there for ten more minutes, watching Dane's chest rise and fall, before finally taking a breath and getting out of the bed. The last thing she wanted was to act like the stalker and freak he'd accused her of being. But she knew the moment she left his house, the real world would intrude on the feeling she had right now.

He most likely wouldn't remember anything that had happened tonight, and if and when she did see him again, he'd be back to thinking she was a weirdo he wanted nothing to do with. She knew she'd hold the experience of his finger on her skin and his beautiful words close to her heart for a long time to come.

Moving around the house, Bryn did what she could to make his morning a little easier, knowing scientifically what alcohol did to the human body, and then left the house through the garage. She then exited through the door on the side, making sure to lock it behind her as she left.

Bryn walked to the end of the driveway and looked back one last time. She'd left the hall light on but couldn't even make out the shape of the house, other than the slight light shining through the front window. She knew there were trees rising behind the roof and she could smell the fresh, clean air. Dane's house was his getaway from the world. She loved it. It was peaceful and made her feel as though reality was far away. Bringing her hand up to massage her chest over her heart, Bryn closed her eyes and pressed her lips together.

She didn't know how it happened, but she had a huge crush on the man, even after only talking with him twice…and he thought she was a freak. When his guard was down, she saw the gentlemanly, caring, and sensitive man underneath the gruff and scarred exterior, and he'd been nice to her. Had treated her as if she was a desirable woman rather than a stranger or, worse yet, a weirdo stalker.

Squaring her shoulders, Bryn turned away from the house, shoved her hands into her pockets, and started walking back to the bar and her vehicle. Even though it was pitch dark, it shouldn't be an issue. It was only three miles.

Heedless of the dangers a lone woman might encounter in the middle of the night, Bryn set off, trying not to think about what would happen when she saw Dane again.

Chapter Four

DANE GROANED AS he turned over and the morning light shone into his eyes as if a laser beam was aiming directly at his pupils.

"Fuck," he swore as he quickly rolled onto his back and threw his arm over his face. Feeling nauseous, he took a few deep breaths, trying to control the urge to throw up. When he thought he had enough control that he wouldn't vomit all over his sheets, he slowly turned his head to see what time it was…and blinked.

Sitting next to the clock on the little table next to the bed was a glass of water, two large tablets and two small. There was also a note. Dane reached out slowly, careful not to jostle his head, and picked it up.

I'm sure you feel like crap. Put the Alka-Seltzer tablets in the glass and when they dissolve, drink it all down. It has sodium bicarbonate, which will help settle your stomach and make you not wanna throw up, and the aspirin will help your headache.

That was it. It wasn't signed and had no other information about what the hell he'd done last night. Dane closed his eyes and tried to recall anything past arriving at the hole-in-the-wall bar he'd impulsively pulled into. He'd been driving home from Post Falls, where he'd gone to grocery shop.

The trip had been a disaster. It was too early, there were too many people, even in the small town northwest of Coeur d'Alene, and he'd been too damn keyed up to finish his shopping. After going up and down three aisles, he'd simply put down his basket and left. The storm that had roared in as he was driving home didn't help the feeling that he'd never be normal again. Even though storms didn't usually send him over the edge, every clap of thunder made him flinch and the lightning reminded him of the flashes of light from the bomb that had killed his friends and ruined his life. Feeling defeated and sorry for himself, he'd stopped at the bar on the outskirts of Rathdrum and proceeded to get shit-faced drunk.

Other than a bartender who needed an attitude adjustment and a waitress who had seemed to want to go home with him—until she'd seen his stump—the rest of the night was a complete blank.

Feeling sick, now for more reasons than the leftover alcohol in his bloodstream, Dane forced himself to scoot upright in the bed. He picked up the tablets and dropped them into the glass of water, watching dispassionately as they bubbled and fizzed. When it looked like they were done releasing their hangover cure into the water, he drank it in three large gulps.

Dane couldn't remember how he'd gotten home. When he first woke up he figured the bartender had probably called a cab or something for him. But after seeing the note and medicine on the table next to him, the cabbie idea was out. He sighed, trying to figure out how he was going to get his truck. It was most likely sitting in the parking lot of the bar. At least he hoped it was.

Thinking it was a good sign that he didn't hear anyone in his small house, Dane eased his legs over the side of the mattress and carefully stood.

He wavered, but remained upright. Deciding that he'd need coffee if he was going to be remotely human in the next four hours, he stumbled out of his bedroom and down the hall into the living room. Focusing on the kitchen, he grabbed hold of the granite countertop as soon as he neared it. Thank God for open floorplans. He reached for the coffeepot—and paused with his hand in the air as if frozen.

Another note.

I figured you'd need coffee first thing. Just hit start. It's ready to go.

After pushing the green "on" button, Dane picked

up the second note to examine it. The writing was slanted slightly to the right without any embellishments. It looked like a man's handwriting, but somehow Dane knew it wasn't. How, he couldn't have said, but there was a memory at the edge of his mind that told him whoever had brought him home, and left him notes, had been a woman.

He looked down at himself. He was wearing a pair of boxers and that was it. Feeling self-conscious for the first time, Dane scratched the stump on his left arm absently. He never went to bed without wearing a shirt anymore. Ever. But here he stood. Practically naked.

Without waiting for the coffee to finish, Dane went back to his room and looked around. The clothes he'd been wearing yesterday were nowhere to be seen. Fuck. Having a feeling what he'd find, he went to his dirty clothes hamper. Empty. Except for another fucking note.

Your hamper was full, and your clothes stunk from all the cigarette smoke, so I started a load. Don't forget to move the clothes to the dryer, otherwise they'll mold and smell nasty.

Whoever it was had done his laundry.
Definitely a woman.
Had she seen his arm?
His scars?

God, he felt pathetic. First, he'd gotten drunk enough to black out for the first time since he'd gotten back from the mission that had changed his life forever, and now he was bemoaning the fact a chick had seen his scars.

Damn. Had he fucked her? Shit. Had he *hurt* her? Kicked her out? Not used a condom? He'd always been careful. Always. In fact, he hadn't been with anyone since he'd been hurt, hadn't had the slightest urge to get naked with anyone. Had being drunk made him lose his inhibitions enough to get laid? He hoped not. He'd never been a man-whore, and his stomach turned at the thought.

Dane turned toward the bed and ran his eyes over it. There it was—a head-shaped indentation in the pillow on the far side of the bed. The one he never slept on. He felt even sicker than a moment before. Damn, damn, damn.

He opened the drawer next to his side of the bed and looked inside. The box of condoms he'd bought on a whim over two months ago after Truck's urging to get back in the saddle was sitting right where he'd left it. Unopened. The sight of it relieved him a bit, although it was possible he'd been drunk enough to not even think about gloving up. Shit.

As if in a trance, he walked over to the side of the bed where someone had obviously lain the night before, and picked up the pillow. He brought it to his face and inhaled.

The smell of coconut assailed his nostrils, and Dane felt his dick twitch in his boxers. He lifted his head and looked down at himself in disbelief. With a hangover from hell, his head feeling as if someone was pounding on it from the inside, his stomach rebelling against him with every breath, it was almost unbelievable that the scent of a woman on his pillow could still give him a woody. He brought it up to his face once again and breathed in the smell that reminded him of the beach...of suntan lotion and woman.

Smalls.

The name popped into his brain as if the smell of coconut had conjured it up. He didn't know anything about her other than the way she smelled and the nickname he'd bestowed on her, but Dane knew without a doubt that the woman who'd done his laundry, pre-made his coffee, and left him Alka-Seltzer tablets to help his hangover—and had given him a hard-on for the first time in forever—was one and the same.

He had a sudden vision of a woman with brown hair lying next to him on the bed. She'd been fully dressed and he was smelling her hair. He relaxed a bit. He still wasn't positive, but he had a feeling they hadn't had sex. He sighed in relief and a little bit of disappointment. Which was fucked; no way did he *ever* want to take a woman and not remember it. Somehow, he knew to the very marrow of his bones that being inside the mystery woman would be fucking amazing.

Dropping the pillow on the bed, Dane wandered back down the hall and opened the door to the garage. After everything else, he wasn't all that surprised to find Miss May was there, and he walked around his truck, checking for damage. Nothing. There *was* another note stuck to the driver's side window, however.

Miss May is safe. No damage done.

He smirked. She was funny. He had no idea if she was trying to be funny when she'd written the note, but it was obvious they'd had a conversation at some point about the nickname for his truck. He hadn't dated, or even met, one woman who would voluntarily use a ridiculous nickname thought up by a man for his truck.

Dane opened the driver's side door and stared at the seat. It was pulled all the way forward; no way he'd be able to fit behind the wheel with it in that position. He nodded, pleased. So he hadn't driven himself home. Thank God.

Smalls.

The name rattling around in his head made a lot more sense now. If the position of his truck seat was anything to go by, she was probably only a few inches above five feet…if that.

A vision of a slight woman hovered around the edges of his consciousness. Deciding not to push it—he'd remember when he least expected it, hopefully—Dane went back inside. He poured a cup of coffee, smiling at how strong Smalls had made it, and headed into his tiny laundry room. He moved his clothes from the washer to the dryer, as ordered, and started it.

It wasn't until around two in the afternoon that he finally started to feel human again. The woman had been right, the Alka-Seltzer had gone a long way toward making him feel better. That and the coffee, and eventually the pasta he'd made himself for lunch. How in the hell he'd gone thirty years without knowing about the magical hangover cure that was Alka-Seltzer was beyond him.

Deciding to have spaghetti made him think about the woman from the grocery store and their encounter. How, even though he'd been irritated about her following him, he'd somehow thought she was cute when she'd spouted off facts about carbohydrates and his eating habits. Then he remembered the words he'd hurled at her as well. Dane knew he'd been feeling vulnerable and paranoid when he'd met her, but it didn't make the words he'd hurt her with any less fucked up.

Remembering the conversation they'd had while standing in the pancake aisle, where she'd offered her name to try to make him feel more at ease, jogged his memory of the mystery woman from the night before—*also* telling him her name was Bryn.

Bryn was an unusual name. There was almost no chance that there were two women he'd met in the last week in the small city of Rathdrum who had the same name.

Remembering her name was all it took. Everything about the night before clicked into place as if it hadn't been hidden behind an alcoholic daze for the last few hours.

Bryn Hartwell. The woman who'd showed up in the bar, driven him home, examined his stump so tenderly—with fascination instead of disgust—and who had held up her shirt so he could check out her tits—it was only fair, after all—was the same woman he'd called a freak and accused of stalking him.

Dane wasn't sure what to think. He was having a hard time understanding exactly why she'd done what she had for him last night, especially the peep show she'd freely given him, when he'd been such a dick to her.

Before he could examine her actions and try to make sense of them, his phone rang. Glad for the distraction, Dane saw Truck's name and quickly connected.

"Hey, Truck."

"Dane. How's it going? How's your stalker?"

"I swear to God you're spooky sometimes."

"How so?"

"I was just thinking about her, then you call and that's the first thing you bring up. It's uncanny."

"Yeah, that's me. The spook. So what made you think about her? Last time we talked, you said she'd quit her job at the grocery store so you could shop there without feeling awkward. She go back on that? She still there?"

"No. But I saw her last night."

"Where?"

Dane sighed. "I was at the local bar, trashed out of my mind, and she came in and took me home." Nothing but silence greeted Dane. "Hello? Truck? Still there?"

"You all right?"

Figures that Truck wouldn't focus on the fact that his little stalker had apparently found him and brought him home. No questions about what they'd done, if he'd fucked her or not. Truck's only concern was the fact that he'd been drunk. He might be a bit rough around the edges, but when push came to shove, he always showed what a good friend he was. "I'm fine. And no, I'm not an alcoholic. It was a poor decision made on an empty stomach. Once I started, it seemed like a good idea. Believe me, this morning I realized how much of a piss poor one it really was. I'm fine. No need for an intervention."

"Good. Now talk about the chick."

Dane chuckled. Now *that* was the reaction he'd expected in the first place. Then he sobered. He could use a sounding board, and Truck was about as impartial as he was going to get. "Here's the thing, man, I was pissed when I found out what she'd done at the store. I felt cornered, like it was written all over my face that I was just another soldier with PTSD who couldn't manage to walk through a damn store without freaking out. You know what I said to her before."

"Yeah, you said she was a freak."

Dane winced. It sounded so much worse now that he remembered last night and how much he'd enjoyed Bryn's company. "I did. And I felt bad about it, but figured what was done was done. Then in she came last night. She didn't seem to care that I didn't even have on my prosthetic. I hate wearing the thing. It's awkward and looks like shit. She didn't care that my name looks like a first grader's signature because I haven't learned to write with my right hand yet. She could drive a stick shift. And the way she…"

Dane's voice trailed off, not sure he wanted to go into detail about how she'd examined his arm and how it made him feel.

"You sleep with her?"

"No."

"But you want to," Truck correctly surmised.

"No," Dane denied immediately, then snorted and relented. "Maybe."

"Look, I don't know what went on, but it's obvious, at least to me, that she likes you. Women show affection in different ways. Some will ignore you to the extreme, even pretending you aren't in the same room with them. Or they'll pick fights with you because they can't understand or deal with what they're feeling inside. Others will come right out and tell you they're interested. You just have to learn to read her signals."

"She blurts out random facts when she's nervous and takes things really literally."

"What else?"

Dane tried to think about the night before. "She's selfless and generous." He remembered the twenty percent tip she'd neatly written on the credit card bill. He'd found the receipt in his wallet, which she'd left on the dresser in his room.

"Do you think she's playing you? That she wants something from you?"

"I have no clue, but I don't have anything to give her."

"Now *that's* bullshit. You better not be talking about your missing hand. I'll have to come up there and beat some sense into you. I didn't spend almost an hour of my life holding your damn artery between my fingers for you to become a grouchy, whiny shut-in who thinks no one will ever like him because of a little scar."

Dane burst out laughing. "Little?"

"Okay, a big scar, then."

Dane had no idea how Truck had received—or how he felt about—the scar on *his* face. It pulled the left side down into a scowl and, combined with his size, made him one scary dude. But missing a hand was a lot different than having a scar. He wasn't going to compare himself to Truck. No way in hell would he go there, but he figured the other man understood a bit of what was going on in his head. His tone lowered. "No, Truck, that's not what I feel, exactly. Smalls is just so...blunt. It's like she doesn't have a filter and just says what she is thinking. She had no problem looking at my stump. Hell, she seemed excited, in a clinical sense, that she was able to examine it up close. For the first time since it happened, I didn't feel less of a man in front of a woman."

"Smalls?"

"Yeah. In my drunken haze last night, I kinda christened her that. She's only about five feet tall and probably weighs about what our packs did over in the desert."

"Take my advice," Truck told Dane in a serious tone. "Get to know her. *Without* the alcohol in the way. Having a woman say what she means is a gift. You won't have to wonder what she's feeling or try to interpret a 'fine' or 'okay' when you ask how she is. 'Cause I'll tell you, one hundred percent of the time when a woman says she's 'fine,' she's not. But trying to figure out if she has a headache, or if she just had surgery and feels like her guts are being pulled out by a pair of tweezers, is one of the hardest things about caring about a woman. It sounds like Smalls has gone out of her way to try to look after you. The least you can do is say thank you for getting your ass home in one piece last night."

"You're right."

"Of course I am."

"Ass," Dane returned, more comfortable now that they were on familiar ground and not talking about love and feelings anymore.

"Seriously, Dane. Find her. See what you think of her in the light of day. Maybe she *is* a freak. Maybe she *doesn't* give a shit about you, but is trying to simply do a good deed, or maybe she has acrotomophilia."

"Do I want to know what that is?" Dane asked warily.

"It's someone who's sexually attracted to amputees. It's a fetish."

Dane didn't really have a response to that. He didn't truly think Bryn was attracted to him because he was missing part of his arm, but honestly, he had no idea.

The fact that there were people out there who *were* sexually attracted to amputees freaked him out a little, and gave him one more thing to be worried about when it came to getting into a relationship.

"My point is that you should get to know her. You'll figure it out soon enough. You're a smart guy."

"Thanks."

"You're welcome," Truck returned immediately. "Now, I gotta go. I'm picking Mary up from a doctor's appointment in a bit."

"What's up with you two?" Dane asked.

"It's complicated," was Truck's informative reply.

"It sounds like it."

"But I'll tell you this…she's worth it. She's worth every second of sleep I've lost, every moment of worry, and every headache she's given me."

"You and her are a thing?" Dane questioned. "I mean, last I knew, you weren't exactly her favorite person."

"Mary's complicated," Truck repeated. "She's had a tough life. Extremely tough. She's learned that she can't completely trust anyone."

"I thought she trusted Rayne."

"She does. To a point. But I think there's a part of her that's just waiting for Rayne to let her down too. So she does what she's done her entire life. Cuts people out of the important shit she has going on so as not to be disappointed."

"Rayne's not going to be happy."

"I know. But at the moment, she's not my concern. Mary is. I'm working on showing her that I can be trusted. That when I say something, I follow through and mean it."

"Good luck, man," Dane told him.

"Thanks. But I don't need it. I can out-stubborn that woman any day of the week. She means somethin' to me and I'm not letting her push me out. I can help her, with her current *and* past issues. But enough about me. Keep me in the loop with Smalls. You know if you need us, we're there."

"I will, and I appreciate you having my back. Tell the others I said hello." Dane hadn't spoken much lately to the rest of the team, but was appreciative of them all the same. After the shit with Kassie, he'd only gotten closer to them all. It felt good. Really good.

"Will do. Just throwing this out there...the guys and I have been talking about taking a trip to Northwest Idaho in the near future."

"No shit?"

"No shit."

"It's about time. I'd love to see all of you...without the whole, you know, kidnapping of girlfriends and asshole ex-boyfriends and their creepy friends to deal with."

Truck chuckled. "I'll make it happen. And Dane?"

"Yeah?"

"Prepare yourself for a hell of a ride with this chick. If you've given her a nickname, she's already gotten under your skin."

"Later, Truck." Dane didn't bother contradicting the other man. He'd think what he wanted regardless if Dane denied it or not.

"Later."

Dane clicked off the phone and drummed his fingers on the kitchen counter. He was excited about Truck and the others coming to visit, but at the moment he had more important things on his mind. He recalled tracing the edge of her bra, how her little nipples had peaked without him even touching them…and the look of surprise and bewilderment on Bryn's face when she realized how her body was reacting to him.

She'd been confused by her reaction to him, and it was that innocence, that small glimpse of insecurity that made his decision this afternoon easy. He wanted to get to know her. Wanted to know all about her. Why she seemed to be a walking encyclopedia. How she'd known exactly what he needed in the grocery store to feel more comfortable. Why she'd quit.

He had no idea where she lived or what she did as a job, but if she could find him at Smokey's Bar last night, he could certainly find her. He hadn't spent a good chunk of his life as a Delta Force soldier to fail now. Rathdrum wasn't that big...if Bryn worked in the small town, he'd find her.

Pushing off the barstool next to his counter, Dane headed for his room. He needed to change out of the sweats he had on, put on his prosthetic, and head into town. He had some questions for one Bryn Hartwell, and he felt anticipation for the first time in what seemed like forever. He'd figure out what her deal was once and for all. And maybe, just maybe, he'd get a second chance to see, and touch, her delectable body.

A man could hope.

Chapter Five

B RYN PUSHED THE cart around the Rathdrum Public Library and tried not to think any more about the night before. It had been an exciting night, life-changing, one she knew she'd never forget, even if Dane didn't remember anything about it. It felt so good to take care of him and have him trust her. After the long walk back to the bar, she'd gotten home around five-thirty, slept for three hours, then got up to make her shift.

She'd never needed a lot of sleep. Even at a young age, she would go up to her room at the appropriate time, but she'd stay up late reading, doing math problems, and surfing the Internet, trying to quench her ever-growing thirst for knowledge. Typically, she only needed around four hours of sleep but could get by on two or three if necessary.

Her parents were happy to send her off to boarding school when she was nine. Bryn knew they loved her in their own way, and their way was to send her money for birthdays and holidays. The only thing Bryn had ever wanted from her parents was their affection…and it was something they never knew how to give.

Even today, their relationship was distant. They'd call on her birthday and send cards at Christmas, but they hadn't seen each other in years. At this point in her life, Bryn had given up on ever getting more than distant affection from them.

Shaking her head to try to dispel the depressing thoughts of her family, she turned her attention to the books she had to put back on the shelves. Working at the public library wasn't exactly her dream job, but it paid the bills and kept her feeling more like an everyday person. She'd tried to work in a lab when she was twenty-one, but found herself getting bored. Most people would probably never understand if she tried to explain that sitting behind a microscope and doing calculations and research was boring, but it had been.

Bryn wanted to be like everyone else. Talking about advanced quantum physics and solving math problems that had no numbers in them made her an outcast.

So working in small-town Rathdrum and re-shelving books after they'd been returned was perfect…for now. Besides, she had all the books she could ever want, and if once in a while she got the urge to figure out how the wiring in her apartment worked or how to take apart and put back together the garbage disposal, she could indulge her too-smart brain and do it without anyone being the wiser.

She grabbed the next book and looked at the title. *Dangers of Fertilizer.* Bryn's nose wrinkled...she knew people could make a bomb with fertilizer, but didn't know otherwise how it might be dangerous. She flipped through the book and realized that there was a chapter on making a bomb with the kind of fertilizer that could be found on hardware store shelves. But perhaps more alarmingly, there were handwritten notes and highlights in the book...in that specific chapter.

Bryn froze for a moment and bit her lip. She didn't know what to do. The last thing she wanted was to accuse someone of something. Maybe they were like her...simply interested in how things worked.

Undecided, she put the book down and picked up another stack. She'd work on those first, then get back to the fertilizer one. Seeing a couple in a clench on a cover of the romance she was holding, she sighed in relief that it wasn't a book on how to make a bomb or something equally as alarming. She never understood the concept of romance novels, they just weren't realistic, but she *did* get that a lot of women read them. The library was constantly getting requests for specific authors, and Bryn was always restocking the romance shelves.

After an hour of putting the borrowed romances back, she picked up another batch of books. Hardware.

She pushed the cart to the craft section and turned the book over to see what it was about. *Design and Build Your Own Doomsday Bunker*.

Cool was the first thing Bryn thought at seeing the title. Seeing this kind of book wasn't exactly surprising in this part of Idaho, but she hadn't really thought much about it herself. Looking around for the head librarian to make sure the woman didn't see her wasting time, Bryn flipped through the book. There were diagrams on how far down to dig depending on how many people you'd be sharing the bunker with, how to get fresh water, and what do to about human waste while underground.

She was about to shut the book and shelve it, when handwriting in the margin caught her attention.

There were arrows drawn around a few paragraphs and what looked like a shopping list. But it was the words *fertilizer storage*, with an arrow pointing to a small space on a sample bunker on the page, that stood out. Not to mention the handwriting was similar to the notes in the fertilizer book.

It was too much of a coincidence, and one that Bryn knew she couldn't overlook.

Now she was curious, and when she got curious, she couldn't just let it go. It drove her mother crazy when she'd been growing up. Once she got interested in something, she had to see it, hear it, or experience it for herself. When she was only five, after seeing a high schooler's textbook and listening to her talk to her friend about how gross it had been, Bryn had nagged, cajoled, and pleaded with her mom to let *her* dissect a frog, until she'd allowed it...if only to teach Bryn a lesson.

After explaining to the high school anatomy teacher a little bit about Bryn's intelligence and desire to learn, he'd agreed. But instead of the trip being traumatic or a deterrent for her, young Bryn had chatted and hung out with Mr. Adams for two hours one afternoon after classes were over. She still remembered it to this day— and it had been proof for her mom that when Bryn's curiosity kicked in, it was better to indulge her rather than try to talk her out of it.

So seeing the book on fertilizer and the notes in the margin of the one on bunkers made Bryn want to know who had checked them out, why, what they were planning, who else was involved, and how and where they were going to build the bunker in which they wanted to store fertilizer. And, of course, she wanted to see the bunker when it was done.

"Are you done, Bryn?"

She almost jumped out of her skin, but managed to calmly put the book on how to build a bunker face down on the cart and turn to the librarian.

"Yes, ma'am. I only need to finish up these last few

books."

"Good. Story hour just finished and the children's area is a disaster. Can you please go and help put the books back in their proper places?"

Bryn nodded. "Sure."

"Thanks. I appreciate it."

Bryn watched the older matronly woman walk away and sighed to herself. She didn't want to think bad of anyone, but Rosie Peterman was a stereotypical librarian. Probably in her mid-forties, she looked like she was at least ten years older. Her long hair was graying at the roots and usually was held back in a bun at the nape of her neck. She was average height and wore clothes more suited to a woman in her sixties.

But the worst was that she lived alone and had five or six—Bryn could never remember the exact number—cats. It wasn't the living alone thing that bothered Bryn the most, it was the thought that she herself was going to end up being just like the librarian someday. Alone. Set apart from society and not able to integrate.

As she made her way to the children's area, Bryn thought about Dane. He'd called her a freak, but he didn't seem to mind her being weird the night before. Yes, he'd been drunk, but he wasn't a mean drunk, and that went a long way in Bryn's eyes. She'd seen too many men who turned angry and aggressive when they'd had too much alcohol. Not Dane. He was funny, silly, and made her feel like a woman for the first time in her life. He'd hadn't seen Bryn Hartwell, the super-smart outcast. He'd acted like he'd enjoyed her company, and when Bryn closed her eyes, she could see his smile in her head as if she'd seen it every day of her life.

Thoughts of Dane and his embarrassment over his messy signature made her think about his missing hand, which made her want to know more about the science behind his amputation. Determined to quickly put the kids' area back to rights so she could find some books on missing limbs before her shift was over, Bryn moved the two books on fertilizer and bunkers to the bottom of the stack still waiting to be shelved. She'd deal with those later. For now, thoughts of Dane and his missing hand were first and foremost in her mind.

The rest of her shift was uneventful and Bryn managed to find three books on amputees on the library's shelves. She checked them out at the end of her shift and quickly headed out to her car.

Out in the parking lot, not watching where she was going, instead looking through the pages of one of the books, eager to learn all she could about what Dane went through and what it might be like to be missing part of an arm, Bryn didn't notice the car that slammed on its brakes right before backing into her. She also didn't have any idea a man stood watching her intently as he stood against his truck. His hands were crossed over his chest and one foot was crossed over the other.

She didn't notice when he pushed off his truck and headed her way. If she had, she might've been more prepared for what happened next.

"Ah, it's the elusive grocery store chick."

Bryn squeaked in surprise at the voice so near to her and barely managed to keep hold of the book she'd been reading. She looked up and her eyes widened at seeing Dane Munroe keeping pace with her as she walked to her car. For a moment she was speechless, but quickly recovered and said defensively, "I didn't know you were here. I'm not following you."

"I know."

When he didn't say anything else, Bryn stopped walking and just stared at him.

She jerked when he reached out and took hold of her biceps and guided her out of the middle of the parking lot, so a car could get past them. Today Dane was wearing a pair of blue jeans, the same boots he'd had on last night, and another long-sleeve shirt, this one a deep plum color. Flannel. Bryn could also see he was wearing a prosthetic. The three prongs of the hooks that served as a thumb and two fingers were unmoving at his side as they peeked out from the edge of the shirt.

"Seriously," Bryn told him, moving docilely where he guided her out of the way. "I work here. Usually from nine to five-ish. I didn't know you'd be here. I can't quit this job though, 'cause it's how I pay my rent and for food and stuff. I could probably get another job, but it might take a while, and if I had to go down to Post Falls or Coeur D'Alene, my car might not make it and I'd get stuck somewhere...which would be bad. So I—"

"I know you're not following me," Dane interrupted, "because I tracked *you* down this time."

Bryn stood stock still, staring up at Dane in disbelief. Not sure at all what to say. Finally, she got out, "You tracked me down?"

"Yeah. Anything you want to tell me?"

Bryn looked around, hoping someone would rescue her from the extremely uncomfortable conversation. Realizing she and Dane were alone, she finally looked back at him and bit her lip before swallowing hard. "I'm sorry about the grocery store thing?" It came out more as a question than a comment.

"Actually, I should be apologizing to *you*. You took me by surprise, and I don't do surprises well. I realize now that you were helping me, and I should've said thank you instead of making you feel like you had to quit."

Bryn could only stare at Dane, her mouth hanging open.

He chuckled, and put a finger under her chin and lifted it, effectively closing her mouth and tilting her head up so she couldn't look away from him at the same time. "Speechless, Smalls? I wouldn't have believed it if I didn't see it for myself."

The use of the nickname he'd given her last night made the adrenaline race throughout her body. He remembered. How in the hell had he remembered after how much he'd obviously drunk? How *much* did he remember?

Bryn jerked away from him, still silent, and took a couple quick steps backward. Her head whipped around at the raucous sound of a car horn and the screeching of tires. Before she could react, Dane had grabbed her around the waist and pulled her into his body, turning them both out of the way of the now stopped car.

"Jesus, Smalls, you gotta pay more attention to where you're walking."

"S-s-sorry," Bryn stammered, shaking with the additional adrenaline pumping through her bloodstream and ignoring the irritated shouting from the driver who'd almost run her over. First Dane had remembered the name he'd given her last night, when she thought for sure he'd been way too drunk to recall anything about her appearance in the bar and in his home. Then she'd almost been run over, and now she stood in the circle of Dane's arms. It was too much for her overloaded brain to comprehend.

"You okay?" Dane asked, not loosening the hold of

his arms around her.

Nodding, Bryn said nothing, just curled her fingers against the hard chest they were resting on. She could feel his heartbeat under his shirt and see it beating strongly in his neck.

"That nod is akin to telling me you're 'fine,' and I have it on good authority when a woman says she's 'fine,' she's totally *not* fine. Talk to me. You're freaking me out a bit here, Bryn."

"You know my name."

Dane smiled. "Yeah, Smalls. I remember everything."

At that, she closed her eyes and pressed her lips together. When he said nothing more, simply continued to stand there holding her close, Bryn opened her eyes and mouth.

"I wasn't stalking you. I swear. I was at home and the storm came through. It made me think about you. One in six soldiers returning from war suffer from PTSD, and I didn't know if storms were one of your triggers or not. I was only going to check to see if you were at the store. You weren't, but I thought I might as well see if I could find your truck to make sure you were okay. I did. But it was late, and the biker couple coming out of the bar didn't seem to be the kind of people you'd normally hang out with. I only peeked in the door of the bar, but you were the only one there and the bartender wanted you out. He was grumpy. I don't think he makes much in tips 'cause he'd get more if he was friendly. It's a catch-22 though. Did you know that a lot of teenagers don't know what that is? I guess the book is way too old for them, which is a shame, it's really good."

Dane smiled again and pressed his hand into her hip.

Bryn looked up at him in confusion.

"You found me in the bar?" he prompted.

"You were drunk, and couldn't drive, and the bartender assumed I was there to pick you up. So I took you home. Nothing happened," she finished quickly.

"How'd you get back to the bar?"

"Uh…what?" Out of all she'd spewed, that was the last thing she thought Dane would ask about.

"The bar. If you drove Miss May to my house, how did you get back to the bar to get your car? Did you call a taxi?"

"No. There are only two in Rathdrum, and they stop picking people up around two."

He waited a moment but she didn't elaborate. With a raised eyebrow, he asked, "So?"

"So…what?"

"Jesus, Smalls. For such a smart chick, you sure can be scatterbrained. How did you get back to the bar?"

"Oh. I walked."

"You walked."

"Yeah."

"What time?"

"What time what?"

Dane stared up at the sky for a moment, as if praying for patience, and sighed. Then he looked back down at her and enunciated carefully, "What time did you leave my house, and what time did you get back to the bar?"

Bryn shrugged. "I didn't measure it. But I got home around five-thirty. I typically walk around a twenty-minute mile but it was dark, and I couldn't really see where my feet where, so I was probably averaging more like twenty-five minutes. It was around three-point-two miles to your house from the bar. So I probably got back to my car around five-twenty or so. For once, the stupid hunk of junk started with no issues, and I got home around six minutes later."

Dane ran his hand over his face, and Bryn could see his jaw was clenched tight. She had no idea why he was so agitated. "It wasn't a big deal."

"Please don't ever do that again." His words were low and tortured.

"What? Why? How else was I going to get back to my car?"

"Don't put yourself in danger like that again. Anything could've happened to you. You could've been hit by a car. Kidnapped. Raped. Eaten by a wild animal. Walking around this part of the world, in the dark, by yourself, when no one knows where you are…it's not smart."

Bryn was taken aback for a moment. Not smart? Her entire life she'd been told over and over how intelligent she was. It was perhaps the only time she'd ever heard anyone say she wasn't. She wasn't sure how to feel about it.

"Not to mention, if something had happened to you because you helped me…it would've been my fault."

"That's not logical," Bryn protested. "You were passed out back at your house. How could it have been your fault?"

"Because you were walking back to your car, at four in the morning, because of me."

"What should I have done? I needed to get back to my car. I had to work today." Her voice was soft and confused.

"Stayed at my place," Dane returned immediately.

"But—"

"I was passed out; I wasn't going to hurt you. I have two other bedrooms and a huge couch you could've crashed on. In the morning, I would've taken you back to the bar and your car. I would've made sure you got to work on time."

Bryn mulled his words over. She hadn't even

thought about staying in his house. It wasn't polite to invite yourself to stay somewhere you weren't invited. The dangers of walking around the backwoods of Idaho hadn't even occurred to her...especially being assaulted; it wasn't as if she had ever really gained the notice of men before. Not to mention the last time he'd talked to her, when he hadn't been drunk, he didn't exactly like her.

But Bryn understood Dane's point. Appreciating that he'd given her time to turn his words over in her head, she finally said, "You're right. I hadn't thought of the logistics of getting back to my car when I drove you home. All I wanted to do was make sure you got there all right. I should've waited for you to wake up, or for the cabs to start operating. Even if you were pissed I was there."

"Want to get dinner?"

Bryn simply stared up at Dane in stupefaction at the abrupt change in topic.

"You know, the meal that people eat after work, in the evenings? Should I call it supper instead?" He was kidding, but he should've known better than to ask her something like that when she was full of random facts he'd never even thought about before.

"Actually, dinner can be the midday meal, like lunch, and supper has connotations of being in the evening. But ultimately dinner is the main meal of the day, whether it happens in the middle or at the end of it."

Dane's lips curled up into an amused smile. "So? Will you eat an evening meal with me? See, the way I figure it, we got off on the wrong foot. I assumed things about you, and said some nasty and hurtful things that I regret. And now I'm afraid you think I'm an alcoholic veteran who can't function in society."

"I don't think that," Bryn protested immediately.

"So, dinner?"

Instead of answering, Bryn spit out what she *was* thinking. She knew she should shut up, but, especially when she was nervous, she had a habit of spewing random facts. "Getting off on the wrong foot was used by Shakespeare in fifteen ninety-five in *King John*. He talked about a 'better foot.' There's debate about where the saying actually came from, some suggesting that it was ancient Greece, where it was thought to be unlucky to put your left shoe on first. But others think it came about because most people are right-handed. And if there's a right hand, or foot, there has to be a wrong one. And I don't mean that in a bad way...you know...since you're left-handed, or you *were* left-handed. It's just what people think..."

Her voice trailed off and Bryn concentrated on the top button of Dane's shirt. She was an idiot. A complete and utter idiot.

"Hmmm, I didn't know that. Interesting."

Bryn inhaled quickly. He hadn't made fun of her or mocked her strange rambling. She risked looking up at him.

As if he'd been waiting for her to meet his eyes, he said in a low voice, "There's not a lot of choice here in Rathdrum, but if you're up for it, Dairy Queen has great burgers. They're really greasy, but we can wash it down with some ice cream when we're done. And bonus…beef has lots of protein, and you did tell me I should cut down on how many carbs I eat late in the day and consume more protein." His lips quirked up in a grin.

Bryn nodded. She *had* said that. "I'd like that."

"Great." Dane finally took his arms from around her waist and bent to pick up the books she'd dropped when she'd almost been run over. Luckily, they were unharmed and in one piece. "Interesting reading choices."

Bryn blushed again but refused to feel bad. "I don't know anything about amputated limbs or prosthetics."

"You did seem really interested in my stump last night."

"You remember that?"

"It took me a while, but yeah, Smalls, I remember everything."

Bryn wasn't sure what to say to that. She was extremely embarrassed that she'd lifted her shirt and showed him her bra. So she kept her mouth shut.

"Come on, I'll drive."

Dane shifted her until she was on his left side, his prosthetic resting lightly on her hip. She fit against him perfectly, her head only reaching his shoulder. She felt surrounded by his warmth…and safe. Bryn clutched the borrowed books to her chest and shuffled along beside Dane toward his truck.

"Don't worry, this time I'll drive you back here to get your car after we're finished eating. I think I've made it pretty clear I don't like you walking around after dark."

"Before I moved here, I checked out the crime statistics," Bryn informed Dane. "The information was a couple of years old, but there were only six arrests for aggravated assault, only forty-six arrests for drug violations, forty-seven DUIs, two robberies, and only one rape arrest. Overall, Rathdrum is very safe, and there were only three hundred and forty-two arrests the entire twelve months of that year."

Dane stopped at the passenger side of his truck and turned her so her back was to the door. He took her shoulders in his hands and looked down at her. "Be that as it may, it's not safe or smart to press your luck. I don't want you to be the three hundred and forty-third incident in this town for the year. It might be small, but assholes and crazies can live anywhere. Remind me to show you the sex-offender website sometime. The last time I checked, there were twenty-two registered living in this zip code."

"There's a website?"

"Yeah, Smalls. The law says that anyone convicted of a sex crime has to report their address to the authorities. They keep tabs on them and make sure they aren't living too close to schools. Information about sexual predators is online and available to the public."

"Cool," Bryn breathed. "I didn't know."

Dane smiled at her. "Yeah, I got that."

When he didn't say anything further, Bryn shifted. Then finally asked, "Did you change your mind about dinner?"

"No," he said immediately. "I'm wondering how in the hell you were able to follow me around that damn store for so long without me noticing you."

"Oh, I'm good at being invisible."

Dane obviously didn't like her words, but didn't confront her about them. He merely said cryptically, "You're not invisible now."

"Obviously."

"Come on. We've got burgers and ice cream waiting for us." He leaned over and opened the door of Miss May with his good hand and waited as she climbed up into the truck.

Bryn settled herself on the soft leather seat and

watched as he shut her door and stalked around the front to the driver's side. She shut her eyes for a moment and sent a silent prayer upwards that she didn't say anything that would make the amazing man next to her decide once and for all that she really was a freak.

Chapter Six

THE RESTAURANT WAS fairly busy for a weekday
night, and after Dane asked what Bryn wanted to
eat, he sent her to find a table.

Eyeing Dane as she went into the dining room, she
realized that he seemed ill at ease. Of course he was. It
was dinnertime and Dairy Queen was quite crowded.
Making a split-second decision, Bryn walked back to
where Dane was standing in line and placed herself at
his left side. So close her arm brushed his.

"You all right?" Dane asked in concern, looking
down at her.

"Yeah." She didn't elaborate.

"Can't find a place to sit?"

"I'd rather go on a picnic."

"A picnic?"

"Uh huh." Bryn held her breath, hoping he would
go for it.

"This wouldn't have anything to do with what happened in the grocery store, would it?"

Bryn looked up at Dane. She noticed once again

how tall he really was. He was wearing his ever-present leather jacket. When he moved, she could smell the slight scent of the leather waft in her direction. She thought about how to answer him, and decided to simply tell the truth.

"It's crowded. You don't like crowds. There are some booths so you could see the restaurant, but your back would be to a window, which I don't think would make you comfortable. There's a small roadside picnic area about a mile south of the city. We could go there and you wouldn't have to worry about other people, and maybe could enjoy your meal."

He didn't say anything for a long moment. Long enough that Bryn thought she'd gone too far. She'd dropped her eyes and pressed her lips together in mortification, figuring he'd finally realized she was as weird as he'd claimed and would leave her standing alone in the restaurant, when she felt pressure under her chin. She obediently raised her head, loving the warmth of his finger on her skin, and met his eyes as bravely as she could.

"That sounds perfect. Thank you."

Bryn breathed out a relieved sigh but didn't say anything, merely nodded and tried not to shiver when his finger dropped from under her chin.

"Want a Blizzard? It might be a bit mushy by the time we get to the picnic area, but should still taste good."

"I think it's against the law to come to Dairy Queen and not get one," she replied with a straight face.

"Right. Let me guess. Oreo?"

Bryn tilted her head. "Why do you think that's what I like?"

They shuffled forward in the line, and she saw Dane's eyes flick back and forth for a moment before settling back on her. She could tell he was uncomfortable. It couldn't be easy for him to stand in a line with people in front of and behind him. If he didn't like others being in the same aisle as him in the grocery store, this had to be torture. She shifted so she was facing his side, rather than standing next to him. She looked to her right then left, then back up at him.

He understood what she'd done. "Got my back?" he asked in a soft voice, which carried to her ears only.

She nodded.

"Thank you."

Bryn reached out for his hand, only realizing at the last moment that she was on his left side. Mentally shrugging, she curled two fingers around one of the hooks on the end of his prosthetic with her right hand and held on tight. "You're welcome. Why Oreo?"

She could tell she'd surprised him, but he didn't pull away from her grip. "You seem like a black-and-white kinda gal. Classic. Oreo and vanilla ice cream is as classic as it gets."

"Brownie, caramel, chocolate chip cookie dough, peanut butter chips, and Butterfinger."

Dane's brows furrowed and Bryn could tell for the first time since they'd walked inside the small restaurant he was wholly focused on her, and not his surroundings. "What?"

"Brownie, caramel, chocolate chip cookie dough, peanut butter chips, and Butterfinger," she repeated. "In my Blizzard."

"Good Lord, woman. You're gonna go into diabetic shock if you eat that."

She shook her head. "Hypoglycemia is usually only an issue for people who have diabetes, which I don't. It's actually when a person has too much insulin in their bloodstream and indicates a *low* level of blood sugar. *Hyper*glycemia is when the body has too much blood sugar and not enough insulin to balance it out. While healthy people can get hyperglycemic, it's also usually only an issue with people who are diabetic.

"If I have too much sugar in a single meal, it fills me with dopamine, which can give me a false kind of high, but because glucose is digested quickly, the levels of sugar in my bloodstream will fall quickly. I don't sleep a lot, so I usually do something to counteract the sugar when I eat dessert...take a walk, eat something with protein in it, like nuts or peanut butter, or have a cup of green tea or water. That helps me pee and expunge the excess sugar in my body."

"Right." Dane smiled at her but didn't say anything else about her explanation. He merely shuffled forward to the counter when the couple in front of them moved to the side to wait for their food order.

Bryn had no idea what she'd said that was apparently humorous to him, but she wished she knew so she could repeat it at a later date. Dane's whole body had relaxed and it seemed as though he'd forgotten there was a line of people standing at his back. The thought that she'd done that for him, made him relax enough to not care about being out in public, was enough to make a warm feeling blossom through her chest.

Even though she'd been studying his face so intently, she noticed when he reached over with his right hand, unhooked her fingers from around his prosthetic, and then reached around her waist and pulled her into his side.

Bryn felt the strength of Dane's biceps against her back. He didn't look down at her at all, merely kept his eyes on the teenager behind the cash register. She rested one hand on the counter in front of them, and curled the other around his waist and hooked her thumb into the belt at his right side. It felt intimate, but right.

He shook her, bringing her attention to what he was saying. "Make sure I get this right, Bryn," he ordered, then recited the items she wanted in her ice cream.

The teenager's eyes got big with each item Dane ticked off, but she nodded after each one.

"Did I get it right?"

Bryn nodded at him. For once in her life, her mind was blank. All she could think about was how nice it felt to be held against Dane and how good he smelled. The leather of his jacket, the slight scent of cologne, and the underlying scent of sweat. Not enough to be gross, but just enough for her to realize he was a man who would never spend his days sitting in a chair behind a desk. Idaho fit him. Or he fit Idaho, Bryn wasn't sure which was more appropriate.

Dane grabbed his wallet and laid it on the counter. He pulled out his credit card and handed it over, all without moving his prosthetic from around her waist. The teenager ran the card and returned it. He stuffed it into his wallet, shut it, and put it back into his pocket. Then he shuffled them both sideways and leaned up against a wall next to the counter to wait for their food.

"You made that look easy," Bryn commented.

"Made what look easy?"

"The wallet thing."

"It's not brain surgery to get a credit card out, Smalls."

"You didn't think so last night in the bar."

He smiled at her for a moment, then informed her,

"I could've gotten it out of my pocket with no problem."

"Nuh uh. You were drunk."

"I was, but even with my non-dominant hand, it's not that hard, even if it's on the far side of my ass."

"So you were faking it?"

"Smalls, I had the opportunity to have a pretty woman stick her hand down my pants and feel my ass…so yeah, I was faking it."

Bryn was speechless.

"What's going on in that amazing brain of yours?"

"You said I was pretty." The five words tumbled out without thought.

"You are."

"No one in my entire life has ever said I was pretty."

"Bryn, you—"

She had no idea what he was going to say, because an employee called out their order number as he was speaking.

Thankful for the interruption, Bryn stepped away from Dane and grabbed one of the Blizzards and the bag of food. Dane took the other ice cream and they headed toward the exit.

A man stood in front of the door, and, as they got close, his cell phone pealed with an annoying alarm sound.

Bryn felt Dane stiffen next to her, and before she

could do anything, he'd grabbed her around the waist and pulled her forcefully to the side, turning as he moved them so his back was to the man in the doorway and no part of her was exposed to the perceived threat.

It was as if they were invisible to others. No one even noticed what had happened. A woman came up to greet the man in the doorway, and he leaned over and kissed her before following her to a table in the back of the restaurant.

Bryn could feel Dane breathing hard against her. His warm breath wafting over her neck and his chest rising and falling against her back. The cup of ice cream he'd been holding was now lying on the tiles at their feet, melting.

"Don't worry about the mess. We'll get it cleaned up, no worries."

Bryn glanced up and saw one of the teenagers who'd been working behind the counter standing near them, a concerned look on her face.

Ignoring her for a moment, she turned in Dane's arms. At first he wouldn't loosen his grip, holding her to him tightly, but finally he let go. Bryn took one look at the tight, closed-off expression on Dane's face and took charge of the situation.

She turned back to the employee. "Thanks. Sorry about that, we were startled."

"We can replace the Blizzard," the teenager said.

"No, it's okay. We can share this one." Bryn held up the treat she'd managed to keep hold of; luckily it was her fully loaded one. She didn't want to wait for them to make a new dessert. She needed to get Dane out of there. "We're sorry about the mess."

But the young woman had already turned away, probably to get a rag to clean up the spill.

"Come on, Dane. Let's go."

He nodded and swallowed hard, before moving once again to the exit. They didn't say another word, but Bryn could see Dane was on edge. His head swiveled back and forth, checking out the parking lot and the area surrounding the restaurant. They reached the truck and Bryn tucked the bag of food under her arm and held out her hand. "I'll drive."

She thought for a second he was going to refuse, but finally he dropped his key ring onto her palm and took the bag from her, tucking it under his left arm much as she'd done, then took the Blizzard into his right hand. He waited until she'd climbed up. He shut the door with a quick shimmy of his ass and moved around to the other side, getting in without a word.

Bryn moved the seat to where she could comfortably drive and started the truck. The cab was quiet until Dane finally said, "Sorry 'bout that."

Instead of telling him that he had absolutely nothing to be sorry about, somehow knowing he definitely wouldn't agree, she instead said, "A Brownie Batter Blizzard has eleven hundred calories. A cookie dough Blizzard has fifteen hundred calories. I figure with everything in the cup you're holding, I've calculated that it tops out around two thousand. It's good that you're so muscular and buff. The dopamine drop from consuming so many calories and sugar will be less if you help me consume it."

He didn't respond, but sagged into the seat instead of sitting ramrod straight and frantically looked around as they moved down the road.

She kept talking. Telling him random facts about the fat content and how many calories were in popular fast food meals. She moved on to talking about the statistics of how many Americans drove a standard versus an automatic car, and when they were pulling into the small picnic area off of the main road that led into Rathdrum, finished with a one-way discussion of her opinion why more women didn't major in physics or math when they went to college.

Bryn turned off the ignition once she'd pulled into a parking spot at the deserted roadside rest area and looked over at Dane. The lines around his eyes were gone and she could tell he wasn't clenching his teeth anymore.

"I'll come around," he said in a firm voice, not waiting for her response as he grabbed the bag of food and the melting Blizzard and hopped out of the truck.

He came around to her side and opened the door, then stuck out his left elbow, giving her something to hold on to as she awkwardly got out. Once again, she felt the strength in Dane's body as he held rock solid while she used him for leverage and to steady her as she safely got out of the high cab of the truck.

She kept hold of his arm as they headed for the nearest picnic table. She sat and was slightly surprised when he settled in next to her. Bryn wanted to say something, but wasn't sure what. He hadn't seemed overly impressed by her conversation in the truck, and she was pretty much out of ideas.

"I don't know what kind of life you've lived and who you've known, but I'm thinking it's been a bunch of idiots. You're pretty, Smalls. Not just pretty, but beautiful. And you know what makes you that way?"

Bryn shook her head and swallowed hard, emotion climbing up her throat and making it impossible for her to say anything as she realized he was continuing the conversation they'd been having at the restaurant before their food was ready.

"You're sensitive to what people are feeling around you. You don't get embarrassed when people near you do stupid shit. You simply take it in stride and defuse whatever the situation is." Dane paused and reached out for one of her hands. They were in her lap clenched

109

together. He rubbed his thumb over the back of it and finally put it down on her thigh and covered it with his own large hand. "You're small, but your heart and compassion and…being…are bigger than anyone's I've ever met. That's what makes you not just pretty, but absolutely beautiful in my eyes."

Bryn's mouth opened, but nothing came out. She had no idea how to respond to that. None. He went on.

"I'm sorry for saying what I did to you in the grocery store. Seriously. You aren't a freak. *I* am. I have to shop in the middle of the night so I don't lose it. When there's a storm, I have to put on music and listen to it turned up way too high on my headphones. I'll probably go deaf and have to deal with that on top of all my other fucked-up mental issues. And I can't even be in the local Dairy Queen for more than ten minutes without making an absolute ass of myself."

And as if he'd flicked a switch, Bryn found her words. It was much easier to defend him than think about herself. "Bull. So you're a little jumpy. Big deal. Twenty percent of veterans from Iraq and Afghanistan have some sort of post-traumatic stress disorder. That's twenty percent of two-point-seven million people, which is around six hundred thousand veterans. And that's a low estimate." She couldn't read the look on his face, and quickly blurted out, "At least you don't spout random statistics at weird times that no normal person would ever know or *want* to know."

"I like it."

"What?"

"I like it. Believe it or not, it brings me out of whatever funk I'm in. I'm fascinated by what you know, and it's interesting."

Bryn could only gape at Dane. Her? Interesting? No way.

"Anyway, thank you, Smalls. I didn't hurt you?"

She knew what he meant. "No. Not at all."

"All I could think was making sure you weren't in the line of fire."

"You did good. You're so big, I don't think one inch of me was exposed to the guy in the doorway."

"It's not me, it's because you're so little, Smalls."

"I am not," she protested immediately. "You're just Gigantor."

He grinned. And the quirk of his lips was the best thing she'd seen in a really long time. Dane wasn't back to his normal self—whatever that was, she didn't really know him after all—but the twitch of his lips meant he was breaking through whatever hell his mind had gone back to. She'd take it.

He let go of her hand after a small squeeze and reached for the bag of food. "We'd better eat this before it's too cold and the ice cream is too hot. Yeah?"

"Yeah," she agreed.

They chatted about nothing in particular as they inhaled the greasy hamburgers and fries. And when they were finished, they shared the almost completely melted ice cream. Dane even agreed that it was the best Blizzard he'd ever eaten in his life.

When they'd finished, Dane drove them back to town and to the library's parking lot. He unlocked her car for her and stood next to her door, making sure it started all right. Grimacing at her when it took three tries.

Backing away, he nonchalantly said, "See you later, Smalls."

"Later, Dane."

And that was it. She drove away and managed to only look back at him once.

Lying on her couch, watching late-night TV later that evening, Bryn thought over the day and about Dane. It was obvious he was struggling, but it was just as obvious he was a good guy.

She looked down at the open book in her lap and started reading where she'd left off. The information about prosthetics and amputations was fascinating, and she couldn't help but hope, from a purely scientific standpoint of course, that she'd get a chance to examine Dane's stump again, now that she knew a little more about it.

He hadn't indicated that he wanted to see her again.

Didn't tell her he'd call. Didn't ask her out again. But he *had* called her pretty. If she hadn't already been half in love with him, she would've been after sitting with him at a trashy roadside picnic area, talking about nothing, sharing a melted ice cream treat, the word "beautiful" echoing in her brain.

Chapter Seven

"SO TELL ME about Smalls," Truck ordered. "You *have* seen her again, haven't you? That town you live in is tiny."

Dane relaxed back on his couch and smiled as he thought about the woman who'd been on his mind for the last week. He hadn't seen her again, as he'd stayed holed up at his house trying to overcome the nightmares and flashbacks the trip to Dairy Queen had brought about. He felt weak. He shouldn't be so affected by this shit. It was almost as though moving to Idaho had made him worse, rather than better.

"I took her out for dinner," he told his friend, trying to snap out of his morose thoughts.

"Well, fuck me sideways and twice on Sunday," Truck breathed. "You went on a date?"

"I wouldn't exactly call getting takeout at the local Dairy Queen a date."

"It *is* in Rathdrum," his friend returned immediately. "And?"

"And what?" Dane grinned. It was kinda fun mess-ing with Truck.

"Fish," the other man growled impatiently.

"We got food, I let down my guard too much, had a flashback, and we went and ate at a shitty roadside rest area." Dane tried to sound nonchalant about the incident, but knew Truck wouldn't let it slide. That's partly why he'd even mentioned it. He hated seeing the Army shrinks, who always made him feel like they were in a hurry and didn't give a shit about who he was as a person. But talking with another soldier, someone who'd been there when he'd been hurt, and had certainly seen a lot more shit than he ever did when he was deployed, was a whole different thing.

"How'd you let down your guard too much? Is that even a possibility?"

"We were in line, my back was to the door and I was ten seconds from bailing. Then Bryn turned so she was facing me. I saw her eyes go from behind me, to in front of me...assessing the situation. It felt so much like I was back in the desert with a battle buddy at my side, that I relaxed."

"And the flashback?"

Dane took a deep breath. "We were headed for the door and a guy came in. His cell phone went off and the ringtone he had reminded me of the ringing in my ears as I laid under that fucking Humvee, unable to move."

There was silence on the phone line as Dane tried

desperately to keep the vision from taking over his mind. Tried to keep from throwing himself on the floor and covering his head.

"Flashbacks can be a bitch." Truck said in an understanding tone.

"Yeah. I dropped the cup I was holding and grabbed hold of Bryn and spun with her, covering her body with mine to protect her from the shrapnel that I was positive was only moment away from flying through the air."

"What'd she do?"

It took a second for Truck's question to penetrate. When it did, Dane said simply, "Nothing. She stood there in my arms as the guy strolled past us to his family."

"I love her," was Truck's strange response.

"What?" Dane asked in a choked voice. Logically, he knew Truck didn't mean love, as in...*love*, but he unconsciously didn't like the other man even thinking about Bryn like that.

"She didn't panic? Didn't struggle? Didn't lambast you, claiming you embarrassed her? Didn't tell you that you were crazy for your reaction?"

"No. She told the employee we didn't need a replacement ice cream and we left. She even demanded my keys so she could drive."

"Fuck, Dane," Truck said in awe. "I don't know her story, and I'm not saying you should elope with the woman, but she sounds like she's a perfect match for you. I only know a handful of women who would react that way. Not get upset or embarrassed, and who would see that you were in no condition to be driving."

"She's super analytical. Wants to know how everything works. Spits out random facts that I've never even heard of when she gets nervous. She also doesn't have a whole lot of common sense. I don't know if it's a type of autism or what, but she walked back to the bar from my place in the middle of the night. And when I told her that wasn't very smart, she had no clue what I was talking about. It's cute as all fuck, but frustrating as well."

"Sounds like she needs someone like you to keep an eye on her. When are you seeing her again?"

"I don't know. I...I haven't left the house in a week, I'm afraid I'm going to do something else fucked up and hurt someone when I react the wrong way."

"Call her," Truck ordered.

"I don't have her number."

"Pbsst...that's why we have Tex. All it'll take is you telling him her name and he'll have her number in like ten seconds. Seriously, call her. When's the last time you went into a restaurant at dinnertime?"

"Before I lost my hand."

"Exactly," Truck said in a smug tone. "She's good for you, Dane. It sounds to me like you've found the

117

person who was made for you. I think you know it, but you're fighting it."

"Hello, pot, meet kettle," Dane deadpanned.

"*I'm* not fighting shit," Truck said immediately. "I know exactly who I want, and I'm going to do whatever it takes to get her. No matter what."

Dane sighed. He hadn't meant to be an ass. He made a mental note not to say shit about Truck's relationship, if it could be called that, with Mary again. "I don't know, man. I'm still so fucked up in the head."

"How do you thinks *she's* feeling right now?"

"What do you mean?"

"She helped you when you were drunk. You showed up at her place of work and asked her out. You had dinner and now she hasn't seen or heard from you in a week."

"Damn," Dane muttered, realizing Truck was right. He'd seen how surprised and pleased Bryn had been when he'd said she was pretty. It was easy to see that she liked him. *Liked* him. And when he'd left her last week, he hadn't even said he'd be in touch or anything. He just let her drive off without one word of thanks for having his back, for sharing her ice cream, or anything. He was an idiot.

"I'm an idiot."

"Yup. Now, you gonna give me her name so I can call Tex and get her number for you?"

Dane could hear the smile in his friend's voice. "Bryn Hartwell."

"Got it. I'll text it to you within the hour."

"Thanks, Truck. I appreciate it. And I...just thanks."

"You're welcome. As much as this pains me, I won't be able to check in and see how things are going for a while, so don't screw anything up until I get home and can instruct you on how to properly fu—"

"Shut it, asshole." Dane cut off his friend before he could say something that would really piss him off. It bothered him to hear Truck say anything crude in reference to Bryn. "You and the others be careful."

"Always. And Fish?"

"Yeah?"

"Don't be so hard on yourself. There are a lot of veterans out there, and more than that, the majority of civilians are aware of PTSD and what it's done to us."

"Now you sound like Bryn."

"I knew I liked her," Truck said with a laugh. "I'll text you soon with her number and I'll talk to the guys about getting up there when we get back. I expect to meet this amazing woman when we come visit."

"We'll see. Later, Truck."

"Later."

Dane clicked off the phone and sat back in his chair. Maybe it was about time he obtained a library card.

Chapter Eight

BRYN SAT DOWN at the small table in the breakroom in the back corner of the library and opened the book she'd found last week about making bunkers. She'd read it through once already, and found it absolutely fascinating. She knew there were people in the world who thought the breakdown of society was imminent, but she hadn't known how extensive their preparations could be.

Stockpiling guns, building underground bunkers, buying property that had a water source that wasn't hooked up to any city facility...it was all very interesting, and she really, *really* wanted to talk to someone who was prepping for the end of society and get a tour of a real-live bunker.

But more pressing at the moment was the thought that whoever had last checked out the book on bunkers, had *also* taken out the book on how to use fertilizer in a bomb. She'd looked up the person who'd done so. John Smith.

If that wasn't a made-up name, Bryn would be surprised. But there was an address on the library card application form. She had no idea if it was legit or not, but had decided to at least research it. On the satellite images she'd checked out on the Internet, it looked like a house on the outskirts of Rathdrum, but she had no idea if the mysterious John Smith actually lived there—he could've made up the address to go with the fake name—or if there was a bunker being built on the property. The thoughts of the bunker were what really made her want to go.

When she was little, her parents had had her checked by all sorts of medical doctors. Then when her high IQ was discovered, she was constantly tested to see exactly how smart she was. She'd been poked, prodded, and analyzed by so many people…all she'd wanted was to be left alone. It was one of the reasons she'd chosen to live in Rathdrum. There weren't a lot of people.

Something about the prepper lifestyle called to that side of her. Being by herself, living off the grid, with no need to go to the store and deal with people. No need to pay bills. She'd miss the Internet and being able to look up information whenever she wanted, but being able to disappear appealed. Big time.

The itch between her shoulder blades was getting stronger each day. She *needed* to see a real-live prepper bunker. Needed to see if the image in her head was a fantasy, or if she could actually live cut off from society as preppers did. Or at least how they were planning to if the need arose.

Her parents had never understood her extreme curiosity, telling her more than once that it would get her into trouble someday, but Bryn had merely shrugged when they'd tried to curb it. How else would she learn anything?

"Hi."

Bryn jumped in her chair and whirled around to see Dane standing in the doorway of the breakroom. She put one hand on her chest and said breathlessly, "I didn't hear the door open."

"Obviously. And I'm sorry, I didn't mean to scare you. What are you looking at so intently?"

She smiled up at him. "A book on how to make a bunker."

"A bunker?"

"Yeah, one of those underground homes where if society shuts down and everyone turns on each other, you can go and live in it and no one will know you're there. Did you know that people have built these things to sustain them for years at a time? They can get fresh water, grow their own food, and literally disappear from the world without a trace. It's so cool."

While she'd been talking, Dane had settled himself into a chair next to her. Not across from her, next to her. *Right* next to her. He leaned over and used his index finger to turn the book around so he could see what she was looking at.

"I did know. Reading about how to get fresh air in there, huh?"

Bryn nodded, trying to push back the disappointed thoughts she'd had all week that she hadn't heard from Dane since their dinner picnic. "Sometimes people just use a simple tube, but the extreme preppers build an exhaust system involving fans, and make sure they have several different intake and exhaust ports, just in case one gets compromised."

"What else?"

Bryn eyed Dane. She couldn't tell if he was making fun of her or if he really wanted to know what she'd learned. He looked good today. His left arm was in his lap, but she'd noticed he had on his prosthetic. He was also wearing the boots she'd always seen him in, a pair of jeans, a white long-sleeve shirt, and his ever-present leather jacket. The smell of leather would remind her of him forever.

She looked down at the book lying in front of her and bit her lip. She was wearing jeans today as well, and she'd paired them with a navy-blue Rathdrum Public Library T-shirt and was still wearing the apron she used when she stocked the shelves to keep herself from getting too dirty. It was very big on her, but she hadn't cared before today. On her feet were her usual sneakers.

Bryn knew her hair was probably a mess. She'd pulled it back into a ponytail when she'd left the house, but it was probably coming loose by now. She so wasn't in his league. Not even close. She might be clueless about a lot of things, but growing up the way she had, she'd quickly learned that she was an outcast and just didn't fit in with the other pretty, well-liked kids.

"Well, um, there are around three million Americans who fall into the category of preppers. People who are making detailed plans on how to survive when the world as we know it ends. That's only around one percent, but still, I was surprised at how high the number was. There's a really popular website run by a former US Army Intelligence Officer. He says that the government isn't going to be able to care for everyone if anything bad happens, so people should prepare now to watch over themselves."

Bryn thought of something for the first time. "You were in the military, right? What do you think?"

Instead of answering, Dane picked up her ponytail, which had been lying along her back, and ran it through his fingers before bringing it to his face and smelling it.

"Dane?"

"Yeah, Smalls?"

"What are you doing?"

"Smelling your hair."

"I see that, but why?"

"Because it smells good. And it's been a week since I've smelled the beach. As for what I think about preparing for the end of the world…I believe it's a good idea to be ready for emergencies. You've seen where I live, it's not too far from Rathdrum, but it's also a few miles out. There's a stream on my property, where I can get water if I need it, I have about a month's worth of food in my pantry, just in case, and I have a gas-powered generator for power. If you're asking if I have a bunker buried on my property, the answer is no."

"Darn."

He smiled at her and put his elbow on the table and leaned on it. "You want to see a bunker, Smalls?"

She nodded. "I thought maybe you might know someone."

"I don't. But I can see what I could find out for you."

"Really?"

"Really. On one condition."

"Anything."

His grin widened at that, but he stayed silent.

"What? Dane?"

"You should be careful who you tell you'll do anything for. They might get the wrong idea."

"About what?"

He straightened and slowly brought his hand toward her face. He smoothed a stray piece of hair that had been hanging in her face, behind her ear. Bryn shivered at his touch and swayed toward him. God, it had been so long since she'd been touched. It wasn't until this moment that she realized how little contact she had with other people.

"Dinner. At my house."

She blinked at Dane. "What?"

"Dinner at my house. I'll find out if I can hook you up with anyone near here who has a bunker, if you'll come over for dinner. But you have to promise to only meet with him, or her, if I'm with you."

"Why?"

"Because some of these guys are paranoid and a little crazy. Many are veterans who haven't dealt well with reintegrating into society, and their answer has been to wall themselves off from everyone. They have extreme opinions about the government, and even about the role women should play in society. There are also men out there who say they're preppers, but in reality, they're extremists. Either planning against modern society, or working with one of the many terrorist groups in the world. I know you've heard of Ted Kaczynski. The bottom line is that it's simply not safe, Bryn."

"But I only want to see how they've built their bunkers," Bryn protested, furrowing her brows.

Dane put his arm on the back of her chair and leaned into her. "You can't just go tromping out into the wilderness looking for bunkers. The last thing I want is for you to run into some asshole who thinks the government's rules don't apply to him. I researched preppers before I moved here. I wanted to make sure I knew what I was getting into when I decided to live in Idaho. Preppers don't trust anyone, and they're not stupid either. Through my contacts and research, I found out there's a group nearby who say they're in the lifestyle, but no one believes them. They're bad news...and they're out there. The last thing I want is you stumbling across these guys."

"I'm no threat to them."

"Smalls, *everyone* is a threat to them. And it's not just these mysterious bad guys. Think about preppers and their lifestyle. They spend their lives preparing for mass chaos. If you haven't eaten in a week and are starving, what do you think you'd do if you found out someone had months' worth of food hoarded away? What if you were dying of thirst and you stumbled onto a property that had fresh, clean water gurgling away? These guys, and sometimes women too, will protect what they have with deadly force. It's exactly what they're getting ready for. So if they agree to show you their bunker, and that's a big if, you'll not only see what they've done to prepare it's also possible you might be able to find it again, or that you'll tell someone else what you've seen. It's a huge risk for them."

"I hadn't thought of it like that," Bryn said.

"Exactly. So if it's possible, I'll set it up and go with you."

"But wouldn't that just mean *two* people would now know all about their setup?"

Dane looked serious for a moment before agreeing. "Yeah."

"And wouldn't that mean you'd be in danger too?"

He nodded again. "Yeah, probably."

"And wouldn't *you* be more of a threat since you're a guy? I mean, you aren't exactly Mr. Nerd who sits in front of a computer screen all day. You're big, built, and former military. I would think, if you're right, and I'm sure you are, that you'd be more of a threat, and the guy wouldn't want you anywhere near wherever his hidden bunker might be, and—Why are you smiling? I don't understand."

Bryn frowned at Dane. He'd been so serious, but as she'd spoken, his lips had curled up until he'd been almost laughing at her.

"Don't laugh at me," she said in a quiet voice, looking down at the table.

She felt his finger under her chin and raised her eyes back to his as he lifted her face toward him.

"I'm not laughing at you, Bryn. I'm merely amazed at how smart you are. To answer your question, yeah, I'd probably be a huge threat to a prepper. But I'm not going to put an ad in the paper. I know a few guys who can help me find someone who's trustworthy…at least more so than a lot of other preppers. Regardless, it's still a risk."

He dropped his finger from her face and Bryn sighed at the loss. "Okay."

"Now, dinner?"

Bryn nodded.

"Good. Want to go shopping with me?"

"I can do it…if you wanted."

"I appreciate that, but I need to stop hiding in my house and get out there more."

Bryn shook her head. "It's not your fault, it's—"

He interrupted her before she could finish her sentence. "How about if you meet me there around seven."

"Tonight?"

"No time like the present. I hope you aren't opposed to a late meal?"

"No, I think I told you before, I don't sleep much. I usually end up snacking until late."

Dane eyed her for a moment without speaking.

"What?" He made her feel off-kilter, and since she wasn't all that skilled at reading people, she felt like she was constantly questioning him about what he was thinking.

"I'm looking forward to getting to know you."

Bryn shrugged. "I'm just me. Nobody special."

"Now that, I don't believe. Seven at the grocery store, right? I'll wait in my truck for you, if that's okay."

"Of course."

"I'll park in the back of the lot. Just pull up near me and I'll see you."

"Okay."

Dane stood and Bryn looked up at him. Way up at him. Before she could say something she'd regret, he leaned over and put his good hand behind her head. He held her still as he kissed her forehead, then backed off. "See you later, Smalls."

Bryn stayed silent as Dane left the room as quietly as he'd entered. Her mind was racing, trying to understand what in the world had just happened. She hadn't heard from Dane in over a week, and she'd convinced herself that he wanted nothing to do with her...again. Then in the space of—she looked down at her watch—fifteen minutes, he'd not only promised to help her find out more information about bunkers, but he'd invited her to shop with him and eat another meal...at his house.

It was surreal, but the warm feeling in her chest felt good. Bryn shut the book in front of her and stood. As much as she wanted to sit and bask in the happiness she was feeling, she had to get back to work.

As she stocked books the rest of the afternoon, questions she wanted to ask Dane raced through her head. There was so much she'd like to know about him, his missing hand, his time in the military, why he'd picked Rathdrum to live, if he had a family, what he did for a living and, most importantly, what had changed his mind about her.

Smiling as she left work at five, Bryn knew the next two hours would drag by. She couldn't wait to spend time with Dane. She had no idea why he was spending time with *her*, but she was going to try to enjoy it while it lasted.

And she knew it wouldn't last. It never did. Anytime a man seemed interested, it was inevitable that he'd get frustrated with her. She wasn't like most people, but for tonight, at least, Bryn wanted to pretend that she was.

Chapter Nine

BRYN PULLED INTO the grocery store parking lot at exactly seven that night. She'd spent most of the time between when she got home a little after five and before she left trying to decide what to wear. She didn't have a huge wardrobe to choose from, and finally settled on a pair of black jeans and a white blouse she hadn't worn in ages. It was a silky camisole covered by a wispy overlay of lace flowers. It wasn't something she wore often, but she wanted to look more feminine for the first time in a long while.

She didn't own a pair of heels, and resigned herself to wearing her usual sneakers, but hoped the effort she put into choosing her shirt would counteract the lame shoes.

Pulling into the space next to Dane's green pickup, she realized he'd obviously seen her car enter the lot and was standing in front of his truck waiting for her. She got out and pocketed her keys, suddenly shy.

"Hi."

"Hi. You look nice."

"My shoes don't match my outfit." Bryn wanted to smack herself in the forehead for bringing attention to her footwear, but since she'd already been thinking about how they didn't go with her shirt, it was inevitable that it popped out.

"They're fine. Smalls, you live in Idaho, not New York City. I'd be shocked if you were wearing heels. But you probably do need to get a pair of sturdy boots. They're good for rain, snow, mud, or just for looking badass."

Bryn laughed. "I don't think I could look badass if I tried."

Dane stepped closer and picked up her hand and started walking toward the front door of the building. "That's what you've got me for."

Bryn almost tripped over her feet. It was only the strong grip Dane had on her hand that kept her from falling flat on her face. Had him? What was he talking about? Before she could ask, they approached the door—and she gasped.

To the side of the automatic sliding doors was a man sitting on the ground. He had a small, scruffy dog with him and a cardboard sign that said: *Homeless Veteran. Spare some change?*

Bryn couldn't take her eyes off the man. He had a long beard and was wearing a red beanie pulled low on his forehead. It was obvious he had on several layers of clothes, all of which looked dirty and ripped. His legs were crossed and he kept hold of a short leash with one hand and held the sign with the other. He looked up at them hopefully as they neared.

"Spare some change? I'm hungry, but I'm trying to feed Muppet here before I eat anything. He hasn't eaten in two days."

Bryn's hand immediately went to her pocket. She always threw a handful of coins into her pockets before she left the house. It was a habit left over from when she was young and her mother had told her to always carry change for a pay phone, "just in case." She had no idea what that meant, but it was a habit she'd started and hadn't ever been able to break.

She pulled it all out and let go of Dane's hand to walk over to the man and his dog. She leaned over and dropped it into the cup in front of the man. "I'm sorry it's not more this time." Bryn petted the extremely friendly dog, who tried to jump on her as she got close. She immediately backed away from him, closer to Dane. She felt him grab hold of her hand again as they went toward the entrance.

Finally, when they were inside, she looked up at him. "I can't stand to see our veterans treated so badly. And his poor dog." Bryn shook her head sadly. "I'm such a sucker for homeless people. I feel guilty that I have a safe, warm place to sleep and they don't."

Dane stopped in front of the carts and turned to face her. "Smalls, Oliver isn't homeless."

She looked up at him in shock. "Yes, he is," she protested. "Why else would he be sitting out there with his poor dog, begging for a few coins?"

Dane smiled, but it didn't reach his eyes. He brought his hand up and brushed her hair behind her ear as he'd done earlier that day in the library. "How many times have you given him money?"

"Every time I've seen him. I feel so bad. He put his life on the line for our country and now doesn't have anywhere to live. It's a disgrace, and it's up to people like us, who he spent part of his life protecting, to help him out now."

Dane put his hands on her shoulders and leaned close to her. "I agree with you that homeless veterans are a societal problem that the government is still working on, but Smalls, I'm telling you straight up, that man is neither a veteran *nor* homeless."

Bryn looked up at Dane in shock, wondering if she'd been completely wrong about the kind of person he was. "Yes, he *is*," she repeated forcefully. "I saw him yesterday outside the library, and earlier this week he was at the gas station. He has that camo jacket with all those patches on it that show his unit."

"He lives a block from here. I saw him at Smokey's Bar the other week, before I got drunk. He was talking with the waitress and they were making plans to get together later…at *his* place. Apparently he was using the money he'd panhandled to buy booze. He was already mostly shit-faced, and was bragging to the waitress about how much he makes by impersonating a veteran and how, since he'd adopted the dog, he was getting twice as much."

Bryn could only stare at Dane in horror. "He's lying?"

Dane's lips quirked, but he didn't smile. "Yeah, Smalls. He's lying."

"His name is Oliver?"

"Yeah. I heard him introduce himself to the waitress. Does it matter?"

"No, I guess not. But the name 'Oliver' doesn't exactly scream con artist."

Dane didn't say a word, just stared at her with a compassionate look on his face and his eyebrows raised.

Bryn didn't think, she simply leaned forward and put her head on Dane's chest, letting her arms dangle at her sides. "I'm an idiot."

"No, you're not," Dane reassured her, running his hand from her head to the middle of her back then up again. His other arm went around her waist to pull her closer.

Bryn brought her hands up and rested them hesitantly on his waist and looked up at him. "I literally can't walk by any homeless people without giving them some money. I feel so awful that they don't have a safe or warm place to sleep that I feel obligated to do what I can for them. I'm fortunate in so many ways, and it hurts to think about what they might be going through. When I lived in Seattle, I had to start taking the bus to my job because there were so many lined up on the route I normally walked to work."

"It's not a bad thing that you're tenderhearted."

"They aren't all lying, are they?"

"No, Smalls. You just have to learn better ways to help them out, other than giving them your money."

"How?"

"How about we talk about it later. Can we get this shopping thing done first?"

At that, Bryn straightened up and took a step away from Dane. "Of course. Sorry! Yes, come on. You don't like it here, so we have to get what we need and get out of here."

"Hang on a sec, Bryn."

She shivered at her name on his lips. He usually called her Smalls, which she loved, but there was something about her name said in his deep, sexy voice that made her want to do whatever it was he asked of her. "Yeah?"

"Thank you."

"For what?"

"For your support of veterans. For caring about them…us. It means a lot."

She leaned forward and wrapped her arms around Dane without thought. Her head barely reached his chin, but she held on tightly for just a moment, then pulled back. "You're welcome. Now come on. What are you making me for dinner?"

THE TRIP THROUGH the store was relatively quick and Dane was thankful for Bryn's presence as they made their way up and down the aisles. He probably could've handled it without her, but watching her do her best to make *him* feel at ease was one hell of a distraction.

She positioned herself on his left side and wrapped her arm around his. He hadn't worn his prosthetic, deciding that Bryn had seen his stump more than once anyway, and hopefully they'd be back at his house before too long. She didn't seem to care at all that he hadn't worn it either.

As they went through the store, she kept up a steady stream of conversation, keeping his mind on what she was saying rather than who else was in the aisles with them. Bryn couldn't reach the groceries on the upper shelves, and grumped and bitched about the layout of the items. Even though she'd only worked there for a short time, she'd obviously taken pride in making sure the layout was "shopper friendly," and the changes that had been made after she left weren't sitting well with her.

She chose the checkout line with the most people, telling him that since there were more people in line, it would mean there would be fewer behind them. When someone did get in their line, Bryn hadn't said anything, just shifted until she was facing his side and could keep her eye on them.

Shopping with her was an amazing experience. From watching her mumble about the number of carbohydrates that were in the dish he was buying the supplies to make for her, to seeing her run interference with other shoppers for him, to the satisfaction deep down that she was doing everything she could to make him more comfortable in the crowded store…it all added up to a sensation of contentment and satisfaction that Dane hadn't ever felt before.

The kicker was that he somehow knew if he pointed it out to her, she'd deflect, saying it wasn't a big deal, or that she was doing it to make her own life easier. Not once had she even mentioned his missing hand or acted like it in any way repulsed her. He had no idea how he'd managed to get so lucky, but Dane had a sudden epiphany that he needed to do whatever it took to make sure Bryn didn't slip through his fingers.

"Thank you."

She looked up at him as they walked back through the parking lot with the groceries. "For what?"

"For not treating me differently. For having my back. For agreeing to come over for dinner. For all of it."

She looked confused, but nodded anyway.

Dane clicked the locks on his truck and they put the bags on the floor of the backseat. He shut the door and turned to Bryn once more. "Ride with me?"

She bit her lip and looked away from him.

"What's going on in that head of yours?" Dane asked.

"It's not that I don't want to, but it's not logical. My apartment is that way," she pointed back into town, "and your house is that way," she pointed the other direction, "so you driving me now means that when we're done eating, you'll have to bring me back here so I can get my car and go home. It makes more sense for me to take my car to your place so when we're done, only one of us needs to make the trip back into town."

Dane smiled. He'd never get tired of how her brain worked. "Smalls, it's not *that* far. Besides, if you drove your car, I'd follow you back into town anyway, so you'd be saving gas if you let me drive us both now."

"Why would you do that? Now that *really* isn't logical."

Dane leaned into her and slid his hand behind the nape of her neck and said, "Because I wouldn't be much of a man if I let you drive home in the dark in that piece of crap and didn't make sure you got home safely. It's my responsibility to make sure nothing happens to you."

She looked confused. "I'm not your responsibility, Dane. I'm an adult. As you said, it's not that far from your place to town, and I've been taking care of myself for a long time now. I don't understand."

He licked his lips and leaned into her before answering. "I like you, Bryn Hartwell. I'd like the opportunity to talk to you for several hours tonight. It's going to be late when you leave. I'm not comfortable sending you off into the dark night by yourself. You could get a flat tire, or your transmission could die. A serial killer could be waiting for a lone woman driving on the back roads of Idaho to kidnap and bring to his lair deep in the mountains." When she opened her mouth to speak, he quickly continued, not giving her the chance.

"I know, it's illogical and the odds are extremely low of it occurring. But I wouldn't be able to live with myself if anything happened to you when you were leaving my house." He shrugged. "Call it a weird Dane quirk. Or a result of being a soldier. I don't care. But it is what it is. Now...do you want to ride with me or drive your car to my place?"

"If I promised to call when I got home, would you let me drive and not follow me home?"

Dane shook his head, but stayed silent.

She sighed hugely and pursed her lips, mumbling, "I don't understand you." Then she raised her voice, and her eyes went back to his. "I'll go with you."

Dane leaned forward and brushed his lips over her forehead. "Thank you, Smalls."

Neither of them said another word as he helped her into the passenger side of his truck then walked around the front to the driver's side. They stayed silent as he drove down the winding roads to his house. It was a comfortable silence, however, and Dane smiled to himself. He loved how comfortable he felt with Bryn and couldn't wait to learn more about her. Tonight would change their relationship from almost strangers to hopefully something more.

Dane knew he had to go slowly with Bryn. In some ways, she was like an untried virgin, and in others she was an old soul. It was a fascinating contradiction and he was excited to learn what made her tick and what her hopes and dreams were.

For the first time in a long while, he wasn't worrying about his missing hand and what a woman might think about it…he was wholly focused on learning as much as he could about Bryn, and when he could convince her to see him again.

Chapter Ten

"THERE WAS A Roman general who lost his hand in one of the Punic Wars and had a new one made out of iron. He did it so he could hold his shield and returned to battle to continue fighting. About fifteen years ago, researchers in Cairo unearthed what they think is the oldest documented prosthetic. It's a toe made out of leather and wood. And believe it or not, it was found on the three-thousand-year-old foot of a mummy believed to have been a noblewoman."

"Really?" Dane murmured the word, knowing Bryn was too lost in her recollections of ancient prosthetics to really hear him.

"Yeah. It's amazing how little prosthetic limbs have advanced over the years. I mean, doctors are still using leather to hold them to people's bodies. And in the Dark Ages, two thousand years after the age of that Egyptian woman with the missing toe and the Roman general, the knights were using metal limbs made by the same people who made their armor and weapons.

"Oh, then the pirates came along. Everyone knows

about their hooks and peg legs. The first major break in the design of functional arms and legs wasn't until the sixteenth century. A French doctor…shoot, I can't remember his name, I'll get back to you on that, anyway, he was the first person to make a hinged mechanized hand.

"Did you know that the National Academy of Sciences established the Artificial Limb Program in 1945 because of how many veterans there were who came home from World War Two with a missing limb? Their purpose was to try to make advances in what they're made of, how they work, and surgical techniques to make it easier for the person to use a prosthetic when the limb was removed."

They were sitting on the couch after eating the chicken parmesan Dane had made for dinner. They'd been talking as if they'd known each other for years rather than only a week or so. Dane had thought for a moment that Bryn would be reluctant to open up to him, to talk about herself, but he'd been completely wrong.

It was as if she had no concept of what might be the socially right or wrong thing to say on what was basically a first date. They'd talked about all the normal things two people getting to know each other would discuss, things like family, jobs, and when and why they'd moved to Idaho, but the conversation had eventually taken an odd turn...but Dane didn't mind.

He'd known she was fascinated by his stump and prosthetic, but hadn't known exactly how much. When, at her request, he'd shown her the prosthetic he was currently using, she'd gone off on her most recent soliloquy.

"Does your arm still hurt? Do you feel phantom pains? I think that would be weird, to have your hand hurt and look down and realize that it's not even there. I mean, how does that work, anyway? And you said that your friend had your brachial artery clamped in his fingers and that's how you didn't bleed out? How could he walk and do that? Did it hurt? Duh, of course it did. Your prosthetic is pretty good, even though it's essentially just a step up from a pirate hook, but I bet you could get on a list to get a bionic one with all the bells and whistles, so to speak. Those companies are suckers for a good veteran story...and you're good looking to boot, so they'd love to show you off, I'm sure."

When she paused to take a breath, Dane quickly interjected, "It truly doesn't bother you that I'm missing part of my arm, does it?"

She looked at him in confusion. "No. Why would it?"

There were a hundred and one reasons that Dane could think of why it would bother her, but if she didn't already know them, he wasn't going to inform her of

SUSAN STOKER

any. "Come here."

"Where?"

Dane grinned and put his arm on the back of the couch and gestured to his side with his other hand. "Here."

"Why?"

Dane couldn't deny that her questions amused him. He wouldn't have to worry about her keeping her thoughts to herself like a lot of other women did. When she had a question, she asked it. No beating around the bush or hiding what she was feeling or thinking.

"Because I'm tired and I'd like to hold you while we talk…unless it would make you feel uncomfortable."

She considered his words for a moment then asked, "Is this a prelude to making out and us having sex?"

Dane nearly choked, but kept his composure, barely. "Tonight? No. I'm simply enjoying your company and would like to have you closer while we continue to get to know each other."

"So not tonight, but maybe later?"

"Yeah, Smalls. If you think you might want to."

Bryn cocked her head and thought about his answer before saying, "Yeah, I think I might like that."

"Then come 'ere."

Relaxing when she moved the few feet over on the couch and settled against him, Dane answered her questions. "I sometimes feel phantom pains. It *is* a bit weird to hurt and look down and realize it's all in my head. I have no idea how it works though, sorry. And yeah, Truck saw that I was bleeding out and stuck his fingers right inside the mangle that was my arm and held my artery together until we got someplace safer. A lot of the details about that day are hazy, but I can honestly say, I have no idea how he kept hold of me while we walked. And I'm not sure I want to be someone's poster child for missing an arm. While I might like a more responsive prosthetic, I've found that it's more comfortable to simply go without it."

"Wow."

"Wow, what?"

"I can't believe you remembered everything I asked," Bryn told him, relaxing into his side even more.

"You're not the only smarty-pants around here, Smalls."

She giggled then slowly moved her arm around his stomach, as if afraid he'd complain.

Dane rested his stump over her arm around him and laid his head back on the couch. "I've always been pretty good at remembering things. I'm not a genius, like you, but if someone says it, I tend to be able to recall it."

"Cool." Bryn paused, but then said, "I'll look up the thing about phantom pains and get back to you."

Dane picked his head up off the couch and leaned over to kiss the top of hers. "Thanks." After a moment of silence, he asked, "Want to watch TV?"

Bryn shrugged. "If you do."

"What do you usually do when you get home from work?" Several moments went by, and when she didn't answer, Dane asked, "Bryn?"

"You were right, you know," she said weirdly instead of answering his question.

"About what?"

"I'm a freak."

Dane felt his heart sink. He knew what he'd said would come back to haunt him. "I didn't mean—"

"No, it's okay. I am. I'm old enough to know it by now. It shouldn't really bother me anymore."

"But it does," Dane said knowingly.

She shrugged. "I eat dinner. Then I'll look through any interesting books I picked up at the library that day. That could take twenty minutes, or three hours, it all depends how into them I am. Then if I have more questions, I'll research whatever I've been reading on the Internet. Sometimes I get lost in what I'm doing and realize it's past midnight."

Dane realized she was answering his question about what she did after work, and didn't interrupt, but tightened his hold on her, hugging her to him as she continued.

"If nothing interests me at the library, I'll do cross-words. Or I'll look at the most recent dissertations posted online at the ProQuest library and decide if I think the research was flawed in some way. Sometimes I'll email the author and tell him or her what I thought. Every now and then I'll get into a good discussion with one of the approving professors about the research. I told you before, I don't need a lot of sleep. My parents had me tested when I was little and it was decided that my brain just never shuts down. That, and I have a mutated hDEC2 gene in my DNA, which has been proven to exist in people who can function on less sleep than the normal population."

"Cool," Dane told her honestly.

Bryn's head came up at that. "Cool?"

"Yeah. Do you know how much that would've come in handy when I was in the Army? There were so many nights I was on duty that I struggled to stay awake."

"You're just trying to make me feel better for being weird," Bryn grumbled.

"A little, but, Smalls, you amaze me. So you're smart? BFD."

"BFD?" she asked with a frown.

"Good to know I can still teach you some things," Dane teased. "Big fuckin' deal. BFD."

She giggled, and he felt his stomach clench that he'd been able to make her smile when she'd felt so bad.

"I think it's awesome that you know so much. My friend, Truck, would love hanging out with you."

"I want to meet him," Bryn demanded, settling back against Dane. "I want to thank him."

"He wants to meet you too. He said that he was going to make a trip up here with some of the other guys he works with. My friends."

"Great." Her voice was low and unsure.

"What's wrong?" Dane asked, immediately seeing her unease.

"I don't usually get along with people. And I'm afraid they'll act like you did in the store. I always say the wrong thing, I'm too smart, and I don't want to make you look bad."

"Smalls, if anything, *I'm* gonna be the one who looks bad. They're gonna love you. In fact, if I'm not careful, they'll try to steal you away right from under my nose. As far as being smart goes, you think I want to date someone who doesn't know how many ounces are in a gallon?"

"One hundred and twenty-eight."

"Exactly." Dane reached up and gently removed the elastic holding Bryn's hair in a ponytail. He carefully ran his fingers through it until there were no tangles, then he continued to caress her, loving the scent of coconut that came from her hair. "Bryn, how smart you are has nothing to do with what kind of person you are. For instance, I've known a lot of really smart terrorists...men who would shoot me or the guys in my platoon on sight without hesitation. Or who take pleasure in coming up with different ways to torture soldiers. On the other hand, I've known a few dumb people who were the nicest human beings I've ever met. What I care about, and what I like about you, is that you're generous, you care about people and animals, and you go out of your way to help others, even if they're assholes to you."

"Most people don't agree," Bryn mumbled into his chest.

"Then *they're* the weirdos, Smalls, not you. Look at me." Dane waited until she lifted her head and met his eyes. "I'm the one in this relationship who should be worried. You're so out of my league it's not even funny. I'm a medically retired soldier who only earned an Associate degree because it would look good on paper for the promotion board. I'm scarred and missing a hand. I can't function well out in public, although I'm working on it. My friends are a group of soldiers who are so super-secret, I couldn't even tell you where they are right this second. I spent most of the money I saved while deployed to buy this house and I have no idea what I want to do with the rest of my life. But I'll tell you something. I've never wanted someone to overlook all of that and see *me* more than I want you to."

"Dane..."

"Don't feel bad for what you like to do, Smalls.

Don't let anyone else make you feel bad about it either. Do what feels right and good and to hell with everyone else. Truck and my friends are gonna love you. I've already told him all about you, so I'm not just talking out my ass here. Yeah?"

"How do you seem to know just what to say to make me feel normal?"

"I'm just callin' it like I see it."

Bryn put her head back on Dane's chest and squeezed him around the middle. "What do *you* like to watch at night?"

"I'm partial to documentaries...oh, and *Mythbusters*."

"*Mythbusters?*"

"You haven't heard of the antics of Jamie and Adam?"

"No."

"Settle in, sweetheart. You're in for a treat. Although I have no doubt you'll already know most of the science involved."

"There's science on the show?"

"Yeah, Smalls. There's a *ton* of science. It's what drives the entire show."

Hours later, Dane woke up. Bryn was lying on his chest sound asleep. They'd shifted on the couch until they were both lying down. Bryn's legs were tangled with his and her head was lying on his shoulder. One hand was resting over his heart and the other was scrunched up under her body. His arm was hooked over her hip and his good hand was resting over hers on his chest.

He'd nodded off sometime in the middle of the second *Mythbusters* show, and he could see the TV was now turned off.

Bryn hadn't left in the middle of the night. She'd turned off the television and made the decision to stay right where she was.

Dane wasn't a man who believed in love at first sight, but he cared more for the woman lying so still and peaceful on his chest than he had for anyone in his entire life.

He made a vow right then and there to be the kind of man she'd be proud to stand beside. The kind of man she could rely on to stand next to her, not behind or in front of her. She made him feel like nothing was impossible, even for a disabled former soldier with very little formal education, like himself. She was a miracle. *His* miracle.

Chapter Eleven

ONE DAY THE following week, Bryn woke up at her usual five-thirty and immediately reached for her phone. Scooting until her back rested against her headboard, she dialed Dane's number. She'd told him she would research why phantom pains occurred and how they worked, and she had. All week. She'd even finagled a phone call with a doctor who specialized in the rehabilitation of adults who had lost a limb as a result of trauma or disease. The doctor worked at the Rehabilitation Institute of Chicago in their amputation and limb deficiency department.

Personally, Bryn thought it was an awful name for a department, but what did she know? Doctor Soriano explained that phantom pain used to be thought of as a psychological issue that stemmed from the person not coming to terms with the loss of a body part, but she further explained that through research it was now recognized as a sensation coming from the spinal cord and brain. She went on to describe the symptoms, causes, which weren't hard to figure out, and treatments.

Bryn had gone to sleep thinking about Dane and what he might be experiencing and had woken up after having dreamed about him. Not thinking about the time, only talking to Dane about what she'd found out, she dialed his number.

"Hello?"

"Hey, Dane, it's Bryn. I talked to Doctor Rachna Soriano at the Rehabilitation Institute of Chicago, which is the number one rehabilitation hospital in the entire country when it comes to amputations. Anyway, she said that the phantom pain you have in your hand is normal, that most people who've lost an arm, leg, hand, foot, even sometimes their tongue or penis—can you imagine needing to have your tongue removed and what that must be like? Yuck. Anyway, most people who've lost a limb or whatever sometimes feel like it's still there, and the pain part is only felt by people who had a limb, but lost it. It doesn't happen with those who were born without an arm or foot or whatever. I mean, that makes sense…if the brain didn't know it was there in the first place it couldn't really send signals to the brain that it *was*.

"Anyway, some people have continuous pain, which would suck. At least you only have it now and then. And it sounds like your pain is actually good…well, not good, 'cause any kind of pain sucks, but you said your hand just throbs sometimes, but others say their pain is like, stabbing or burning pain. Ugh. I can't imagine! Sometimes stress can bring it about. Are you stressed? You shouldn't be. I mean, you need to work on that if you are. I hate that you're in pain."

"Bryn?"

She ignored him, and continued on excitedly. "The coolest thing is that she said the brain can actually remap itself to another part of the body. So since your hand can't send signals back to your brain, the information is referred somewhere else...like to your chest. So when you touch your chest, it can wig your brain out because it knows you're touching your chest, but it's also like your missing hand is being touched. And it can result in pain because your sensory wires are crossed. Of course, phantom pain can also be caused by other, not as interesting reasons, like damaged nerve endings in your stump or scar tissue there."

"What time is it?"

Dane's question startled Bryn for a moment, but she glanced at her clock beside her table. "Five thirty-nine. Why?"

"Do you always get up this early?"

"Yeah."

"I don't. Not anymore."

"Oh." Bryn bit her lip. "Were you sleeping?"

"Yeah."

Bryn didn't say anything for a moment, then ventured to ask, "But you're not anymore...right?"

He chuckled, then confirmed, "No."

"Right. So treatments. You can either try drugs, or something more non-evasive like acupuncture, or something called TENS, transcutaneous electrical nerve stimulation. The doctor discussed the kinds of drugs some of her patients take, and I don't really think any of them sound very fun. Things like antidepressants, which would modify the chemical messengers that make you think your hand hurts, or anticonvulsants...they quiet the damaged nerves. Some people also take narcotics like morphine, but I really don't think that would be good for you. And besides, I don't like the thought of you being drugged to the gills. The most interesting treatment she told me about is something called a mirror box. And I think I can set one up at your house without too many issues. I mean, it's just a bunch of mirrors, but essentially you'd put your right hand in one side and stick your stump in the other. The mirrors make it look like you have *both* hands in the box. You then do exercises with your right hand and watch it in the mirror, thinking that it's your missing hand doing them. It sounds ridiculous, believe me, I laughed when Dr. Soriano told me about it, but she said it really does help with the pain. There's so many other—"

"What time did you go to sleep?"

Bryn frowned at the interruption. "Around three I think. Why?"

"You want breakfast?"

"Breakfast?"

"Yeah. The meal most people eat when they get up in the morning."

"I know what breakfast is, Dane. And yeah, I want breakfast. I'll make it when I'm done talking to you."

"You want company?"

"For breakfast?"

"Yeah, Smalls. For breakfast. You want me to come over and share breakfast with you?"

"But you saw me last night."

Bryn heard Dane chuckle. The sound went right through her, making her shiver. She'd seen Dane almost every day since he'd made her dinner. One time he'd brought lunch to the library and they'd shared it in the breakroom, his back to the wall and facing the door. Another evening he met her at the library—refusing to let her give twenty bucks to Oliver, who'd set up shop outside in the parking lot, probably waiting for Bryn to exit—and they came back to her apartment and watched more *Mythbusters* and ate ramen noodles. Yesterday he'd called when she'd been walking into work and their conversation was very short since Rosie Peterman, the head librarian, gave her the evil eye for speaking too loudly in the library. He was waiting in the parking lot at five once again. She'd invited him to dinner, but he'd merely handed her a single rose, said he'd been thinking about her, and had followed her to her apartment, watching her park and enter the building before driving away.

And now he wanted to know if she'd like to have breakfast with him.

"I did," Dane said. "And now I want to see you again. Since I'm awake now, and it seems like every time I'm awake I can't stop thinking about you and wanting to see you, I thought I might stop by…if it's okay with you. I can stop at the doughnut shop and bring some over."

"Doughnuts are bad for you."

He chuckled again. "A lot of things are bad for you, but most of the time those are the things that can bring you the most joy."

"Doughnuts bring you joy?"

"Yeah, but more so than the sugar is you. *You* bring me joy."

"Wow. That was…um…nice." Bryn scooted down on her mattress until her head once again rested on her pillow. His voice was deep and scratchy and she could almost picture him lying in his bed, one arm behind his head as he talked to her. It was sexy as hell and with every word he spoke, the slickness between her legs increased. "Are you in bed?"

"Yeah. You?"

"Um hmmm." Bryn's hand edged along the T-shirt she always slept in, down to her belly, where she hesitated, then pressed it farther, edging her fingertips under her panties and brushing against her folds. She inhaled deeply.

"Are you all right, Smalls?"

"Yeah." She brought her index finger to her clit and slowly massaged it, closing her eyes and imagining it was his finger on her body instead.

"What are you doing?"

"Nothing." Bryn kept her eyes closed and her finger moving as she caressed herself.

"Are you touching yourself?"

Dane's voice had lowered even more and Bryn breathed out a small moan as she pressed against her clit harder. Too lost in pleasure to filter her words, she said, "Yeah."

"Jesus, Smalls. You're killin' me. I can picture it. Laying there on your bed, stroking yourself as you talk to me. I bet you're beautiful…and soaking wet. Are you naked?"

"No," Bryn managed, moving her finger quicker. It was as if he knew what his voice did to her, because he kept talking, pushing her faster and faster toward her peak.

"That's so sexy. I can just imagine what you look

like, your hand pressed inside your panties, flicking over yourself. If I was there, I wouldn't be able to see anything but your hand moving under your clothes. Fuck, that image will be burned in my brain forever. You close, Smalls?"

She was. Really close. "Keep talking," she ordered Dane, wanting his deep voice in her ear to push her over the edge.

"You like the sound of my voice? Like knowing that you're driving me crazy imagining what you're doing right now? The luckiest day in my life was when you saw me in the grocery store, Bryn. I'm so fucking thankful you gave me another chance. You've inserted yourself into my life so deeply, I can't imagine you not being there. You make me want to be a better person. I can't wait to—"

Bryn groaned softly as she flew over the edge. She kept stroking herself as her orgasm peaked. She vaguely heard Dane still speaking through the phone into her ear, but had no idea what he was saying. It wasn't until she took a deep breath to try to get herself under control that she understood him.

"God, that was so fucking hot, Bryn. You're so sweet. Thank you for sharing that with me."

"You're welcome?" It came out more a question than a comment.

"Yeah. I know we haven't been dating for all that

long, but you trusting me enough to share that with me means the world. But you should know something."

When he didn't say anything else, Bryn tentatively asked, "What?"

"I'm gonna want to *see* you do that sometime. Now, you want doughnuts?"

Bryn cleared her throat and moved up until her back was resting against the headboard again. She knew she was blushing bright red, but she couldn't bring herself to entirely care. She hadn't planned on masturbating over the phone with Dane, but when she'd pictured him lying in his own bed, and hearing his voice, she couldn't stop herself.

"Yeah, I want doughnuts."

"Get up and get dressed, Smalls. I'll be there in a little while."

"Okay."

"I mean it. Dressed. Jeans, bra, T-shirt. Maybe even a sweatshirt. I'm strong, but I'm not sure I could handle it if you came to your door in your sleep shirt and panties."

"Are you going to kiss me?"

"Yeah, Bryn. I'm going to kiss you. When the time is right for both of us. Then I'm going to make love to you."

"I'm ready," Bryn insisted.

"I'm not," Dane retorted immediately. "I want to be

the kind of man you can be proud of. The kind of man who can take you out to eat and not freak out. The kind of man who doesn't give a shit if he only has one hand. I'm not there yet. I'm trying, and you make me want to try harder. But sweetheart, listening to you breathe my name as you came just now gave me even more incentive to get there. Knowing you spent the time to research phantom pain and talk to an expert about it gives me even more. And knowing that the first thing you did when you woke up this morning was lean over, pick up your phone and dial my number so you could share what you learned, was the best wake-up call I've ever gotten in my entire life. So, yeah, I'm gonna kiss you, Smalls. I'm gonna kiss every inch of your body and let you kiss me the same way."

"Okay." Bryn wanted nothing more than to stroke herself at his words, but knew that wasn't why he was saying them.

"So…thirty minutes? You'll put clothes on?"

"Yeah, Dane. I'll be here."

"Thank you for the wake-up call, Smalls. I'll see you soon."

"Bye."

"Bye."

Bryn clicked off the phone and closed her eyes for a moment. She was mortified, turned on, and scared out of her mind all at the same time. Taking a deep breath, she twisted her body and put her feet on the floor. She needed a shower if she was going to see Dane this morning. Smiling, and feeling more feminine than she ever had before in her life, Bryn entered her bathroom more than ready to start her day…with a doughnut and spending time with Dane. Life was good.

Chapter Twelve

DANE LOOKED OVER at Bryn and smiled. They were sitting on his couch, taking a break from another episode of *Mythbusters*. They were into season four and her interest hadn't waned one bit. Rosie had given Bryn the afternoon off after seeing her talking with Dane. He'd been a regular visitor to the library, and the older woman had obviously recognized that he was doing his best to court Bryn.

Bryn was an intriguing woman to get to know. Most people tried to pretend they didn't see his prosthetic...not Bryn. When she saw people staring at him, she called them on it. When kids would make comments, she'd engage them in conversation and even pull him over to them so they could see his prosthetic up close and personal.

She made him feel like there was absolutely nothing wrong with him, until he'd started to believe it himself. They hadn't repeated the incident from two weeks ago, when she'd masturbated to the sound of his voice, but he could see the desire in her eyes every time she looked at him.

He'd been holding back because…he wasn't sure exactly why. Maybe it was because he was afraid sex between them would be awkward. He hadn't tried to be with a woman since his accident. Figuring out where to put his hand and elbows would be strange.

But if he was honest with himself, he knew exactly why he was going slowly with Bryn. As much as he wanted inside her, he was enjoying the anticipation a hell of a lot. He hadn't ever put this much energy into courting a woman before, and the longer he waited with Bryn, the better it was going to be. He knew it.

"Are you sure you don't need to go down to Coeur D'Alene today?" Bryn asked. "We could go to that grocery store and get you some organic stuff. I know you liked the gluten-free bread I served with dinner the other night."

"I did. But I'd rather spend the time with you."

Bryn cocked her head and examined him. "Is it still bad?"

Dane would never get used to the way Bryn didn't just look at him, she *looked* at him. She saw things no one else had bothered to see before…other than Truck. "It's better. Slowly but surely, it's getting better. I appreciate you shopping with me every weekend. It helps."

"Well, I get more out of it than you, I think. I don't

have to worry about my car dying when I'm down in the city and you keep me from giving all my money to the beggars. Win-win for me."

Dane smiled and ran his index finger down her cheek.

"Do you have any friends?"

"Friends?"

"Yeah," Bryn said easily. "I mean, I know why I don't have that many. I'm too weird. People can't stand to be around all my babbling and facts. But you? You're beautiful, smart, and a hero. But I don't see you with anyone."

"I'm not beautiful. Women are beautiful, men are handsome."

"Nope. You're beautiful. You're all like," Bryn waved her hand in front of him, encompassing his entire body, "hard where you should be hard and scruffy and...simply beautiful."

Dane wasn't exactly sure how to respond to that, so he let it go. "I have friends, Bryn. Just not here. Truck calls me when he can."

"Who else? You have to have more than one friend."

"Yeah. The group of men who died in the same explosion that took my arm were my friends. I hadn't realized how much I'd miss them. But then Truck and his close-knit team kinda browbeat me into life again. So now they're my friends too."

"Do they have fun names like Truck?" Bryn asked.

"I'm not sure 'fun' is the word, but yeah, they have nicknames. Ghost, Fletch, Coach, Hollywood, Beatle, and Blade."

"Cool. Do you?"

"Do I what, Smalls?"

"Have a nickname?"

"Yeah. It's Fish."

"Fish…hmmm, you a good swimmer?" Bryn asked.

With no conceit, Dane said, "The best."

"I'd like to see that sometime."

"When the weather gets warmer, I'd be happy to go swimming with you, Smalls."

"Me too."

"And getting back to the topic, you're my friend now too. Aren't you?"

Bryn didn't respond right away, merely kept her intense gaze on his for a beat. Then she smiled. One so big that Dane almost flinched from the brightness of it. "Yeah. I'm your friend."

"Good. And Bryn. You're not weird. I thought we've been over this."

"Different then."

"Different *maybe*. But anyone who can't see past your differences to the amazing woman you are underneath, doesn't deserve to have a friend like you. You're the kind of friend who only comes along once in a blue moon. The kind of friend who would drop everything if someone called for help. Unselfish, caring, kind, and interesting. I've learned more being around you than anyone else I know. I love that about you."

Bryn bit her lip, then smiled shyly. "Thanks."

"You're welcome. How long have we known each other?"

"Thirty-seven days."

Dane smiled. He should've guessed Bryn would know to the day how long it'd been. "Right. And in all that time, through all the time we've spent together, has there been anything you've wanted to ask me, but haven't?"

Dane loved the way Bryn always spoke whatever she was thinking about, but lately he had a feeling she was holding something back. And he hated it. It was getting harder and harder to go slow with her, but he'd promised himself he wasn't going to rush their relationship...but with every day that passed, he wanted her more and more.

When she continued to stare at him, he coaxed, "Come on, Smalls. We're friends. I want you to be honest with me."

"Whyhaven'tyoukissedme?" The words were all jumbled together, so it came out as one word. Then she went on. "I mean, I see the way you look at me sometimes, and that one morning on the phone...I thought

169

maybe…" Her voice trailed off and she lowered her head and picked at a thread on the bottom of her jeans.

"Look at me, Smalls," Dane ordered. When she didn't lift her head, he put a finger under her chin and pressed upward lightly. When she finally met his eyes, he continued, "I haven't kissed you because I don't trust myself."

"What?"

"I don't trust myself," he repeated. "You are so amazing and I've never been attracted to someone as much as I am to you."

"Then why?"

"Because I know once I get a taste of your lips, I'm not going to be able to hold back any longer. I'll want more. I'll want you under me, over me, and I'll want to lose myself in you. I'm trying to go slowly. I've enjoyed hanging out with you. Watching TV, shopping, sitting in the library, watching you work."

"How's that working? Is it helping you be more comfortable in public?"

Dane smiled at her change in subject. It was typical of her. She was always worried more about him than herself. "Yeah, Smalls. When I have you to concentrate on, it helps keeps me grounded."

"I'm glad."

"So, to answer your question straight out, I want to kiss you. And I will. And so you know, once I finally have your lips on mine, it's only a matter of time before I'll take you to bed."

"Okay."

"Okay."

"Dane?"

"Yeah, Bryn?"

"I don't want to rush you or anything, but I'm ready for that. As soon as you are, I am too."

Dane smiled, picked her hand up and kissed her palm. "Good to know. Want to start another episode?"

"Yeah. Next up is the steam cannon episode…where they try to figure out if Archimedes could've made one. I love how they make sure the shows aren't too deep for people by mixing the more science-y myths with funny ones. I can't wait to see the results of whether the cardboard the cereal box is made of is more nutritious than the sugar crap that's inside it."

Dane chuckled and leaned back into the corner of the couch and picked up the remote. "Come 'ere, Bryn."

She scooted over and leaned against him, pulling his left arm around her until his stump rested on her hip. Her eyes were fixated on the screen as the opening credits of the show rolled.

Dane sighed in contentment and ignored his hard-as-nails dick. He lowered his head to inhale her unique scent and smiled when his cock twitched once more. One sniff of her coconut shampoo and he was up and rarin' to go.

Paying more attention to the woman at his side and how she felt against him rather than the television, Dane thanked his lucky stars that he was sitting there with Bryn. He knew as well as anyone that if he hadn't met her, his life could've been very different. She'd helped him deal with his post-traumatic stress and made him feel like a man again. The fact that she didn't see him as less than a man was a miracle. One he wasn't going to let slip out of his hands.

Chapter Thirteen

BRYN PICKED UP the phone absently, her mind still on the math problem she was trying to solve. She'd found it online in a chat room where everyone was talking about how it was impossible. Saying that had been like waving a red cape in front of a bull.

"Hello?"

"Hey, Smalls. What are you up to?"

"Math."

Dane chuckled in her ear. "Can you take a break?"

"I'm able to. But don't really want to."

"Truck and his friends are coming over. They'll be here in about twenty minutes or so."

Bryn's mind suddenly snapped to Dane. "What? Here? As in *here*, here?"

"Yeah. Here in Rathdrum. They'll only be here for a day and a half. So I'm having a cookout tonight to celebrate. Want to come over and meet them?"

Bryn's first thought was to say yes immediately, but a part of her was still very scared that his Army buddies wouldn't like her. That she'd say something totally off the wall and alienate them. And if his friends didn't like her, then maybe Dane would have second thoughts.

As if he could read her mind, Dane said in a soft voice, "Bryn. Trust me."

"Okay. What time?"

"I'll come get you."

"I can drive out there."

"I know. But I'll come get you anyway."

"Dane, seriously, your friends are on their way, it's not cool to leave them there while you come into town to get me."

"Smalls. They're adults. The Army trusts them with multimillion-dollar equipment and they're responsible for the lives of hundreds of other men and women they fight with. I think they'll be okay in my house for the thirty minutes it might take for me to come into town, get you, and return."

She heard the smile in his voice and gave in. "Okay. Now's good. Because if you give me time, I'll get lost in this equation I'm trying to solve again and then I'll be grumpy if you interrupt me."

"I'm on my way."

"Dane?"

"Yeah, Smalls?"

"What should I wear?"

He didn't make fun of her for asking. "Jeans, sneakers, T-shirt with a sweater, or sweat-shirt, or something.

It's chilly outside."

"Okay. I can do that. See you soon?"

"Yeah. I'll be there as quickly as I can."

"Drive safe."

"Always."

"Bye."

"Bye, Bryn."

Bryn hung up the phone and sat at the table, looking off into space. She didn't know much about Truck or his friends, because she simply hadn't asked. She wanted to know all about them, but was afraid if she knew too much, and they ended up not liking her, it would hurt knowing what she was missing out on.

Pushing back from the computer, Bryn hurried to get changed. She wanted to be ready when Dane got there.

Twenty minutes later, she was in Dane's truck and they were headed back to his house.

"Tell me their names again," Bryn demanded. "And a little about each one."

Without seeming to get irritated with her, Dane said, "Ghost is the leader of the group. He's the most watchful out of all the guys, but he's also not afraid to jump in when the shit hits the fan. Fletch recently got married to a woman he met because she was living in the garage over his apartment. They have a six-going-on-eighteen little girl, Annie. She reminds me of you in a lot of ways."

"She does?"

"Yeah. She's smart. Really smart. And quirky. She wants to be a professional soldier when she grows up, just like her daddy. Everyone she meets loves her on sight."

"I love that for her," Bryn said a little wistfully. When she was growing up, people just seemed to be irritated and weirded out when they met her.

As if he could read her mind, Dane reached over and squeezed the back of her neck briefly, then put his hand back on the stick shift. "Then there's Coach. He's tall, slender, and almost had his face bashed in by a bird when he was parachuting with the woman who would become his girlfriend."

"God. He's okay though?" Bryn asked.

"Yup. He and Harley are doing great. Solid. Then there's Hollywood. He'll be the one who looks like a fucking movie star. But don't say anything about it. He's kinda sensitive."

"Oh. Uh…I don't understand."

Dane chuckled. "I'm teasing. He's always been the guy in the group all the women hit on. His looks have continually been a thing with him. But he's recently off the market. I didn't think he'd agree to make the trip up."

"Why not?"

"Because he recently got married…and his woman was literally stabbed twice in the back. She's okay now," Dane hurried to reassure her, "but she's had a long recuperation."

"That sucks. Hope they caught the guy who did it," Bryn told him firmly.

"Oh, they did. And I made sure the asshole who was behind all of the shit Kassie went through will never hurt her again."

Bryn put her hand on his thigh and merely nodded. "Good."

"Okay, wrapping this up…Beatle and Blade are also here. They're still single. And of course, Truck. I've told you about him. He's also single, but not."

"What do you mean?"

"Just that he's got his eye on a woman back home. She likes him too, but she's going through some health issues and doesn't want to tie him down or some bullshit."

"But she's going to be okay?" Bryn asked.

"Can't lie…I don't know. She doesn't talk about it and neither does Truck. But I know my friend. If there's anything he can do to make her fight easier, he will."

"I can't wait to meet them," Bryn said, shifting so her back was to the door on her side of the vehicle.

"They all can't wait to meet you," Dane told her.

"Can we give this a time limit?" Bryn asked, looking

at her watch.

"What do you mean?"

"It's just…I really was in the middle of something. And if I know I only have to stay and try to make your friends like me for a certain amount of time, I'll do better. Like, if I know it's only two hours, then I can deal. But if it's open ended, and I don't know when I can go home and back to the math problem I was working on, it'll just…it'll be hard," she finished lamely.

They'd reached his house, and Bryn bit her lip in agitation at seeing the three vehicles parked haphazardly around the driveway. Dane turned off the engine and reached for Bryn. "Come 'ere, Smalls."

She scooted closer to him, and when he continued to urge her farther, she carefully swung a leg over his hips until she sat in his lap. He took her chin in his hand and held her still in front of him. The elbow of his other arm wrapped around her and rested in the small of her back.

"Bryn. They're going to like you."

"Okay."

Dane studied her for a long moment, then said, "You need this, don't you?"

She nodded jerkily and tried to explain. "I was twelve. I was invited to a party. I didn't want to go, but my parents thought it'd be good for me. I went. It was awful. The girls all sat around and giggled and the boys were downright mean. I didn't know when I could leave. I was stuck there. If I knew when my parents were coming back, it would've made it easier. I couldn't tell myself…only two more hours, only one more hour because I didn't know when my parents would be back for me. So I had to sit there and take it and the party lasted forever. I don't like meeting people. If I know how long I have to stay, I'll be better."

"Okay, Smalls. No problem. How about this…we'll say two hours. In two hours, I'll check in with you and see how you're feeling. If you want to go, I'll take you."

"Thank you, Dane," Bryn said softly, looking down at her watch to mark the time. "I can do a hundred and twenty minutes. For you."

"For me," he echoed.

Bryn nodded.

"You ready?"

"No. But you said they wouldn't make fun of me, and I trust you, so I guess I have to be ready. Besides, it's only two hours. I can do anything for that length of time."

Dane's hand went from her chin to the back of her neck and pulled her into him and kissed her forehead. Then he tilted her head up and brushed his lips against hers.

Without thought, Bryn opened her mouth and invited him to deepen the kiss.

He lazily licked her bottom lip, then tilted his head, giving him better access to her mouth.

She felt him press into her back with his stump and she grabbed hold of the sides of his shirt and held on as she shyly mimicked the movements of his tongue. She tasted his lips, then sighed when his tongue swept into her mouth.

He took his time, learned what she liked and never got aggressive with the kiss. Bryn whimpered in her throat and tried to pull him harder into her. But Dane simply eased back, nipping at her lips teasingly as he did so.

Then he gathered her into his arms and hugged her.

Bryn melted into his chest, feeling her heart rate slow just by being close to him.

Their first kiss had been everything she'd dreamed about and more. He didn't try to maul her. Didn't shove his tongue into her mouth without thought as to what she might like. He took his time. Teased. Tasted. It was simply perfect.

After several moments, he said, "One hour and fifty-seven minutes, Smalls. Let's do this."

Bryn nodded and opened his door. She awkwardly climbed off his lap and, using his arm for leverage, hopped out. He followed her, pocketing his keys as he shut the door with his hip. He wrapped his left arm as far around her waist as he could get it and they started walking toward his house.

Bryn licked her lips, tasting Dane there, and glanced at her watch. One hour and fifty-six minutes. Piece of cake.

"I SWEAR TO God, I've never seen anything like it. There was Fish, with only one and a half arms, and Tex with only one and a half legs, and they kicked the shit out of that guy before he had any idea what was coming at him!" Kassie said enthusiastically.

Dane sat in his living room, with Bryn sitting on his lap, while Hollywood's woman told Bryn all about how Emily and Fletch's wedding reception had been robbed. Kassie hadn't been there, but while she'd been recuperating from the stab wounds she'd gotten from her ex-boyfriend's psycho minion, Emily had entertained her by bringing over the security tapes from the entire incident.

He'd been surprised to see Kassie at his house with Hollywood. They'd arrived, as planned, after he'd left to pick up Bryn. Apparently, Hollywood didn't want to leave her at home, even for the short time he'd be visiting, and Kassie refused to stay back in Texas anyway.

It had been exactly what Bryn had needed though.

She was nervous to hang out with him and all his guy friends, so having another woman had broken the ice. As he knew they would, they all loved Bryn. They'd been fascinated by how smart she was, and had given him the side eye several times. He knew what they were thinking. She'd be excellent to have as a researcher for their missions, but there was no way he was going down that road with Bryn. With her curiosity, she'd want to know more information, and he never wanted to put her in danger like that. Because he knew without a doubt Bryn wouldn't be able to stop. It'd be up to him to shield her from herself, if necessary.

"I would've liked to have seen that," Bryn said easily.

"I'll totally get Em to send you a copy," Kassie told her. Then she pushed away from Hollywood, who she was leaning against on the couch, and said, "I'll be back."

"Anything wrong?" Hollywood asked, immediately alert.

"No," Kassie told him, rolling her eyes. "I just need to use the restroom."

"I'll show you where it is," Bryn said, and struggled to get out of Dane's lap.

"You good?" Dane asked her, helping her get her feet on the ground.

"Yeah. I'll be right back," she reassured him.

"It's been three and a half hours, Smalls. You good?" he asked again. He'd taken her aside after two hours and loved that she'd been surprised at the amount of time that had passed. Her eyes had widened and she'd stared at her watch as if she couldn't believe it. She'd reassured him that she was okay and that she liked his friends. So she'd stayed.

"I'm good," Bryn said. "I just need a break."

"You got it," Dane told her, not offended in the least. She'd taken a few breaks throughout the evening. Little walks to clear her mind. And when she'd returned, he'd seen that she seemed to be more relaxed. It wasn't that she didn't want to be with him and his friends, she just needed time to recharge here and there.

He kept his gaze on her as she and Kassie disappeared around the corner.

"Like her, Fish," Truck said as soon as they were out of hearing.

He smiled. "Thanks. Me too."

"You said she was stalking you?" Blade asked, smirking. "Wish I could get a stalker like that."

"Shut up," Dane groused, throwing a balled-up napkin at the other man.

"You look better," Ghost said easily. "More relaxed. Less keyed up."

"Feel it," Dane told him. "She sure keeps me on my toes. Her curiosity is worse than Annie's."

"Jesus, you're doomed," Fletch deadpanned.

Dane smiled, then elaborated, "Not in a bad way. It's cute as fuck, actually. I love how she can get lost in her research for hours at a time. But lately she's been engrossed by the prepper lifestyle."

"That's dangerous," Coach said.

"Tell me something I don't know," Dane returned. "I don't mind the preppers so much. They're secretive and shit, but when push comes to shove, I don't think they'd actually hurt her. It's the others, the survivalist extremists, that I don't like. I'm trying to steer Bryn away from the bunker-and-prepper thing, but once she gets her mind set on something..." He trailed off.

"You need us, you call," Ghost ordered. "I don't give a shit what it is. We can be here in two hours, tops."

Dane looked down at his lap for a moment and fought for composure. He'd thought he'd lost this in the explosion that took his arm and his friends' lives. They'd had each other's backs. He'd more than once flown to help them out when it was needed. It wasn't that he'd lost only his arm, he'd lost that connection. That sense of security that came from knowing he had a group of men who would drop everything just to be at his side if it was needed.

And now he had it back. This group of Deltas hadn't known him before that fateful day in the desert, but they'd pulled him into their tight circle without blinking.

"After what you did for Kassie, hell, even before that, you should know we've got your back, man," Hollywood said softly.

"Can't repay you, Fish," Fletch put in. "Emily hasn't ever talked about it, but I know she was worried about the day that asshole would get out of prison. You takin' that worry off our plates means the world."

"You know I didn't do it for repayment," Dane growled.

"You got it anyway," Fletch returned immediately.

"Whatever," Dane said. "What else you guys been doing?" he asked, trying to change the subject.

"Things have been quiet, lately," Beatle answered for the group.

Immediately, he was pelted by balled-up pieces of napkin, a pencil, and an empty plastic cup by the men sitting around the comfortable living room.

"I can't believe you said that, you ass," Blade told him. "What's the first rule of the teams?"

"Never comment on how bored you are or how slow things are," Ghost said unnecessarily.

"Exactly. Jesus, if we get sent to the Sandbox for six months, I'll never forgive you," Hollywood told his teammate.

"Something you want to tell us?" Truck asked,

smirking.

"Yeah, Hollywood, you got something going on?" Ghost asked.

"Fuck off," Hollywood mumbled.

"Oh now, see? Now we *know* you've got something you want to tell us. Go on. You might as well get it off your chest. You know we've got ways of making you talk," Fletch chimed in.

Dane loved this. It reminded him all too well of his fallen friends. For once the memory didn't hurt as badly.

"Remember that one time when we were on a mission and we heard Beatle scream? We all hotfooted it over to where he was, but he wouldn't tell us what had made him make that girlie-ass sound?"

"Shut the fuck up," Beatle told his friend.

Blade ignored him, and continued, "So we got him drunk, duct taped him to a tree, and threatened to leave him there overnight if he didn't cave?"

"You didn't see the size of that fucking bug!" Beatle griped. "It was huge. And had three-inch fangs!"

"It's fucking hilarious that everyone thinks his nick is due to his last name being Lennon. But it's really because he's scared of bugs! Little teeny beetles make him lose his shit!"

Beatle didn't continue to protest, he merely crossed his arms over his chest and glared at his friends.

"Oh, and when he heard my sister was an entomologist, he swore right then and there he never, ever wanted to meet her!" Blade cackled. "As if I'd let you anywhere near her anyway."

"You don't think I'm good enough for your sister?" Beatle asked.

"Oh, you're good enough for her, but she wouldn't have you in a million years," Blade told his friend.

"Why not?"

"Because she loves bugs. *Loves* them. Has them in little containers all over her apartment. She never kills them, even flies. Catches them and lets them go. I think she even has a few hissing cockroaches she keeps as pets."

Beatle shuddered but Blade continued. "I would take you as a brother-in-law in a second, Beatle, but unfortunately, you'd never make it with her. Casey is a die-hard bug lover. You'd be like oil and water. In fact, she's currently down in Costa Rica with three of her students from the university she works at. They're studying ants. Don't ask me what kind, 'cause I don't know, but they're spending every day in the jungle looking for, collecting, and cataloging fucking creepy-crawly ants. We've spent our share of time in the jungle, but you'd never spend time there voluntarily. I know you."

"Whatever. It's not like I'd ever even *meet* your sister

anyway. But can we get back to the question at hand?" Beatle asked, pinning Hollywood with his gaze. "What secret is Hollywood keeping and how do we get it out of him?"

Dane laughed along with the others. It was obvious Beatle was desperately trying to change the subject.

Hollywood glared at his friends for a moment, then his lips twitched and he said matter-of-factly. "I don't want to get sent to the Sandbox *or* the fucking jungle for six weeks because Kassie is pregnant."

There was silence around the room for a half second before everyone spoke at once.

"Fuck yeah!"

"Hooah!"

"Way to go, stud!"

"Congrats!"

Hollywood held up his hand to quiet everyone down. He looked nervously at the hallway, where his wife and Bryn had disappeared. When he had their attention, he told them, "But you can't say anything to her, *or* your women," he looked at Ghost, Fletch, and Coach as he said it. "Or anyone else. We aren't announcing it officially until she's hit the twelve-week mark. That's another month or so. I told her that I'd keep it a secret."

Everyone laughed.

Hollywood shook his head. "Yeah, she even believed

me when I told her that, since we were one of the most clandestine government agencies, we could keep secrets better than the average person."

Once again, all his friends laughed. It was an inside joke. There were things they'd done that they'd take to the grave with them and never tell a soul, but when it came to everyday things and their personal lives, no one had any problem sharing. It came with the job. When you'd literally lain in shit together, or killed another human with your bare hands so your buddy could live, secrets in everyday life meant jack squat.

They all knew that anything they shared with the group would stay with the group. Period. No questions.

"Congrats, man," Fletch told him. "I'm doing the best I can with Emily, but she hasn't conceived yet. But it's a fuck of a lot of fun trying."

The guys all grinned at each other before going back to the earlier topic...making fun of Beatle for his hatred and fear of creepy-crawlies.

Bryn and Kassie came back into the room and joined in the good-natured haranguing. But what Dane loved best was the fact that Bryn had come straight to him and crawled back into his lap, as if it was the most natural thing in the world. He loved holding her. Loved listening to her inform Beatle that the cockroach was the most fascinating of all creepy-crawlies, and that the biggest ever was the rhinoceros cockroaches from

Queensland, Australia. They were apparently more than three inches long and could weigh up to half a pound.

As the lively discussion continued around him, Dane kissed the side of Bryn's head and relaxed into the chair when she wrapped her hand around his stump, her finger absently rubbing back and forth, while she continued bantering with the people who meant the most in the world to him.

LATER THAT NIGHT, after Dane had returned from taking Bryn home, Truck met him in the kitchen. Everyone else had settled in for the night. Hollywood and Kassie were in one guest room and Fletch had taken the other. The rest of the guys were sleeping wherever there was room…they were used to bunking in all kinds of conditions, so the floor or couch at Dane's house was almost luxurious compared to, say, the jungle floor.

Everything was quiet and still when Dane returned.

"She get in all right?" Truck asked.

"Yeah. She's good," Dane told him.

"I like her."

"Good."

"No, Fish. I *like* her," Truck reiterated.

"What the fuck, man?" Dane asked, crossing his arms over his chest. "Don't you have enough on your plate with Mary?"

Truck didn't get offended, instead he chuckled. "I don't mean I want her for myself. I only meant that I think she's absolutely perfect for you."

"How do you figure?"

"She'll keep you on your toes. You are not a man who does well with being bored. I mean, you're living in the middle of nowhere Idaho with nothing to do. You're used to being in the thick of things. I've been worried about you wallowing and sinking deeper into your head. She won't let you do that."

Dane didn't want to grin, but couldn't help it when his lips curled up anyway. "No, she won't," he agreed.

"Right. So I like her," Truck repeated.

"She's quirky," Dane said.

"Didn't miss that, Fish. Again, she's exactly what you need."

"I agree. She makes me feel good. Like I can breathe again." He looked down and shook his head. "Now I gotta tell Akilah she was right."

"About what?"

"She told me the night of Fletch and Emily's wedding that when I went to where the land fed my soul, I'd find a woman who doesn't see what's missing, but instead sees me."

"Smart kid," Truck commented.

"I shouldn't like it so much."

"What?"

"Looking out for Bryn. Being protective of her," Dane said. "It makes me feel as if I have a purpose again. Making sure she eats. Gets home all right. Isn't doing any research that can get her into trouble."

Truck put his hand on Fish's shoulder. "It's the kind of men we are. It's what we do. We look after those we love. Make sure they get what they need. We stand behind them, keeping watch, so they can blossom."

"What if she gets tired of me doing that for her?"

"Sometimes you gotta be sneaky about it. Make her depend on you so much that she can't imagine her life without you in it," Truck said matter-of-factly, dropping his hand.

Dane looked at the man who'd saved his life for a long moment before asking, "Is that what you're doing?"

"Tryin'," he said immediately. "But I have a feeling it'll work out for you long before it does me."

"Thanks for not making me feel like as asshole for wanting to protect her…even if it's from herself."

"You're not an asshole, Fish. You're a man who's found the purpose of his life. Life sucks sometimes, that's no lie, but if you've got your eyes open, she'll present you with just what you need. Sometimes it takes more work than you'd like, but if you persevere, she'll show you as much beauty as you can take."

"You're sounding awfully philosophical," Dane said with a smirk.

"Yeah. I better go drink a beer and crush the can on my head or something," Truck returned immediately.

"I'm heading to bed," Dane informed his friend. "I gotta get my sleep in when I can. I never know when Bryn is gonna call me at three in the morning to tell me about something she found on the Internet."

"Enjoy the ride, Fish," Truck told him. "And remember that you've got friends if you need 'em."

"Appreciate that. More than you know."

"I know," Truck said. "See you in the morning."

"Later."

Dane headed to his room, his heart and mind full. He didn't like that he lived so far from his friends, but he loved Idaho. The fresh clean air, the lack of people...and Bryn. Even though the guys were halfway across the country, he knew, without a doubt, they'd drop everything if he needed them. Just as he would for them.

Chapter Fourteen

"COME ON! LET'S go already." Bryn wiggled in the seat next to Dane in his truck.

She still had a hard time understanding what Dane saw in her, but she loved every second they'd spent together. After the visit with his friends, she'd relaxed even more around him. She actually liked them…and they'd liked her back.

Having Kassie there was a surprise, in a good way. The other woman had instantly made her comfortable by asking a thousand questions about Idaho, and had let Bryn blab on and on about all the facts she'd stored up regarding her adopted state.

When they'd gone to the bathroom, Kassie had actually admitted she was pregnant, and that was why she always had to pee. Bryn had been floored when Kassie had said no one else knew yet. The simple act of confessing something that she hadn't told anyone aside from Hollywood, almost made Bryn cry. She hadn't had a true girlfriend her entire life, and while she might not know Kassie well, the admission that she was having a baby went a long way toward soothing any anxiety she'd still held about the visit from Dane's friends.

Not only that, but Dane seemed to actually *like* her weird way of spouting random facts, and was doing so much better at being out in public. She liked to think it was partly because of her. They'd gone back to Dairy Queen one day and met a man named Steve. He'd been there trying to fix one of their ovens. He owned his own business, servicing industrial appliances, mostly in restaurants, and they'd struck up a conversation while waiting for their food.

It turned out that Steve was way busier than he really wanted to be. He'd moved to the Rathdrum area with his wife and two small kids from Colorado Springs, in order to enjoy the outdoor activities the area offered, but found that he actually had less time now than he did before to spend with his kids.

Even though Dane didn't have any experience working in the business, Steve was desperate, and had said that even with one hand, Dane could be trained in some of the basic maintenance that didn't take a lot of fine motor skills, and he'd be a big help, even if he only worked part time.

So Dane was looking into licenses and what he might need to do in order to work for the man. Bryn had brought up working at the grocery store again, but had conceded that she much preferred to spend her nights hanging out with Dane, and had quickly put aside that thought.

The only thing Bryn wasn't happy with as far as her relationship with Dane went was that he still seemed reluctant to kiss her. *Really* kiss her. After their conversation at his house a couple of weeks ago, when she asked why he hadn't kissed her yet, he'd started pressing his lips to her forehead all the time.

They cuddled together when they watched TV, and he held her hand all the time, but he'd only kissed her, truly kissed her, a few times since the night she'd met his friends. And those always left her wanting more. It was starting to give her a complex, especially since he'd told her once he *had* kissed her, he wouldn't stop. She liked Dane, and was pretty sure he liked her too. But she didn't want him as a friend. Or *only* a friend. She wanted in his pants. Bad.

Dane turned sideways in the driver's seat and said in a serious tone of voice, "I want to go over what we talked about one more time before we leave."

"Dane, I *know*. We've been over it a hundred times already," Bryn whined.

"It's important, Smalls. I know you're excited, but the guy who's letting us see his bunker is only doing it as a favor to someone I know. He's not that thrilled about it. I know you have a million questions, but you need to tone it down. Don't ask how much or how many of anything he's got. Don't ask where he obtained the things you might see in his bunker. He's not going to want to tell you details about any of that in case you try to horn in on his sources."

"I wouldn't—"

"*I* know that. And *you* know that. But *he* doesn't know that."

"I'll just tell him when we get there."

"He won't believe you. Bryn, preppers are great people. Most have normal jobs, they function in society like any other person. But that doesn't mean that they aren't paranoid or super suspicious of people who ask too many questions about what they're doing and why. Okay?"

"Okay, okay. I got it. But you should know, it's gonna kill me to keep my mouth shut."

Dane grinned at her. The kind of smile she loved because it filled his face. The wrinkles around his eyes deepened and she could swear she saw a twinkle in his eye. "How about some incentive?"

"What kind of incentive?"

Dane brought his hand up to her face and brushed his fingers across her cheek. Then he moved it behind her neck and pulled her closer to him. "I've been dying to take our relationship to the next level, you know that, but I wanted to make sure it was what *you* wanted. I want to feel your heartbeat against my chest as we make out. If you're good today, and don't get us in trouble with Mr. Jasper, I'll see what I can do about making that happen."

Bryn held her breath and locked her eyes onto Dane's lips. His proposal was a bit presumptuous and even a little condescending, insinuating that he held all the power and control in their relationship, but since it was what she'd wanted for a while now, and hadn't acted on, she supposed he was right in bringing it up. She wasn't going to pass up the opportunity to get what she'd been dreaming about for weeks.

"Deal. On one condition."

"Name it."

She saw that Dane's breathing had increased, and felt sexy knowing it was the thought of kissing her, *really* kissing her, that had done that to him. "I want a preview of what I'll get if I behave myself."

Without a word, Dane's head lowered to hers. His lips touched hers once, then again, then finally came down over hers as if he couldn't hold himself back anymore. The hand at her neck tightened and Bryn brought her own up around his nape, holding him to her.

The angle was awkward, as they were in his truck, but Bryn couldn't think about anything except the feel of Dane's lips on her own. She immediately opened her mouth, wanting more, and wasn't disappointed when his tongue brushed against hers.

She followed his lead, curling her tongue against his, enjoying the taste and feel of his kiss. When he retreated, she followed, brushing her tongue against his teeth and tangling with his inside his mouth. He pulled back a fraction, only to nip and suck at her bottom lip. Bryn moaned and tried to push herself harder into him.

Dane gentled their kiss and ended it by brushing his lips against hers once more. He nuzzled her neck by her ear, and said, "For the love of God, Smalls, please be good today. I need more of that. I can't keep away from you anymore."

She smiled and pulled away, ignoring the goosebumps that had risen on her skin when the warm air from his words brushed over her sensitive neck. Suddenly understanding how much power she actually had over Dane made her feel giddy inside.

She brought a hand up to her mouth and pantomimed zipping it shut. "Not one extra question will pass my lips today. Promise."

"Fuck, you're cute," he murmured, covering her mouth with his for one more short kiss before pulling back.

Bryn smiled as Dane sat back in the driver's seat and adjusted himself in his pants before smiling sheepishly over at her.

"Why do guys do that?"

"What?"

"Fondle themselves in public."

"We're not fondling ourselves, Smalls. You got me so turned on my dick got hard. It's uncomfortable and pressing on the zipper of my pants. So I'm adjusting it so it's lined up next to the zipper instead of right on it."

"Oh." Bryn's voice was small and she couldn't take her eyes away from Dane's lap. He did look bigger down there, now that she thought about it. She licked her lips, wondering what he'd look like.

"But most of the time we adjust ourselves when our balls get stuck below our ass when we sit, or when they stick to our skin. It's not usually a sexual thing at all, just a comfort thing. But if you don't stop licking your lips and looking like you want to take my pants off right here in this truck, I'll never get comfortable, we'll never leave, and you'll never get to see a bunker."

Bryn brought her eyes up to his. "You're big." She wanted to comment on the other things he said, but couldn't stop thinking about his size. "None of the other men I've been with looked as big as you."

"First, please stop talking about other men. It makes me crazy. Second—"

"Why?" she interrupted him, not understanding.

"Why does it make me crazy?" he clarified.

Bryn nodded.

"Because I'm finding that I'm possessive when it

comes to you, and I can't stand the thought of anyone else being with you and doing the things to you that I'm dying to."

"But if I hadn't been with them, I'd be a virgin. I'd be even more shy than I am now, and I'd have no idea what to expect, which would make me reticent to sleep with you. Besides which, I wouldn't know the first thing about making it good for you."

"Smalls," Dane said, shaking his head. "Take my word for it, okay? It's not that I care that you've been with other men…okay, that's a lie, I *do* care, but only because I want to be only man on your mind when you're thinking about sleeping with someone."

"You're the only man on my mind when I think about having sex, Dane."

"Good."

"What's the second thing you wanted to say?"

"I'll fit. I might be bigger than what you've had in the past, but women's bodies are built to be able to take any size cock. I'm not just going to shove myself in, I'll make sure you're ready for me, and you can't imagine me *not* being inside you."

Bryn's mouth opened and shut then opened again. She wasn't sure what to say in response to that. Finally, she simply said, "Thank you."

Dane laughed and leaned toward her, propping himself up on the seat with his good hand. "Kiss me,

Smalls. Then we'll go take a look at this bunker you've waited so long to see."

She did as he asked, copying his position, leaning on her hands and stretching her face up and touching her lips to his in a chaste kiss.

"Now, buckle up and let's do this."

She did as Dane asked and settled back on the seat, her mind switching gears from kissing and making love with Dane to their destination.

"How did you hook up with this guy again?"

Dane pulled out of the parking space in front of her apartment and turned left to head through town. "I have connections from my time in the Army. Basically, I know a guy who knows what seems like everyone. I contacted him, and he arranged for us to visit this prepper. From what I understand, Mr. Jasper wasn't that thrilled about our visit, but he was talked into it with the promise of a shipment of materials that are usually only available to people in the government."

"What materials?"

"Stuff that he can't simply order on the Internet.

"How long is our tour gonna last?"

"No clue. I figure probably about as short as the guy can make it."

Bryn nodded; she'd expected that. "Can I take pictures?"

Dane snorted. "I'd have to say no on that one. We

can play it by ear though."

"Do you think he's dangerous?"

"Not really," Dane replied immediately. "But I don't want to test him either. You remember how we talked about the different kinds of men in this area? How some are harmless and only want to be left alone to do their thing, and the others could actually be dangerous because they're against the United States and all it stands for?"

"Yeah."

"Good. I'm fairly certain this guy is the first kind. But I don't want to do anything that might make him decide he doesn't like us being in his space, or to become the second kind." He looked over at her intensely. "Just play it smart, okay?"

"Hey, I'm the smartest woman in the state. I can do that." She was rewarded when Dane chuckled at her response. She was getting used to making fun of her intelligence rather than putting herself down because of it.

They made small talk as Dane drove through the back roads surrounding Rathdrum. Bryn was lost within a couple of turns, but Dane continued on as if he knew exactly where they were going. And he obviously did, because twenty minutes later, he pulled onto a gravel driveway between two large hills.

He stopped the truck in front of a house that had

seen better days. It was brown with wooden siding. Bryn could see marks on it from where the snow in the winter had piled up, leaving behind a white residue. The porch, if it could be called that, looked as if a stiff wind would blow it over. But she couldn't deny the land around it was beautiful.

They stepped out of the truck and Dane came around to her side to take hold of her hand. She studied their surroundings as they headed to the door of the house. The grass was long and there were wildflowers everywhere she looked. Large trees surrounded the property, throwing their shade over the house. There was a garden planted off to the side and Bryn could hear a stream gurgling in the distance somewhere.

The sound of a shotgun being cocked brought her out of her happy Snow White place, where everything was singing birds and happy dwarfs, and into the present with a thud.

"Stop right there and identify yourself."

Chapter Fifteen

THE VOICE WAS hard and angry and Bryn froze. Her mouth dried up and she wouldn't have been able to say a word if her life depended on it. Luckily, Dane wasn't as affected.

"Dane Munroe and Bryn Hartwell. We're here to see the bunker." His explanation was short and to the point. Bryn squeezed his hand and was relieved to get a squeeze in return. He didn't take his eyes off the house, but he didn't look especially worried either.

A man stepped out from behind a fence at the side of the house. Now that she looked more carefully, Bryn saw a hole had been cut out in it…just big enough for the barrel of a rifle.

He was tall and slender, a few inches shorter than Dane. He was wearing a worn pair of jeans and a black T-shirt. His arms and face were tan, as if he was used to working outside, and his dark hair was oily, slicked back away from his face, and looked like it hadn't been washed in a couple of days. His eyes were narrowed, making it hard to see what color they were. His nose was crooked, as if it'd been broken several times. It was hard to tell exactly how old the man was, but if Bryn had to guess, she'd assume somewhere in his fifties or sixties.

"Mr. Jasper, I presume," Dane said calmly, holding up his left arm and raising the hand holding Bryn's, to show him he didn't have any weapons.

"Humph. You're late," the man grumbled.

"Sorry." Dane didn't elaborate.

"Well, come on then. Let's get this over with." The man rested his rifle in the crook of his arm and gestured for them to follow him with the other.

Bryn could tell Dane wasn't thrilled that the man hadn't put down his weapon, but he didn't say a word, just walked toward the man slowly and carefully, as if afraid any sudden movements would spook him. For the first time, Bryn understood what he'd been trying to tell her. He hadn't been blowing smoke up her ass.

Mr. Jasper was jumpy and uncomfortable with them being on his property. Whatever the incentive for him to allow this was, it had to be huge. Bryn made a vow to herself to keep her mouth shut as much as possible. She could take everything in and research it later. There were a few chat rooms she'd found when she'd been surfing the web for prepper info, where she could ask questions.

They stopped in front of the man and he held out a

pair of blindfolds. The kind that people wore to sleep in. "Put these on."

"Oh, but—ow!"

Bryn's words were cut off when Dane squeezed her hand so hard she couldn't help but cry out in pain. He didn't say anything, merely held out his hand for the material.

He turned to Bryn and looked down at her. "It's fine. He just doesn't want us to be able to find his bunker in the future. The only way we'll get to see it is if we wear these. Mr. Jasper isn't going to hurt us. He's protecting his family." Dane glanced over at him as if to confirm his words, but the man stayed silent. "Trust me, Smalls. I'm not going to let anything happen to you."

Bryn nodded, even though she wasn't happy about it. She realized that Dane knew this would happen. He didn't seem surprised or even upset at the blindfolds. Even as she figured that out, she understood why he'd not told her. She wasn't happy about it, not at all, but she trusted Dane.

"Okay." He nodded and leaned down to brush her lips with his before using his prosthetic and other hand to lift the elastic around her head and settle the material over her eyes. When her world went dark, Bryn panicked for a moment, before sighing in relief when Dane curled her fingers over the waistband of his jeans.

"For what it's worth," Mr. Jasper said to Dane, "I

don't mean to be so jittery about this, but there's been some talk amongst my friends and I about outsiders trying to worm their way into our community. We don't mind others who have our same mindset moving in, but when someone comes in and starts asking odd questions about law enforcement presence and how we stay under the radar, we get nervous. I might be a prepper, but I do love my country. Outsiders talking shit about the good ol' US of A make us nervous. You got me? I want nothin' to do with that, and I'll protect me and mine from anyone and everyone who tries to take my freedom away. I'm doing this for my protection, and that of my way of life. Okay?"

"Yes, sir," Dane responded immediately.

Bryn heard him shuffling next to her and was relieved when his hand curled around hers once again.

"Hold on to me and I'll hold on to the rope, Smalls. I've got you. No worries."

"Lead on, oh fearless warrior of mine."

He huffed out a laugh but didn't respond. Within moments they were on their way. It was temping to use her facial muscles to try to wriggle the mask up a bit so she could see, but Bryn didn't want to do anything that might piss off Mr. Jasper. He was jumpy enough as it was. Besides, she really did want to see the bunker. If the man was this worked up about it, it had to be amazing.

They stumbled their way for about ten minutes until

they reached the area where the bunker was.

"Keep those blindfolds on until I tell you to take 'em off. I'm gonna open the door. I'll tell you where to step."

Bryn had really wanted to see the bunker from the outside, but she wasn't going to say anything at this point. She was so close to seeing a real-live prepper hideout and didn't want to screw it up now.

She heard a loud creak, and then she and Dane shuffled forward. She gripped his hand harder and held her breath as he stepped down. Bryn followed behind him, putting her free hand on Dane's shoulder as they descended ten steps.

The door slammed shut behind them and Mr. Jasper said, "Okay, you can take 'em off now."

Bryn brought a shaky hand to her face and pushed up the material. She kept hold of Dane's hand, not wanting to lose contact with him, and absently noticed he'd also pushed up his blindfold. Blinking at the bright light from the lanterns set up around the area, she squinted at her surroundings.

It looked like a lot of the survivalist shelters she'd seen online. They'd entered at one end of the space. Her first thought, and it was one that popped out of her mouth without her thinking, was, "It's not as big as I thought it'd be."

To her right was a surprisingly comfortable-looking

sofa. To her left was a TV in the corner and a table with a bench seat. In front of that was a kitchen area, complete with a sink. There was a small hallway-looking space farther in, with a room walled off to the left of it.

"It's ten feet by fifty feet," Mr. Jasper told her with what sounded like pride.

"It doesn't look fifty feet to me," Bryn said honestly.

"That's because there's a hidden room."

Bryn took a step forward, then stopped. "May I look around?" she asked the gruff older man.

"Yeah."

It wasn't exactly said politely, but Bryn didn't hesitate. She walked over to the sink first and opened the cabinet under it. It looked like it had regular plumbing. The questions came to her mind fast and furious, but she bit them back. She wanted to know so many things, but she'd promised Dane…and wanted to be rewarded. It was incentive enough.

She opened cabinets and saw stacks and stacks of MREs, Meals Ready to Eat. Dehydrated food that could be stored for years without going bad. There were books, filters, and boxes of ammunition as well. Plates, cups, utensils, soap, shampoo…the stacks of things were endless.

She opened a small closet and saw winter clothes vacuum packed in storage bags, along with piles of blankets and towels. There was a large section of the closet allocated to storing first-aid supplies as well.

She opened the bathroom door and was amazed at how modern and sleek everything was. This wasn't a do-it-yourself job. Mr. Jasper had spent quite a bit of money on making sure he and his family had a safe place to escape to in case of nuclear war, the apocalypse, or even a zombie attack. She figured there had to be storage tanks for the clean water and waste water, but would look up how it all worked when she got home.

Dane hadn't moved from the door as she'd explored, examining every inch of the bunker but not saying anything. Finally, she asked tentatively, "May I see the hidden room too?"

Without a word, Mr. Jasper went to the wall next to the bathroom and moved a picture that hung there. Behind it was a digital lock. He punched in a code, making sure to stand in front of it so neither she nor Dane could see what numbers he used, and the wall folded back to reveal the hidden room.

Bryn stepped inside without a thought to her safety and looked around. There was a queen-size bed behind another open door against the back wall, and a set of bunkbeds to her left and right. The "master bedroom," so to speak, had some privacy with the door. She walked forward and looked inside. There was a closet to the left and what looked like a big hose tucked away in the corner.

"What's that?" The question popped out before she could recall it.

"NBC air filtration system, with blast valves and overpressure valve as well. The toilet is composting and the doors are bullet resistant. There's a tankless hot-water heater and a pump to evacuate the gray water. The stove is alcohol-burning and the water comes from the stream on the property. I hooked up a pipe to travel from there to here. It's stored in a large tank under the bunker."

Bryn was impressed, and more eager than ever to get home and look up everything he'd just mentioned, but managed to merely nod.

"You done?"

No. She wasn't done. She wanted to open every cabinet, look under every bed, turn on every gadget, take a shower, watch a movie and cook a meal…just to see how it all worked…but she'd promised Dane. So she nodded.

Dane's lips quirked up, but he merely said, "Thank you for showing it to us."

Mr. Jasper grunted in response, having seemed to blow his conversation wad moments earlier.

Bryn walked back to Dane and looked up at him. She mouthed, "thank you," then turned to the older prepper. "Thank you, Mr. Jasper. Seriously. I know you didn't have to show this to us."

"I didn't do it out of the kindness of my heart, girly. When will I get my shipment?"

His question was directed at Dane.

"As soon as I get home, I'll arrange it."

Without a word, the older man locked the secret room and recovered the keypad with the photo on the wall. He went to the other door and turned back to them. "Masks on."

Bryn didn't hesitate this time, and pulled the black blindfold over her eyes again. With her hand tight in Dane's, she followed him up the stairs and back to the main house. There they exchanged a few more words with Mr. Jasper, thanking him once more, then Dane opened her door and waited until she got settled before closing it and walking around the front of his truck and climbing in.

Without further ado, Dane backed the truck up, turned it around and headed up the gravel driveway toward the long, winding roads that would lead them to Rathdrum.

"You gonna explode, Smalls?"

Bryn huffed out a huge breath and exclaimed, "Maybe."

For the first time in the hour or so they'd been on Mr. Jasper's property, Dane relaxed. He laughed heartily and smiled over at her. "I'm proud of you."

"Thanks. But, um…do you think we can postpone

my reward until after I've had some Internet time? There are a few things I need to look up as soon as possible."

Dane continued to smile at her. He hooked his prosthetic over the wheel and reached out to her with his other hand. He lay his warm hand on her thigh. "Yeah, sweetheart. I'll be waiting for you whenever you're ready. But do you think I can get a kiss to hold me over when we get to your place?"

"Yeah, I think that can be arranged," Bryn told him, bringing his hand up to her lips and kissing the palm. "Thank you for arranging this for me. It was amazing."

"You're welcome. Anything you want to ask me while we head to your place?"

Bryn nodded. "Now that you mention it, yeah." She took a deep breath and started talking. She asked questions all the way back to her place, and for ten or so minutes while they were parked in front of her apartment building.

When she'd wound herself down, Dane told her, "Go on. I know you're dying to look up the things I couldn't answer. Call me later?"

"I will," Bryn told him, then bit her lip.

"What?"

She looked over at him shyly. "Do I get a kiss?"

"I thought you'd never ask. Come here." Dane reached down and pulled the lever to move the seat all the way back. She scooted over on the truck seat and got up on her knees next to him. He turned her and she plopped down on his lap. She'd gotten really used to him hauling her around and being in his lap. She felt comfortable there. Protected.

Before she'd gained her balance, Dane was kissing her. His hand wrapped around her waist to keep her steady and his lips devoured hers. His tongue plunged into her mouth without any warm-up. Bryn opened wider to facilitate his exploration. Her head rotated back and forth, changing the angle of the kiss, but her lips never broke free from his.

Finally, he pulled back. Dane rubbed his nose over hers.

"Call me when you're done."

"Okay."

She sat without moving on his lap and stared at his lips. They curled into a grin.

"Up you go." Dane helped her sit up and scoot back over to the other side of the truck. When she was sitting normally on the passenger side, he asked, "You good, Smalls?"

"I'm more than good, Dane. Thank you again for today. It meant a lot to me that you humored me like this."

He nodded. "Later, sweetheart."

"Later."

She opened the door and hopped out. Knowing he wouldn't pull away until she was inside the building, she closed the door and waved, then backed away, keeping eye contact with him as she went.

When she reached the door, she opened it and disappeared inside. She brought her fingertips up to her mouth and smiled, remembering how good his lips felt against her own and how amazing it felt to be in his arms. She'd never felt so content anywhere in her entire life as she was when he had his arms around her.

She locked her apartment door, and headed straight for her computer, her mind switching gears almost instantaneously as she thought about Mr. Jasper's bunker and how it'd been set up. It was genius, and she wanted to find out as much information about it as possible. She'd just get a few searches in to assuage her immediate need for knowledge, then she'd call Dane.

Chapter Sixteen

B RYN WOKE UP slowly, groaning as every muscle in her body stretched when she sat up. She was sitting at her desk, laptop in front of her, still open to the prepper forum she'd visited the night before. The people she'd met had been overall very nice and open to answering her questions. She'd gotten the impression from Mr. Jasper and Dane that all preppers were paranoid and close-mouthed. That hadn't been her experience at all. Of course, the more questions she got answered, the more she'd thought of.

She yawned and put her arms over her head to stretch. She'd had weird dreams all night. About bombs, and mobs of people trying to get into her house, and—

Shit!

Dane!

She looked at the clock on the computer and groaned in exasperation when she read it. Six-thirty. She didn't remember what time she'd finally fallen asleep, but it had been late...or early. She'd logged into the forum and had been chatting with several different preppers at the same time. It had been fascinating, and all thoughts of Dane and how she was supposed to call him had disappeared.

She took a moment and logged out of the website, trying not to think about when she might have more time to talk again to the preppers she'd met online, and headed into the living area of her small apartment. It would be a while before the sky started lightening with the morning sun, so she clicked on the entryway light and went to the small table just inside her door and grabbed her cell.

There were three text messages. All from Dane.

Dane: *I had a good time today.*

Dane: *Still researching?*

Dane: *I'm going to assume you're still sitting at your computer and lost in information on how to save our hides if the end of the world comes and not purposely avoiding me. ;) I'll call tomorrow. I hope you got some sleep.*

Bryn stared at the texts for a moment, a funny feeling in her chest. He'd checked up on her and didn't sound mad that she'd forgotten all about him. The last time she'd done that to a man she'd just started dating, he'd been so pissed that he'd "wasted his night," and had told her he didn't want to see her again.

Dane got her.

And didn't seem to care that she was scatterbrained

sometimes. That she gave money to the homeless. That she didn't seem to see the bad in people. That she could get lost in searching for information and block out everything around her.

Glancing at her watch again, and seeing it was only four minutes since she'd last looked and too early to call Dane, Bryn headed for her bedroom. She'd shower and change and go see him. She didn't have to work today, but she wanted to stop at the library and look for a book one of the preppers had recommended. The title was, of course, *Surviving Doomsday*. She wanted to see if the library had it already, or if it could be ordered.

One of the things a man had told her last night in the forum was that it was important to get hard copies of instruction books. If the infrastructure fell after a nuclear bomb or mass chaos, the Internet would be tough to get connected to. So having the actual books made sense rather than relying on the Internet or other electronic devices.

After showering, Bryn killed time by baking muffins from scratch for breakfast. She didn't want to get back online because she knew she'd just end up sucked into the knowledge on the screens.

Finally, at ten minutes to eight, she headed for the library. They typically opened early for people who liked to read the newspaper and generally start their day relaxing with a book or magazine.

Bryn waved hello to her coworker behind the circulation desk, but didn't go over to make small talk. She headed for the computer and searched for what she wanted. As she was searching, she remembered that she hadn't returned the two books she'd found about bunkers and fertilizer.

The thought stopped her in her tracks. Finding a prepper wasn't exactly easy. Heck, it took a friend of a friend of Dane's, who had some sort of pull with the government, to find Mr. Jasper. But thanks to those two books, she'd already found someone else she could talk to in person. Whoever had checked out those books was obviously an extreme survivalist.

Bryn thought about if she should try to check out the address where this John Smith person lived. She remembered one had been listed, but the question was whether it was real or made-up. He'd be fascinating to talk to. She could find out a ton of information from him. It'd be like having a prepper forum come to life right in front of her.

She thought back to what Dane had said...and their experience with Mr. Jasper. He'd been willing to show them his bunker, but only because Dane was giving him something in return. She totally got that preppers could be dangerous. She didn't think they *all* were, but knowing who was and who wasn't was the tricky part.

Bryn recognized the feeling inside her. It was just

like when she'd been young and had wanted to dissect the frog to learn more about it. She knew it could be dangerous to talk to someone who'd checked out both a prepper book and one about explosives, but she was having a hard time letting it go.

But more than curiosity was the alarming notion that there might be someone out there who was actually dangerous. Who might hurt other people. People like Dane. Dane didn't live in town, he could be vulnerable at his house by himself. What if this John Smith guy was truly dangerous? Shouldn't he be stopped before he hurt someone?

Bryn struggled with what she should do. She really wanted to see another bunker. Wanted to compare them. Note the similarities and differences between the two. But she couldn't just walk up and say, "Hi, I'm Bryn and I want to see your bunker." She knew that wouldn't fly. But what if she discovered more information about the man without physically going to see him? She might be able to find out if she should report this John Smith guy to the authorities.

But if she wasn't able to find out any other information and she did go and see him, she'd just reassure him that she didn't care about where he lived and she wasn't going to come back if the world ended to steal his stuff. She just wanted to pick his brain.

Deciding right then and there to see what she could

find out about John Smith the next time she worked, Bryn turned her eyes back to the computer screen and the books the library had on preppers and survivalist training. Luckily there were a few, not the one the guy on the forum suggested, but Bryn decided she'd start with what was available and go from there.

She wasn't surprised at the level of interest she had, which bordered on obsession, because that was how it usually worked with her. A topic would resonate with her and, once it did, she had to completely exhaust all avenues to get information about it. In the past, she'd researched everything from roller coasters and how they were built and maintained—which ended with a trip to Cedar Point in Sandusky, Ohio, to observe them and get a VIP tour—to the use of pesticides on farms in the Midwest.

There was no rhyme or reason as to what she got obsessed with, but Bryn had learned over the years that the only way she could get back to "normal," whatever that was, was to learn as much as possible about the topic. Once she'd satisfied her curiosity and felt like she had a good understanding of the issue or topic, she could drop it.

The trip to Mr. Jasper's bunker had only piqued her interest. It'd started with the bunker book she'd found in the library and now she was fully in the midst of an obsessive need to know more. She didn't tell Dane about her chats with the preppers she'd met on the forum, but the more she talked to them, the more she wanted to know.

But as much as she wanted to know more about bunkers and the prepper lifestyle, she had another obsession...Dane. She liked the man. Really liked him. Was fascinated by his prosthetic and the man himself. Not to mention how much she enjoyed kissing him. It was unlike her to have more than one obsession at a time, but she was well and truly hooked by both Dane *and* the survivalist lifestyle.

As if her thoughts of Dane were a magnet, she felt compelled to hear his voice. To apologize for not calling him last night. To connect with him.

Pulling out her phone as she walked to the stacks of books where she'd find the books on the prepper lifestyle, Bryn clicked on Dane's number.

"Hey, Smalls."

"I'm really, really sorry I didn't call. I wanted to. It's not that I didn't want you to come back over or that I didn't want to make out with you. It's just that once I logged on, I started to research survivalist shelters and they're all so different. Did you know some people have to drive like two hours to get to theirs? They're up in the mountains, hidden so well no one would ever be able to find them. Even they have to use a GPS to find them. And they range from the really expensive ones that are put in by professional companies—did you know there are organizations that specialize in making shelters like that?—to Conex containers people have buried in the ground. It's completely amazing. But I got distracted and meant to only message a few people, but I lost track of time. I'm sorry."

When Dane didn't say anything, Bryn tentatively asked, "Dane?"

"Where are you?"

"The library. Why?"

"I'll be there in ten minutes."

"Uh…okay?"

He chuckled but didn't elaborate. "See you soon, Smalls."

Bryn clicked off the phone, her brows drawn down in confusion. She'd never really understood men, but she *really* didn't get Dane sometimes. Shrugging, she tucked her phone into her pocket and perused the shelves. If she only had ten minutes, she needed to find the books she wanted and check out before Dane arrived. The last thing she wanted was to forget about him again. It seemed like he wasn't all that mad…this time, but she didn't want to push her luck.

Exactly ten minutes later, Bryn was thanking Bonnie, who had just handed her the two books she'd checked out, when she felt a hand at the small of her back.

Turning, Bryn saw Dane standing behind her, smiling down at her.

"Hey."

"Hey back," he returned. "Ready to go?"

"I guess. Not that I know where we're going."

"My place."

"Oh, okay. Is everything all right?" Bryn asked. He was acting weird, and she wasn't sure exactly what to think.

"Yup." He led them out to the parking lot and to his truck.

"I can drive out to your place."

"Nope."

Climbing inside, Bryn waited until Dane was belted in and had started driving through Rathdrum to speak. "I really am sorry, Dane. I didn't mean to lose track of time. But you should know, it happens more often than not. I can't help it."

"I know."

Bryn huffed out in exasperation. "Then what's going on? You aren't saying more than two words at a time. Do you need coffee? Is your blood sugar low? I'm kinda freaking out here."

"I'm not upset at all, sweetheart. I knew when I dropped you off that I probably wouldn't hear from you. I know how you are. And it doesn't bother me. But I didn't sleep that well last night."

"Why?"

"I was worrying about what was going on in that pretty head of yours. Were you arranging to fly to Wyoming to meet with a man you met online who offered to show you his bunker? I wondered if you were going to get any sleep or not. I worried about if you were going to try to hack into the FBI's database to find out more information about what I might have arranged to send to Mr. Jasper for agreeing to meet with us."

"I don't know how to hack. Although I'm sure I could probably figure it out, it can't be that hard, I'm just not interested in computers that way. Science and math are more my thing."

Dane grinned, but kept his eyes on the road. "I also didn't sleep well because I couldn't stop thinking about seeing you without your shirt on again, this time *not* while I was drunk, and how much I couldn't wait to get my hands, and mouth, on you."

"Oh."

"Yeah, oh." He finally turned to look at her then, and Bryn almost felt burned alive at the heat and desire she saw in his eyes. "I want you, Smalls. Every way I can get you. I swear to God I've never felt this pull I have to you with any other woman."

"You haven't had sex in a long time," Bryn blurted.

"Nope," he agreed immediately. "But just because I haven't been with anyone since before I was hurt, doesn't mean that I haven't been around attractive women. Women who would've taken me home and let me fuck them if I'd only given them a sign I wanted that. But I had no desire to even think about it. None. Zero. I was too busy having a pity party for myself. Thinking about how broken and fucked up I was.

"I think part of the reason I was so mean to you in the grocery store that night was because I was attracted to you at first glance. It threw me for a loop and I reacted badly. I'm happy as I can be that you seem to have forgiven me, but I haven't forgiven myself yet. I'm working on making it right."

"So we're going to your house so you can take off my shirt and make out?"

He laughed and shook his head in amusement. "You really say it like it is, don't you, Smalls?"

She shrugged. "Yeah. It's too confusing when people say things they don't mean. I don't always get sarcasm either...although I think I'm getting better at it."

"Then yes. I'm taking you to my place so we can make out and I can see those beautiful breasts of yours without your bra covering them up. I want to see what you look like when you come, and I'd kill to feel how hot and wet you are inside. Was that clear enough?"

"Uh...yeah. Dane?"

"Yes, sweetheart?"

"Will I get to see you too? Make *you* come?"

"You can do whatever you want with me."

"Okay then."

"But I'm not just gonna jump you the second we go inside. I want to know what you learned last night. I want to see the books you just checked out, and I want to feed you. I like taking care of you, listening to you. Then you can ask me what I did after I got home and we'll have a pleasant conversation. I'll touch you while we're doing it. Maybe hold your hand. I'll probably kiss you a time or two. Then when we're both comfortable, and we've drawn it out as much as possible, I'll take you to my bedroom and lay you on my sheets and we'll go from there."

"So we'll have sex?"

Dane shook his head as he turned down his driveway. "I don't think so. I mean, I'm sure we could change our minds if we get so excited and turned on we can't resist…but that's not my plan."

He parked the truck and turned it off. Dane hopped out and strode around to the other side and opened her door. Before she could get out, he stepped closer and blocked her exit. Putting one hand on her hip and his stump on her other thigh, he leaned in and looked into her eyes.

"I want you, Bryn. I want to bury myself so far inside you that I can't tell where you end and I begin. But if I'm being honest, I've enjoyed getting to know you over the last few weeks. You're funny, smart, and I learn something from you every day. I'm not hanging out with you simply to get laid, and I hope it's the same with you."

Bryn huffed out a laugh. "No, Dane. No guy has wanted to hang out with me before the way you have. If he wanted to have sex, it usually came up in our second date."

"So I want to make out with you. I want to make you come, but I also want to prove to you that you mean more to me than a quick lay. Okay?"

"You don't have to prove it to me."

"Then I want to prove it to myself. Now, come on. I'll see what I've got inside that I can make for a late breakfast. I know you probably ate already, but you'll want to eat something to keep up your strength. I don't want you passing out on me later." He grinned, then continued, "I ordered seasons five through eight of *Mythbusters* and they were delivered yesterday. We can start where we left off and work our way through them."

"Today?"

Dane helped her out of the truck and closed the door behind her. "Yeah, Smalls. Today. But not too many. I've got other plans for us too…remember?"

She glanced up at him as they walked to the front door of his house. "Yeah, I remember."

Bryn let go of Dane long enough to let him unlock

his door, and took a deep breath. She was tingling with excitement, and she knew without a doubt that when she walked through the door of Dane's house, her life would change forever. But she wanted it. She wanted Dane.

Chapter Seventeen

D ANE MADE THEM each a small veggie omelet and they watched a couple episodes of the science show Bryn had grown to love. But Dane could tell Bryn wasn't really concentrating on the show.

Wanting to keep her off-kilter, Dane ran his hand up and down her arm, loving the goosebumps that arose in its wake. He took out her hair tie and brushed his fingers through the silky tresses. He leaned down and inhaled the smell he'd forever associate with her, and made sure his nose brushed the sensitive nape of her neck as he did so.

He could tell Bryn was ready to either stand up and rip all her clothes off or run screaming out of the house because she wasn't ready for what he wanted to do to her. If he had a vote, it'd be for the former rather than the latter. He had to tread carefully; the last thing he'd ever do was anything that would knowingly hurt the amazing woman by his side.

When the second episode had ended, Dane stood up and held out his hand to her. "Come with me?"

She nodded and grabbed hold of his hand as if she were drowning and he was the only person who could save her. He led the way to his bedroom and kicked off his shoes. She followed his lead and did the same. Dane wasn't wearing his prosthetic, which she'd said she preferred when they were alone together at either of their homes. He also felt more normal when he didn't have it on, so was glad she felt the same way.

"Lie down, sweetheart, before you fall down."

Bryn jerkily scooted up on the bed and lay down, her head on the pillow, and held her breath, her hands twitching at her sides. He could tell she was worrying about what exactly they were about to do.

Just as it seemed she was starting to panic, Dane ordered, "Breathe, Smalls. Deep breaths. I'm not going to do anything that doesn't feel good...for both of us."

Bryn let out the breath she'd been holding in a whoosh. "I'm not good at this," she blurted out. "I like you a lot and I don't want to be a disappointment."

Dane leaned over and rested his weight on his elbows on the bed next to her upper arms. He trailed the fingers of his hand along her arm lightly, trying to gentle her. He felt her hands come up and fist his T-shirt at his sides. "I can promise you, I'm not gonna be disappointed. If anything, I'm the one who should be nervous."

"You? Why?"

"You know this is the first time I've done this since I

was injured."

"Yeah, so? It was your arm that was hurt, not your penis."

Dane resisted the urge to chuckle at hearing her call his dick a penis. He loved the way Bryn always said whatever was on her mind. It should make their love-making interesting, to say the least.

"True. But in the past, when I was with someone, I never had to worry about where to put my hands. I could support my weight wherever and however I needed to without having to think about it. But that's impossible now. I've only got one hand. I can only do one thing at a time. If I want to make sure you're wet enough to comfortably take me, I can't simply reach down and caress you like I might've in the past."

Dane could tell she was thinking over what he said.

After a moment, she said simply, "I can see how that might be an issue. But I know you, I'm sure you'll compensate somehow."

Dane felt his stomach unclench at her words. She had such confidence in him. It was a heady feeling. "So relax, Smalls. Yeah?"

"I talk too much."

Dane couldn't stop the smile that spread across his face that time. "You don't."

"I *do*," Bryn insisted. "The last time I did this, the guy put his hand over my mouth and said that he couldn't come when I was blabbering."

"Fucker," Dane said as he frowned down at her. "Bryn, I've hung out with you long enough to know this about you, and think it's cute as all get out how you say exactly what you're thinking. Not only that, but I *like* it. I don't have to worry about whether I'm screwing something up or saying the wrong thing. You'll either tell me or I can take one look at your expressive face and figure it out. It's refreshing, and it honestly makes me more comfortable. Especially here in bed. The last thing I want is to hurt you, or do something that you don't enjoy. Knowing you'll speak up and tell me, and not make me guess what you like, is an incredible turn-on. So nothing you say while I'm inside your hot, wet body, will have any effect on whether or not either of us orgasm…except maybe to speed it up."

"I told him that the average man ejaculates anywhere from a teaspoon to a tablespoon when he orgasms."

Dane put his weight on his left elbow and moved his right hand to the hem of her T-shirt, slowly moving it up her belly and chest as she spoke. He saw her take a deep breath and felt her back arch into his hand as he cupped her left breast. "Interesting. What else?"

"When masturbating, seventy-five percent of men reach orgasm within two minutes."

"Sounds about right," Dane murmured as he pulled

the cup of her bra down so he had better access to her nipple. He plumped the tissue and caught the small bud between his fingers, rolling and tugging on it until it was stiff and hard. "Like that, Smalls?"

"Yeah. Oh yeah. Every time you do…that…I feel it between my legs."

Dane swallowed hard. Fuck, she was amazing. "What can you tell me about nipples?" He didn't take his gaze from her face, wanting to make sure everything he did to her was still arousing and not making her uncomfortable.

"Some people find that the tops, sides, or bottoms of their breasts are more sensitive than their nipples."

Dane could tell Bryn wasn't really thinking about what she said, which made the fact that she could still recite random facts even more amazing. "Like this?" he asked, moving his fingers so they were lightly brushing around her nipple, but not touching it directly. Then he trailed his index finger around the bottom and side of her tit, testing her reaction to his touch.

"Dane," she protested, arching her back, trying to get him to touch her nipple again. "It feels good, but not like…" Her words trailed off as she whimpered, obviously wanting his fingers back where they'd been before.

"Guess we figured out what you like best, huh? Nipples for you all the way. Good to know." Dane moved to her other breast, pulling the cup down on that side as well. "I'm figuring out how best to please you as I go, but I can tell one thing that's gonna be tough…" He purposely let his sentence hang in the air.

"What?" Bryn breathed.

He smiled and waited a beat, pinching her other nipple until it peaked against his fingers as its twin had. "I don't have two hands to please both these babies at once…so I'll have to use my fingers on one side and my mouth on the other if I want to stimulate them both at the same time."

"God, Dane," she moaned.

"Take your shirt off for me, Smalls," Dane ordered. "I can't do it with only one hand…and even if I could, I'm a bit busy at the moment." He didn't stop his caresses as she moved. Her hands unclenching from his sides to grab the hem of her shirt and draw it upward.

Dane propped himself up as far as he could on his elbow as she stripped for him. Her hair got caught in the shirt as she pulled it off and ended up spread out on the pillow under her. Distracted, Dane leaned down and buried his nose in the brown tresses.

"Fuck, you smell good, Smalls. I swear I get a hard-on anytime I smell coconut anymore. If we ever go to the actual beach it's gonna be torture, because all I'll be able to think about is you on my bed, your hair spread out on my pillow."

Her hands came back to rest on his sides and pushed under his T-shirt. "Your shirt too," Bryn demanded, ignoring his commentary about the beach and her hair.

"My hand is busy. Take it off for me," Dane ordered.

She didn't hesitate, drawing her hands up his sides, taking the cotton material with her as she went. Dane shivered as her warm hands caressed his sensitive skin. He let go of her nipple long enough to hold up his arm so she could get the material off, then immediately dropped his gaze to her chest.

"Dane, lift your other arm up so I can get it off," Bryn demanded after the shirt had cleared his head.

"Leave it," Dane said absently, relieved when she did as he asked. The shirt fell to the mattress. He hadn't wanted to take his right hand off her chest long enough to prop himself up so the shirt could be thrown to the side.

He looked into Bryn's wide, glassy eyes. "Beautiful, Bryn. I've never seen such perfection. Tell me what else you know about nipples."

"Um…they show up on a fetus before the sex organs do… God…Dane!"

He barely heard her as he lowered his head and latched onto her right nipple with his mouth. He felt it peak even more as his teeth gently closed around it and he sucked with a light, steady pressure and caressed it at the same time with his tongue. His good hand plumped and caressed the other mound as he concentrated on the nipple in his mouth. Bryn squirmed under him, but wasn't moving away. Finally, he pulled back from her and murmured, "I've wanted to do this since that night I was drunk and you lifted up your shirt just to be fair. I knew you'd be this responsive. I somehow fucking knew it."

Dane didn't give her a chance to respond, but moved his mouth to the other side and worshiped that nipple, using his hand to plump the fleshy mound higher up to his eager lips.

He pulled back when he felt her hand caressing his rock-hard cock under his jeans. He pushed his hips farther into her palm and threw his head back for a moment, enjoying her touch through the thick cotton material of his pants more than he'd liked other women's hands on his bare skin.

Bringing the hand that had been at her breast up to her face, he palmed it and forced her eyes to his. "Are you sure, Smalls?"

"Men need more sex than women."

"What?"

"Men need more sex than women," Bryn repeated.

"Maybe so. But I've been masturbating on a regular basis since I met you. I can wait until you're ready."

"You were left-handed."

Used to her seemingly random comments, Dane leaned closer to her and rubbed his chest over hers. "I was. And?"

Bryn's breath hitched, but she asked, "Is it difficult to masturbate with your right hand?"

"Ah." Dane smiled and answered her question honestly. "It was at first. It frustrated and pissed me off at the same time. I felt like I was twelve years old, trying to learn the best way to get off again. But it got easier with practice, and I've had *lots* of practice over the last two months."

He didn't think she understood at first, but then her eyes closed briefly and she moaned. Her eyes met his again and she shifted under him, dragging her erect nipples over his chest. "I've never come with a man. I have a vibrator, and I can orgasm with it if I hold it against my clit, but men haven't seemed to know what to do."

"I'll give you permission to tell me exactly how you like, and need, to be touched if I can't figure it out. How about that?" Dane moved his hand from her face to the back of her neck. "I want to be the first, Smalls. The first to feel your hot body clench around my dick as you explode. The first to watch you get yourself off. The first to show you how women can more easily have multiple orgasms than men."

"You're awfully sure of yourself," Bryn observed.

"Most men have no idea how the female body is made or where to touch and how."

"That's why you can teach me." He saw the interest in her eyes, so he continued. "Call it research. You can see if it's possible to teach a one-handed former solder exactly where and how to touch you to get you off. Yeah?"

"Okay," she agreed immediately. "If you'll teach me how to touch you too. I've never given a guy a blow job...or gotten him off with my hands."

"Damn, this is gonna be fun," Dane declared, shifting until he was kneeling over her. "Take off your bra, Bryn. Then unbutton and unzip your pants, but don't take them off. That's my job."

She nodded and immediately arched her back and moved her hands so she could undo the hook of her bra. Dane didn't look away from her squirming body as his hand went to his own waistband to unfasten his pants. His cock hurt, pressed against the zipper as it was, but he didn't dare release himself yet. He needed the pressure to keep control over his body. No matter what he'd told Bryn, it'd been a long time since he'd had sex, and he knew he wouldn't last long at all once he got inside her.

After she'd done as he asked, Dane ordered, "Put your hands over your head."

"I want to touch you," Bryn pouted.

"And you will. But the second you do, I'm gonna explode. Let me take care of you first. Please?"

She nodded and slowly lifted her arms until they were resting on the pillow over her head.

Dane didn't wait for her to get settled, but immediately moved his hand and eyes to her stomach. He flattened his hand on her belly and ran it up between her breasts, then all the way back down so the heel of it pressed against her pussy. Then he ran it upward again, this time running his calloused palm over her right breast, then the left, before dragging it back down her body.

"Dane…"

"Speechless, Smalls? I'm shocked," he teased, keeping his hand moving over her body, getting her used to his touch and at the same time, stimulating her nerve endings.

"I can't think," she moaned as he leaned over her, using his thigh muscles to hold him upright, and ran his scarred stump lightly over her nipple. "Oh!"

"Was that a good oh, or a bad one?" Dane asked, freezing in place. He hadn't thought about what he was doing, he'd actually forgotten about not having a hand on his left side. He didn't want to do anything that would make her uncomfortable, but thankfully using his stump seemed to turn her on rather than off.

"Good. Definitely good. More." Bryn squirmed under him, using her motions to rub herself against his stump.

"Yeah, Smalls. God, that's so fucking sexy." Dane couldn't take his eyes off the sight of her rubbing her nipple against the scars on his left arm. She'd told him over and over again that she didn't see him as handicapped and wasn't repulsed in any way by his amputation site, but her actions right that moment made it finally stick in his mind. She was fully in the moment, wanting nothing more than to feel good, and *he* did that for her. It didn't matter that he was missing a hand, or that he was scarred, or even that he was jittery as all get out when he was in public.

As she continued to squirm against him, Dane used his hand to push her panties and jeans down until his thumb could reach her soaked folds. He looked down and inhaled a deep breath. Her pubic hair was soft as his hand brushed over it, but her pussy itself was slick and smooth.

"God, Bryn. You shave?" He looked up at her face as his thumb lazily caressed her, spreading her wetness over every inch of her pussy.

She shrugged, meeting his eyes and only stuttering once said, "It's cleaner and m-more aesthetically pleasing to the eye."

Dane pushed his hand down so the tip of his thumb pushed just inside her body, then pulled it out and moved up to her clit and swiped over it once. "It's *very* pleasing to the eye. But one other pro...more sensitivity without the hair."

Bryn's hips pushed up into him and she inhaled deeply. "More," she demanded.

"Are we entering the instruction phase of our love-making?" Dane asked with a smile.

"Yes."

"And you're gonna tell me where and how you want me to touch you if I don't do it right?" Dane pushed her underwear down farther and twisted his wrist so his thumb once again rested at her opening. He pressed it into her slowly, but this time didn't stop with just the tip. He kept going until it was inside her as far as it could go, and his index and middle fingers rested over her slippery clit.

Bryn nearly came up off the bed when he eased his thumb out, then back in, making sure to rub her clit with his other fingers as he did. Her hands came down from over her head and gripped both his biceps, her fingernails digging into his skin. Dane didn't care that she'd moved, the small pain in his arms somehow increasing his pleasure of the moment. Neither of them was completely naked, but it was the sexiest and most erotic experience he'd ever had in his life.

Her hips lifted again until her back was taking all her weight. Dane shifted closer to her, letting her rest her raised ass on his upper thighs. He leaned over her, putting his left arm on her belly and resting his stump between her breasts to help hold her still.

The position opened her more to him, and Dane wished he'd had the foresight to take off her pants before getting this far, but he couldn't stop now to save his life. He needed her orgasm like he needed to breathe. He moved his hand in and out of her folds. Then again. For once he was the one talking, and Bryn was silent.

"You're not telling me what to do, so maybe I'm doing all right, hmmmm? You like that, Smalls? Feels good, doesn't it? You're so wet, you're dripping all over my hand. I can feel you clenching my thumb...it's not big enough, is it? You need something larger in there, don't you? We'll get there, promise, but for now, show me how beautiful you are when you come. I want to witness what no other man has had the good fortune to see before. It's mine. Let go, Bryn. Trust me to bring you there. Stop thinking and feel. Just feel, sweet Bryn."

Dane could tell she was on the brink of her orgasm, and the next time he pushed inside her, he stretched his thumb just a bit farther and curled it up, feeling the spongy wall of tissue behind her clit. When she jerked in his grasp, he smiled.

"That's it, Smalls. Right *there*, huh? *That's* the spot, isn't it? Feels *good*, doesn't *it*?" With each emphasized word, Dane thrust against her G-spot with his thumb. "*Come* for me, Bryn. You can *do* it." With one last thrust, Dane pressed hard against the spot inside her and used his other two fingers to press hard against her clit.

Holding her down and loving the jerky, uncontrolled movements she made, Dane kept the pressure on her clit as she had the largest, messiest orgasm he'd ever had the privilege to witness. He slowly eased his touch as she became more sensitive and helped her come down from her sexual high.

He slowly pulled his thumb out from between her legs and brought it to his lips. He waited until Bryn's eyes opened to slits, then opened his mouth and licked every drop of her juice off his fingers.

"Female ejaculate is mostly water and there aren't many, if any, calories in it. Semen, on the other hand, has five to seven calories per teaspoon."

Dane chuckled and scooted back, letting Bryn's hips rest on the mattress again before leaning over her and kissing her. Their tongues tangled together and it was several moments before he pulled away. "Good to know that I can eat you out and make you come as many times as I want and won't have to worry about my caloric intake."

Bryn blushed and licked her lips nervously.

"You like the way you taste?"

She shrugged. "I hadn't thought about it before. But I like the way *you* tasted just now. With me still on your tongue."

Dane couldn't stop smiling.

"I came. With you. And I didn't have to tell you what to do."

"Nope."

"That was my G-spot, wasn't it?"

"Yup."

"The G-spot is short for Gräfenberg spot...named after Ernst Gräfenberg, who was a German gynecologist. It hasn't been proven to exist at all, some people say it's merely an extension of the clitoris."

Dane couldn't help it; his head went back and he roared with laughter. Getting himself under control with difficulty, he leaned down and rubbed his nose over hers. "I'd say it exists, Smalls. Want me to prove it again?"

Bryn bit her lip and looked adorably indecisive before she finally stated, "Maybe later. It's my turn to do that to you."

"That?"

"Make you come."

Still grinning, Dane rolled off Bryn to his back next to her and put his good hand behind his head as if he were relaxing on a beach in Tahiti. "Go for it."

Bryn slowly got to her knees next to his hip and

took her time looking him up and down before asking, "Can I take off your pants?"

"Yes." When she reached for them, he hurried to add, "I have a feeling this is gonna be really quick. I'm so turned on right now I'm not sure I can hold off for long. And before you get nervous, anything you do is gonna be perfect. You can't mess this up, Smalls. Swear."

"You're in shape," Bryn stated as she pulled off his jeans. "It typically takes men anywhere from one minute to an hour to get hard again once they orgasm...with your age and body type, I figure you're probably on the low end of that scale."

"Thanks for the vote of confidence, but we'll play it by ear. It's not a contest, and there's a lot more I want to do with you before we actually have sex." He reached up with his good hand and put it behind her neck, pulling her gently down to him so they were eye to eye. "Relax, Smalls. We've got all the time in the world. Yeah?"

Bryn nodded jerkily and Dane let her go. He lifted his hips and reached down and pushed his boxers off awkwardly with his right hand, using a foot to help kick them all the way off. He lay back, completely naked, and not feeling self-conscious for the first time since he'd been injured. He instinctually knew that Bryn wouldn't find him repulsive. It was a heady bit of knowledge that made him even harder.

He watched as Bryn took in his naked body for the first time. If he hadn't expected it, he might've been concerned at the clinical look in her eyes. He'd realized it a few weeks ago, but she processed her world differently than anyone he'd ever met. Her brain was constantly in motion and, almost like a computer, needed continuous input.

After several moments, she looked him in the eye and licked her lips. "Is anywhere off limits?"

"Jesus," Dane exclaimed breathlessly. Then took a deep breath and told her, "No. Touch me anywhere you want, Smalls. I can take it."

Chapter Eighteen

B RYN LICKED HER lips then bit the bottom one. Anywhere, he'd said. But she had no idea where to start. He was absolutely beautiful, from his head all the way down to his toes. She could see a few scars here and there, but it was as if they just made him even better. He was a complex man, and the imperfections of his body seemed to make him more approachable and interesting. Closing her eyes, she leaned down and put her nose in the space where his neck met his shoulder and inhaled deeply.

Dane moved his head to the side to give her more room, and Bryn nuzzled the skin there. He smelled a bit musky, with a hint of the soap he'd used that morning. Moving down his body carefully, Bryn moved her nose to his chest, then his belly, then lower. Using her hand to lift his erection, she inhaled his scent at the base. Definitely muskier than the rest of his body, but it didn't turn her off in the least.

Shifting until she was sitting between his legs, Bryn opened her eyes and glanced at Dane. He was watching her with an indescribable look. She froze. Shit, was she being weird? Should she not have smelled him like she had? He'd said nothing was off limits, but maybe he'd just been saying that.

"Go on, Smalls. Keep exploring."

She huffed out a breath and noticed a bead of semen appear on the tip of his cock. "You smell good...interesting...you don't mind?"

"No." His answer was short and to the point, but it was all she needed to hear.

She breathed out again heavily, and was rewarded by the semen drop getting bigger. "Pre-ejaculate is made in the Cowper's gland and sperm is made in the testicles. It's a fallacy that precome doesn't contain sperm. Approximately forty-one percent of men have active sperm in their pre-ejaculate and can impregnate women from that alone."

"Is that right?"

Dane's voice cracked, but Bryn was so fascinated by what she was witnessing, she didn't process it.

"Yeah. Studies show that pre-ejaculate and semen taste similar. Salty and bitter, but it can depend on what kinds of food the man has eaten." Her eyes came up to Dane's as she took one of her fingers and swiped over the liquid at the tip of his cock.

"Oh, Lord," Dane breathed, but didn't take his eyes off of her.

Bryn put her finger in her mouth and wrapped her tongue around it.

After several moments, Dane asked, "Well? What's the verdict?"

"It's…not that good."

He chuckled, and Bryn's attention went back to his dick as it bobbed with his movements. "Some people love it, others don't. It's okay if you don't, Bryn."

"You won't be upset if I don't want to swallow it?"

"Not at all. Nothing we do when we're together will upset me. If you don't like it, you don't like it."

"I can still give you blow jobs…as long as you don't make me swallow."

Dane almost choked but said, "God, Smalls. You have no idea how fucking sexy the image in my brain is right now. You leaning over me, or kneeling in front of me as you take my dick into your mouth. I can just see your lips closing around me…fuck…I will never complain about getting to come in your beautiful pussy rather than your mouth. I'm putty in your hands, sweetheart. Whatever you want, I'll make sure you get. But I hope you won't get upset that I love how *you* taste, and plan on getting up close and personal with your pussy on a regular basis."

"Uh, no, I don't think I'll mind that at all."

Bryn licked her lips and studied Dane's cock. She hadn't ever had a chance to get this close with one before. In the past, the men she'd been with had been all about putting their cocks inside her as fast as they could and not letting her explore. She didn't want to waste this chance…still afraid that she'd do or say something so off the wall, Dane would realize that she really was the dorkiest dork on the planet and run as far and as fast as he could from her.

She leaned forward, pushing his dick up toward his stomach so she could look at his balls. They were slightly hairy and dangled, what looked to her, uncomfortably between his legs. Putting a finger against one and pushing, she was somewhat surprised at how soft it was.

"Take them in your hand," Dane ordered. "Don't grab them, but feel their weight."

She did as he asked. "They're a lot softer than I thought they'd be."

"Right before I come, they get harder."

"Are they always this big?"

Dane snorted. "No. You should see them when I'm cold or scared. They shrivel up practically to the size of grapes."

Bryn nodded. "Yeah, it's the cremasteric reflex, which shortens the muscles to bring them closer to your body to keep them warm. Do they hang lower when you're hot?" Her hand wrapped around his balls carefully, getting used to the size and weight.

"I guess."

"Can you feel them jostling around down there when you walk?"

Dane laughed outright at that. "No. Not really. They stay pretty contained in my boxers. They'll shift around sometimes when I sit and need to be adjusted, but for the most part, I don't really notice them...unless I'm about to get kicked down there or if I'm around a pretty woman...like you."

Bryn nodded, her mind already moving on to the next topic. "Guys have a G-spot too, research says it's about two inches inside your anus and is approximately the size of a chestnut. Most people call it the prostrate, but I like thinking of it as a guy's G-spot instead." She moved her index finger down toward his ass—and brought her eyes up to his when he grabbed her wrist.

"How about we save that for another day?"

"You don't like it?"

"Never tried it, sweetheart."

"Oh." She liked that. Liked that there was something he hadn't done, that maybe she could share with him. Their eyes stayed locked on each other and Bryn couldn't tell what Dane was thinking. "Will you show me what feels good for you? I don't want to do anything wrong."

"With pleasure. But I don't think you could do anything to me that was wrong. Give me your hand."

Bryn held her hand out to him and he wrapped it around the tip of his dick, making sure to get his precome on her hand. He smoothed it down his shaft, lubricating it, then back up. He kept his grip tight on hers, but not so much that she felt as if she was hurting him.

"The best way is to start slow, speed up after a while, then end slow." Bryn concentrated on their joined hands on his body as he spoke, soaking in each word and committing it to memory. "I'm already rock hard, but when it hasn't been quite so long since I've been with you, it'll take a bit longer for me to get to this point. You could use just one hand to get me off, hell, it's how I have to do it now, but it would be more interesting if you changed it up...using one hand, then both, then back to one. Alternate your pattern and your touches...it'll keep me on edge longer."

Bryn nodded and brought up her left hand, grasping his length under where he was guiding the other, smiling when he groaned in enjoyment.

"I can feel you flex under my hand. It's hot," she told him, not taking her eyes from his cock as their hands continued to stroke up and down the hard length."

"Yeah, like that. Don't neglect my balls. They're really sensitive. You can either take a break from your hand that's stroking me, or use your other hand to softly fondle them. You can squeeze them, but keep your grip light…God…yeah…just like that…perfect…"

Bryn used her fingernails to lightly scratch the sensitive skin and was rewarded by another drop of precome leaking out of the top of his dick.

He continued in a hoarse tone, "The tip of my cock is very sensitive, it's got the most nerve endings. Put your thumb and fingers in the shape of an O and move it up and down over the tip…not so far down…yeah, fuck, just like that. God, Bryn, your hand is so much softer and coordinated than mine."

Bryn glanced up into Dane's face and felt her heart rate increase. He'd closed his eyes and tilted his head back. The hand that had been guiding hers had fallen to the side and was clutching the sheet next to him. She'd never felt as powerful as she did right at this moment. The strongest, most take-charge man she'd ever met in her life was putty in her hands. It felt amazing.

When he didn't say anything for several moments, she asked in a soft voice, "What next?"

"Use your free hand to press against the base of my dick, there's a piece of skin that meets…"

His voice trailed off as Bryn found exactly where he was describing and caressed it. She moved her other hand from just the tip, down to the base, then went back to caressing just the tip again. She added in some twists of her palm and altered the strength she was using to grip him.

He was leaking fluid almost constantly now, lubricating his length and making it easier for her hand as it caressed him. Bryn licked her lips, enjoying being able to pleasure him.

"I'm close, Smalls. Real close. No...don't speed up...the closer I get to orgasm, the more sensitive I'll be. When I shoot, point the tip toward my stomach to catch my come and hold my cock tightly...don't stroke me...it'll hurt more than feel good...you ready?"

"Yes. Please. I want to see you come."

Bryn felt his hand come up and clutch her thigh where it sat between his legs, the stump of his other arm came up as well and he curved it as best he could around her right forearm.

"Oh yeah...squeeze my balls a little more...fuck, exactly like that...when I say, press hard at the base of my dick...ready? Here it comes...now! Fuuuuuuuuuuuck!"

Bryn hardly heard Dane swearing because she was too engrossed in the semen shooting from the tip of his dick. She stilled her hand as he requested and felt him jerk under her palm as he orgasmed. His come spurted out in several long, milky-white jets, coating his lower stomach.

He moaned a few times, and when she moved her hand slowly up and down his softening shaft, he pumped his hips up into her grip. More come leaked out the tip, lubricating her palm and making his cock extremely slippery. Keeping in mind that he said he got really sensitive after orgasming, Bryn let go of him and laid his cock down on his lower stomach, covering it with her palm.

"What are you doing?" he whispered.

"It seems wrong somehow to just let go," she replied somewhat sheepishly.

He chuckled and lifted his hand to hers. "Give me your other hand."

Bryn did, and swallowed hard when he brought it to his stomach and placed it over his release.

"It's not a thorough scientific experiment if you don't follow through, Smalls."

"This wasn't in any way scientific," she retorted, smiling, but not taking her eyes off their hands smearing his release over his stomach. "We didn't have an official hypothesis."

"But jacking me off provided you some insight into cause and effect, didn't it? And I do believe it's not only reliable, but valid too."

Bryn smiled up at him at that, happy he was talking her language. She mimicked his words, "I do believe you're right, Mr. Munroe. If I conducted this same test again, I think I'd most likely achieve the same results."

"Damn straight. And did it measure what it was

supposed to?" he asked lazily.

"You mean, if I figured out just the right way to stroke your cock, you'd come?" Bryn returned.

"Yeah."

"Then yes, the validity of my research was proven."

"Come here," Dane ordered, reaching up with his left arm and hooking his elbow over her hip.

Bryn moved up his chest, purposely brushing her hard nipples over his release as she went. She collapsed onto him and lowered her mouth to his at the same time he raised his head to meet her.

This wasn't a nice polite kiss like they'd shared in the past. This was passionate and almost desperate. Bryn's nose rubbed against Dane's and she impatiently turned her head, trying to get closer. Her mouth opened wide under the onslaught of his and she welcomed his tongue as it curled and dueled with hers. Her hands started flat against his upper chest, but inched their way up until her fingertips caressed his lower jaw and neck as they made out.

His hand shoved itself under her loose waistband to clamp onto her ass and grind her lower body against his. His other arm wrapped around her upper back, keeping her flush to his chest.

The smell of his release only turned Bryn on more. She wasn't a fan of the taste, but loved how he smelled like sex...how *they* smelled like sex. Her fingers were still wet from his release and she realized she'd smeared it on his chest and neck as they'd kissed. It was a tactile and olfactory turn-on. She inhaled deeply as they kissed, lost once again in a haze of sexual satisfaction.

Dane pulled back and bit lightly on her lower lip before sucking it into his mouth. She whimpered and breathed as hard as if she'd run two miles.

She opened her eyes and saw Dane's looking into hers. As soon as he noticed her watching him, he closed his eyes and tilted his head again, once more crushing his lips to hers. This time when she licked over his tongue, he sucked on it. Bryn moaned into his mouth. She'd never, not once, felt this overwhelmed in her entire life. Not even right before she took the GRE exam.

Finally, when they both needed to breathe, they pulled their heads apart, but didn't move their bodies even an inch from where they were plastered together. Without a word, Bryn put her head on Dane's shoulder and relaxed into him bonelessly.

His come was sticky between them, they smelled like she imagined a porn shoot would after it was completed, and her panties were soaked with her earlier release and her excitement at being able to please Dane, but Bryn didn't ever want to move again. She tried to memorize every second of what had just happened, in case she did something to screw up their relationship in the near future.

When her heart rate had finally slowed down and she could breathe normally again, she whispered, "Thank you."

Dane chuckled under her. "I think that's *my* line, Smalls."

She lifted her head so she could look at him. "No one has ever trusted me like you just did. Ever. I had no idea it was so...amazing. Messy. Intense."

"Just wait until I'm inside you and we get to come together."

"You still want to?" She couldn't help the note of vulnerability that leaked out with her question.

"Yeah, Bryn. I want to get inside you more than I've ever wanted anything before in my life. Including when I'd woken up in the hospital in Germany and realized my hand was gone and prayed it had all been a dream."

"Wow."

"Yeah," Dane agreed. "If you thought what we just did was hot, just wait until I'm inside you."

"Lord," Bryn breathed. "I don't know if I'll survive."

"You'll survive. And hopefully become addicted."

"I don't think *that* will be an issue," she commented dryly, then murmured reluctantly, "We probably need to get up."

"We will. In a bit." He didn't sound like he was in a

hurry to move at all. "I'm comfortable. Aren't you?"

"Well, yeah. But you're covered in…" Her voice trailed off.

"I am. And it feels fucking fantastic."

"All right then."

"All right then," he echoed. "And for the record," Dane continued in a soft voice, his hand slowly and easily caressing her ass under her pants, "I've never been as turned on in my life as I was just now. You might be new at this sort of thing, but the passion in your eyes, the enthusiasm and wonder shining through…it was the best gift anyone has ever given me. Thank *you*, Bryn. I've spent the last almost year feeling like only part of a man. You changed all that with one hand job. Crude, but true."

Bryn snuggled back down into Dane's chest, refusing to let him see the tears in her eyes at his words.

"I used two hands," she told him shakily.

He chuckled. "So you did." As if he knew she needed a moment to collect herself, he said nothing more, other than, "Take a nap, Smalls. You're gonna need your energy tonight."

"I don't nap."

"Shhhhhh."

"Bossy."

She heard the puff of laughter come from him but

he didn't say anything else. Merely caressed her bare back with his stump and her ass with his hand. She wouldn't have thought it possible, but within moments, she was sound asleep.

Chapter Nineteen

B RYN PUT BOTH elbows on the table and rested her chin on her hands. She'd been ready, more than ready, to have sex with Dane, but they'd been woken up from their catnap by his phone ringing. It'd been Steve, asking if Dane wanted to go with him on a few jobs to see if working with him was really what he wanted to do.

The look of desire and heat in Dane's eyes as he gazed at her was hard to combat, but Bryn had encouraged him to go ahead and spend what was left of the day with the other man. She wanted to make love with Dane more than she wanted almost anything…even the time she'd had the opportunity to sit down and talk with Stephen Hawking about his latest research. But, he needed to do this to find himself again, and working with Steve could be the first step in doing so. Not only that, but after the haze of her orgasm had worn off, she'd felt unsure again, so she'd climbed out of his arms and grabbed her shirt, gesturing at him to tell Steve yes.

An hour later she was back at her apartment…bored

out of her mind. The crosswords weren't cutting it, nobody was online at the prepper forum to talk to her, and she wasn't finding any information on the Internet about survivalists that she didn't already know.

Looking at her watch, Bryn saw that the library was still open. Once the idea took root, there was no stopping it. Her quest for knowledge was insatiable, and she knew she wouldn't be able to think about anything else until she satisfied it.

Knowing Dane was busy, and would be for the rest of the afternoon, she rationalized that she'd have plenty of time to get to the library and do what she needed to do before Dane got back and came over to her place.

Goosebumps broke out on her arms when she thought about what she wanted to do with Dane later that night. He'd made it more than clear that they'd make love when he got back…and the kiss he'd planted on her only made her look forward to seeing what she'd been missing all the more.

But first things first.

Bryn put thoughts of a naked Dane out of her mind and grabbed her car keys and cell phone. She didn't bother with her wallet because she was just going to the library…it was only a mile or so away, and if she drove within the speed limit, she should be okay.

AN HOUR LATER, Bryn was driving down a gravel road, miles from Rathdrum, intent on her mission. She'd started out just looking at a few of the books on preppers she hadn't checked out previously, and had been reminded about the person who'd taken out the *Design and Build Your Own Doomsday Bunker* and *Dangers of Fertilizers* books.

The longer she thought about it, the more she realized it wasn't a good thing. The people on the online prepper forum had reiterated how dangerous some of the others in the lifestyle could be, mostly because they were paranoid about outsiders finding their bunkers. But not one had talked about the need for explosives in their bunkers. They did some gardening, but kept them small because, again, they didn't want to give away the locations of their bunkers...and having a large garden could lead someone straight to them.

That got Bryn thinking. Why would a prepper want to check out a book on the dangers of fertilizer when there wasn't a good reason to have that much on hand in the first place?

Then she remembered the address she'd looked up before. And *that* got her thinking maybe she could just do a drive-by. See if anything looked suspicious. She wouldn't try to make contact with anyone; she recalled Dane, and the others online, warning her about confronting a prepper.

She'd just find out if the address was made-up, or if someone actually lived there. And if they did, she'd tell Dane what she'd found at the library, about the books, and he could help her decide what to do about it…if anything.

She'd put the address into her phone map app. There wasn't a house showing on the satellite view, but the pin was on a real road. Knowing it wouldn't be smart to go without telling Dane, she tried to call him, but it went to voicemail immediately.

Hey Dane. I wanted to let you know that I'm on my way out to check an address. There were two books checked out by the same person recently and I think maybe this person is up to no good. I don't even know if the address is a real one, the person probably made it up. But don't worry, even if it is real, I'm not going to talk to anyone. I'm just going to drive by and verify the address. I'll tell you more about everything when I get back. I should be home around five. I hope your day with Steve is going okay and nothing has freaked you out today. If it has, don't get sad about it. I'm sure Steve will have your back. Anyway, I'm looking forward to having sex with you tonight. Did you know that when people have sex their inner nose swells up? Scientists think it's because of increased blood flow. I'm interested to see if it's true or not…okay, I'm off. And don't worry, I'm being safe. Bye.

Putting the phone in the holder on the dash, Bryn kept one eye on the small screen, making sure she was turning at the right times.

Heading down the one-lane gravel path that should be the driveway of the house she was looking for, if it existed, and if her directions were correct, Bryn couldn't help but feel nervous. Her quest for knowledge had sometimes gotten her in trouble, but this time she was being smart. She'd told Dane where she was going, and she'd turn around if she saw a house of any sort.

Her car bumped and rattled down the long driveway until she came to a stop in front of a ramshackle building. It didn't really look like a house anyone actually lived in, but it was rural Idaho. It wasn't as if there were mansions down every gravel road. There was also a large garage-type building, built out of what looked like a massive pipe which had been cut in half.

She sat in her car, curiosity warring with her need to be smart and safe. She rolled down her window and didn't hear anything but the sound of the wind through the trees and birds chirping.

She shivered. A feeling of something not being right shooting through her.

Bryn immediately put the car in reverse to get the hell out of there, when the sound of a shotgun cocking had her spinning around.

A man stood next to her open window with the barrel of a shotgun pointed at the ground.

In some ways, he reminded her of Mr. Jasper. His hair was too long, badly in need of a wash, and he was tall and slender. But that's where the similarities ended. While Mr. Jasper looked wary, this man looked bat-shit crazy.

His eyes were narrowed in suspicion and she could see the evil in their depths. His hands and face were filthy, caked with dirt and who knew what else, and the unkempt black beard made him look even more sinister.

He was younger than Mr. Jasper, probably closer to mid-thirties. His voice was low and menacing…and she knew down to the marrow of her bones she was in deep trouble.

"Who the fuck are you?"

Bryn wanted to turn back time, even only if by a few minutes. She shouldn't have turned down the driveway. Once she'd realized there probably wasn't a house at the address she'd looked up at the library, she should've just turned around and gone back to Rathdrum. Told Dane what she'd found. He would've let her know if she was on to something, if the person who'd checked out the books was harmless or not.

But it was too late now.

"Uh…I'm Bryn…I seem to be lost. I must've made a wrong turn somewhere. I was turned around. I'll just be on my way."

"Oh you made a wrong turn somewhere for sure, girly. Get out of the car. Now."

She didn't want to. Really didn't want to. But when he raised the shotgun and pointed it at her, she knew she didn't have a choice. She was smart. Maybe she could talk her way out of this. She wanted to reach across the car and grab her cell phone. Call Dane. But as she moved, the man took a step closer to her and she could see his finger twitch on the trigger.

"Okay, okay. I'm getting out," Bryn said softly, opening her car door and stepping out. She kept her eyes on the man in front of her, and his gun, and didn't dare look at anything else.

She didn't understand the head movement he made…he jerked his head to the left and then nodded once.

Bryn didn't see the person come up behind her, and knew nothing else when she fell unconscious to the ground.

DANE CLIMBED BACK into Miss May with a tired grunt. He was out of shape. Four hours following Steve around, bending and holding pipes while the other man checked fittings and connections and looked for the reasons why a large stovetop or refrigerator wasn't working, had worked muscles he hadn't used in quite a while.

He made a vow to start running and getting back into shape. He knew he'd let himself go for far too long. Truck had tried to tell him to get off his ass, but he hadn't listened. Now that Steve had officially offered him the part-time position, he was excited about returning to his pre-injury fitness level.

Leaning over and opening the glove compartment, Dane grabbed his cell. He hadn't wanted to be distracted while working, and had wanted to put his best foot forward for what might've been his future boss.

Smiling when he saw he had a message from Bryn, Dane clicked to listen—and immediately felt uneasy. It was obvious she truly hadn't understood how dangerous preppers could be. And he knew her. There was no way she was going to be able to simply drive by an address if she thought there might actually be a bunker located on the premises.

He grinned momentarily at her nose comment, and could imagine her wanting to shove her finger up his nose to measure whether or not his inner nose had swelled while they had sex, but his concern for her quickly overrode any amusement he might feel about her quirkiness.

He dialed her number and waited, but it went

straight to voicemail. He left a quick message for her to call him as soon as she got the message, but had no intention of waiting for her to get back to him. He put the truck in gear and headed through Rathdrum toward her apartment.

Bryn's car wasn't in the lot, so he turned his truck around and headed for the library. Her car wasn't there either, but this time he parked and headed inside the building. It was closing time, but he had just enough time to get inside and see if Bryn had talked to anyone before she'd left.

Dane had a bad feeling about the whole situation. It was the same feeling he'd had right before his unit had set out to investigate reports of insurgents in the area before they'd run over the IED. He'd made himself a promise when he'd woken up in the hospital in Germany that if he ever had the feeling again, he wouldn't dismiss it as simply being paranoid.

The door dinged as Dane entered the public building and made his way straight to the circulation desk. He didn't even wait for the woman sitting there, he thought her name was Bonnie, to ask if she could help him. He'd met her a few times, but wasn't interested in sharing pleasantries at the moment.

"Did you see Bryn today?"

"Hey, Dane. Yeah, she was here earlier. Why?"

"She's not answering her phone and I'm worried

about her."

Bonnie looked relieved. "Oh, well, she probably just got distracted by something. She does that a lot."

Dane was shaking his head before she'd gotten halfway through her sentence. "No. It's more than that this time."

Bonnie looked uncomfortable for the first time. Her brow furrowed and she bit her lip before saying, "Maybe I should have you talk to Rosie."

"Yes, please," Dane agreed immediately, knowing the head librarian would be able to help him faster than the college student who usually sat at the front desk.

Bonnie stood up and backed away, keeping him in her sights, until she got to a doorway behind her. Then she spun on her three-inch black heels and disappeared through the door.

Dane fought the urge to pace, barely. He felt the seconds ticking by as if in slow motion. Every second he stood here in the library was one more second Bryn could be in danger. He didn't know it for sure yet, maybe the address she was checking out would turn out to be nothing, but somehow he didn't think so. He had no idea how or when she'd become so important to him, but there was no denying it.

Rosie Peterman came out of the door behind the counter. "Hi, Dane, can I help you?"

"Hey, Rosie. I have reason to believe that Bryn is in

trouble. She's been fascinated lately by the prepper lifestyle. I took her to meet with a man who has a bunker, and I'm afraid it only fueled her quest to learn more. I know this is unusual, but we both know Bryn, she doesn't exactly see dangers when she's lost in her quest for knowledge. Can you help me figure out what she looked up and whose address she found?"

The head librarian nodded regally. "I do know. Her love of information is what makes her an exceptional employee. And yes, I've had to remind her to focus on her job rather than looking through books she's shelving more than once. Follow me. We'll see what we can find. We can start by reviewing the security video…see what she did when she was here."

Dane glanced at his watch as he followed the woman. He instinctively knew he didn't have a lot of time to search for the address, but since it was the only way he'd find Bryn, he'd do it. He just hoped she could hang on until he could track her down.

BRYN PICKED UP her head from where it rested on her chest and moaned at the pain that shot through it. Her neck ached from the odd angle it had been resting and her head hurt…she wasn't sure why, just that it did. She tried to open her eyes, but squeezed them shut again at the bright light that pierced into her pupils, making her head throb even harder.

"The prisoner is awake."

Bryn didn't understand what in the world the voice meant, so she cautiously lifted her eyelids a fraction of an inch, wanting to see where she was and what was going on.

The bright light shining down on her from above and in front of her kept her from being able to see anything. "W-where am I?" she stuttered.

"We ask the questions here, not you. Who are you and what were you doing on my property?"

Swallowing hard, Bryn licked her dry lips in vain, her mouth not able to produce any saliva to bring relief to her parched skin. "I'm Bryn. I was lost." She decided to stick to the story she'd used when she first saw him. "Did you hit me?"

"We ask the questions here." This time the words were decidedly feminine. "Who do you work for?"

"The library. I work at the library."

Bryn screeched as ice-cold water drenched her from head to toe. She tried to wrench her hands up to block the second bucketful, but found her arms tied tightly behind her. Gasping at the second, and just as cold, unasked-for shower, she could only blink the water out of her eyes and tug futilely at her bonds.

"Try again." It was the man's voice.

Bryn squinted, but wasn't able to see anything past the bright light in her eyes. It was as if she was standing on a stage and had a spotlight on her. The room was dark except for the lights. She looked down at herself and saw she was still wearing the jeans and T-shirt she'd put on that morning before heading to the library.

She'd known it when she'd first seen the house, but now her bad decision was being reinforced all that much more. She shouldn't have tried to find out if the address was real or not. She should've gone straight to Dane...or even the cops. She thought back to not only Dane's conversation, but the many chats she'd had with the men and women online, about the differences between a prepper who wanted to be left alone and the dangerous men who could be living in and around their rural town. Guess she'd found out for herself how right they all were.

But at least she'd called Dane and told him where she was going.

She groaned. Shit. She hadn't actually given him the address. She'd told him she was checking it out, but not *where* she was going.

She was in deep shit—and it was all her fault. For someone as smart as she was supposed to be, she sure had been stupid.

"My name is Bryn Hartwell. I really do work at the library," she told the man. "I'm a nobody. I'm a big nerd and I met a prepper the other day and it made me more interested in the lifestyle. I was just driving around the countryside checking out different properties that were for sale and got lost. That's it. That's all it is."

"Who did you meet with? Was it Frank?"

Bryn's mind spun. *Who the hell is Frank?* The man didn't give her a chance to answer.

"Doesn't matter. You're just another government spy who's here to make sure I don't carry out my life's work! It's my destiny. The United States government is brainwashing its citizens. They're watching us all the time. They know every move we make. They won't let us worship who we want and they definitely don't want any other countries to worship the way *they* want. It has to stop. And the majority of the citizens just go right along with it! They don't care, goin' about their business, not caring about the slaughter their country is conducting, all in the name of national security. Who are you working for? The CIA? The FBI?"

"No!" Bryn responded immediately. "No one. I'm just me."

"You're lying."

"I'm not, I swear!" Bryn struggled to get free again, wanting nothing more than to start the day over and not make the incredibly stupid decision to go looking for that address by herself.

"Do you want me to go take care of her car now?"

the female asked in a low, trembling voice.

"Well, Bryn, I don't know who you really are, but I'll find out," the man told her. "I've worked too hard and long to get where I am, and to set up the op I've got planned, to let a nosy female ruin it all. Just goes to show the only thing a female is good for is having babies and keeping house, like my woman does. She doesn't go where she's not wanted and does exactly as she's told. When the Taliban takes over this country, they'll make sure women learn their place. Don't go anywhere, you hear? I'll be back, and you had better be prepared to answer my questions. You don't want to know what I'll do if you don't cooperate."

Bryn heard footsteps then the clang of a door, then nothing.

She had no idea where she was, but knew she was in big trouble. She shivered in the cool air and shook her head, trying to get a piece of wet hair that was stuck to her cheek off her face. It didn't budge. She hung her head in defeat at her hopeless situation.

But then her sense of self-preservation kicked in. She wasn't going to sit around and wait for the elusive Mr. Smith to torture her more.

She spent several minutes trying to get her hands loose from her bonds, but only succeeded in hurting her wrists. Her ankles were also secured to the legs of the wooden chair she sat in. The lights shining down on her hurt her eyes, so she shut them and tried to think.

Her phone was still in her car, as long as Mr. Smith and his wife hadn't found it and smashed it. Maybe Dane could find her that way. She hadn't really told anyone in the library what she was doing, but had logged into the library computer system. Dane was smart. Maybe he could track her activity and figure out the address that way.

She huffed out a breath that was half sob, half laugh. It wasn't as if Dane was a computer genius. He was smart, but she had no idea if he would even think to track her that way. The phone company could follow the pings from the cell phone towers she passed, but by the time he figured out to do that, it might be too late for her anyway. Figured just when she was finally looking forward to spending the night with a man, she'd do something to screw it up.

Relaxing her neck muscles, she rested her head on the back of the chair. She kept her eyes closed and took a deep breath, forcing her tears away. Crying wouldn't help her now. The only thing she had to rely on was her brain. She'd have to talk her way out of this somehow. She hadn't told anyone where she was going. Dane wasn't going to swoop in and magically rescue her from her own stupidity. She should've listened to him, but it was a moot point now. She was on her own.

Chapter Twenty

"SO SHE SPENT some time on the computer, then left." Dane asked, "Is there a way to see what she was looking at?"

Rosie shook her head. "Not really. I mean, all of the employees have a separate login, and I'm sure someone who's good at computers could probably do it, but I don't know how."

"I might be able to help."

Dane turned to the door and saw the woman he'd talked to earlier standing there. He racked his brain for her name and finally remembered it. "Bonnie, right?"

She nodded. "I'm majoring in computer science down at the University of Idaho. I had a class last semester on tracking logins and keystroke monitoring. I'm not sure I can help, I only got a B in the class, but I'm willing to try."

"Anything at this point would be extremely helpful. I'm going to step outside and make a call, but please let me know if you find anything," Dane told the women.

"Of course," Rosie replied, already focused on the

screen as Bonnie started working.

Dane dialed his phone as he stalked out of the quiet library. "Come on, come on," he muttered as the phone rang in his ear.

"Yo! How's it goin', Dane?"

"I need your help." He didn't beat around the bush. If anyone could help him find out what Bryn had gotten herself into, it'd be Truck and his connections.

"Sitrep."

"Bryn's missing. She told me she was checking out an address of someone who'd taken out some books at the library, but didn't tell me where. She's not answering her phone. It goes straight to voicemail."

"You call Tex?"

"No. I wanted to get in touch with you first. I've got a really bad feeling about this, Truck."

"Give me her number and I'll call Tex."

Dane immediately recited it to Truck. Having him talk with Tex would leave him free to concentrate on whatever was going on here.

"What's she drive?" Truck asked.

"A piece-of-shit, nineteen-ninety Corolla. She's been incommunicado for about two hours, give or take fifteen minutes or so."

Dane could hear Truck talking to someone in the background, and he paced while he waited for the other man to get back on the phone.

"Okay, I'm on this, but here's the thing. I'd be out there in a heartbeat if I could, but you caught me at the worst time possible. I literally would do anything for you, brother, but I cannot leave right now."

Dane's stomach dropped. He'd thought Truck would have his back. He'd thought—

"But I'm already getting the rest of the team on this. They'll be wheels up in twenty minutes. They're comin', Fish."

"Everything okay with you?" Dane asked. He was mired in his own worry about Bryn, but couldn't ignore the warning bells that were going off in his head about what Truck had said.

"I've got an appointment that I can't miss. You know I would if I could. But it's literally a matter of life and death. If I don't do this today, I'll lose my chance." His voice dropped. "Kills me. Fucking *kills* me that I can't be there. But I've got your back. I'll be the liaison with Tex and I'll contact the local PD for you while you search."

Dane had no idea what could possibly be a matter of life and death for his friend, but now wasn't the time to get into it.

"Dane? I think I found something."

The words came from the front door of the library, and Dane turned to see Bonnie standing there, motioning him to come back inside.

"Hang on, Truck."

"I'm here listening."

Dane appreciated his friend more than he could say at the moment. He stalked back into the library and into Rosie's office, keeping Truck on the line. "Did you get in?"

"Yeah," Bonnie said. "She looked up two books that had been checked out about two months ago. *Design and Build Your Own Doomsday Bunker* and *Dangers of Fertilizer.* She then accessed the patron database to look at the application of the person who borrowed them. A John Smith."

"Is the address on the application?"

"Yes, of course." Bonnie recited it out loud.

"Get that, Truck?" Dane asked into the phone.

"Check."

"That has to be where she went." Dane turned to Bonnie, who was now looking at him in concern. "Thank you. This is exactly the information I needed."

"Is she all right? You'll find her?"

"I'll find her," Dane said with conviction. "Thanks." He headed for the front door once more.

"I'll call Tex. Give him the info you got there. In the meantime, be smart. Hang tight and don't do anything crazy."

"She's out there," Dane told Truck. "She needs me."

"And she'll get you," Truck retorted. "As long as

you hold on to your shit. You need intel. So hang the fuck on and wait for me to get back to you. Do not head out to that address on your own. Bryn is tough. Whatever is going on, she'll hang in there until your backup can arrive."

"I don't like it." Dane told Truck something he already knew.

"And Hollywood didn't like it when he knew Dean had his woman, but let his team do what they do best."

Dane knew Truck had a point. "I'll hold off, but you call me the second you find out any information."

"I will."

Dane sighed in relief, then asked what had been nagging at him. "You gonna be able to do this and get your life-and-death thing done?"

"Yeah. I might be out of pocket for thirty or so, but I'll make sure the team is there and ready and you have all the info you need before I do."

"I owe you."

"Fuck off," Truck bit out. "You don't owe me shit. I gotta go call Tex."

Dane frowned when Truck hung up on him, but shook it off and stalked toward his truck. He thought he'd head to Bryn's apartment again. Maybe, by some miracle, she'd returned there and he could call Truck back and tell him to call the guys off.

She hadn't. Ten minutes later, Dane sat in his truck

staring unseeingly at Bryn's apartment. He wanted to go to the address he'd been given by Bonnie, but knew Truck was right when he'd said he needed information before rushing into a potentially volatile situation. The last thing he needed was to become a hostage himself.

When his phone rang, Dane impatiently answered, knowing it was Truck. "What'd you find?"

"It's not good," Truck said bluntly. "Tex looked up the address and found out who he really is. I have no idea, more of his computer voodoo shit, but his name is actually Joseph Knox, and he's on quite a few watch lists. Failure to pay taxes, domestic violence, assault with a deadly weapon, and general assholedness. And that's all in the last three years. Before that, he spent time overseas."

"Fuck," Dane swore.

"Yeah. He flew to Paris, then vanished. Surfaced two years later in England. He was deported after being arrested as a suspect in one of the subway bombings they'd had over there. They didn't have any evidence to directly tie him to the blast, so they sent him home."

"Jesus. So he spent time with the terrorists over there?" Dane asked unbelievably. "How in the hell has been allowed to go about his business here?"

"Nothing could be proven. Traveling isn't against the law," Truck noted. "Anyway, he's married, and her parents have filed several reports about the fact they think he's brainwashing their daughter, but there's not much the cops can do because every time they question her, she swears she's not being abused in any way and that her place is with her husband. Sounds like typical Stockholm syndrome to me. This guy's address is literally in the middle of no-fucking-where, and regardless of how you approach, he's probably gonna know you're there before you get within a hundred yards of it."

"You think he's posing as a prepper for cover?" Dane asked.

"Sure of it," Truck told him.

"If he's acting like one, he's probably got the whole setup then. Where's the best place for a bunker on the property?" Dane had a gut feeling if Bryn was there, that's where the asshole would've stashed her...if he hadn't shot her on sight. She'd said she was just going to drive by, but if Knox had surveillance, he would've seen her. The thought of a brainwashed terrorist getting hold of Bryn made his skin crawl.

"Southwest edge of the property. It backs up to a large hill with a stream nearby. There are trees everywhere, clumps of them here and there. Enough for some cover, but not enough that the entire property is concealed. Bryn's car is nowhere to be seen, but there's an outbuilding next to the house. They could've stashed it already. They've had time."

"Got it."

"Wait for the team," Truck ordered.

"You know I can't do that," Dane told Truck in a quiet, determined voice. "Bryn's out there, and I have no idea if that asshole is hurting her. If he feels superior to women, he's not going to take Bryn's intelligence well, and she probably won't be able to keep her mouth shut. It's how she is. Don't tell me to wait."

"He's checked out books on fertilizer," Truck told him urgently. "It's why Bryn felt the urgency to see if the address existed in the first place. But in case you've forgotten your fucking training, it means that he could blow her up before you get anywhere near her if he feels threatened."

"Fuck!" Dane swore.

"Listen to me, Fish," Truck ordered. "I fucking outrank you and you'll do what I say, hear me?"

"He's got Bryn." Dane's words were soft and tortured.

"I know. But you've got six of the men I trust most in the world on their way to you. They aren't going to let anything happen to her, but you have to fucking let them get there to help. Got me?"

"Yes."

"You trust me?"

"Yes," Dane repeated.

"You trust *them*?"

Dane took a big breath and said, "Yes," as he exhaled.

"Good. I've talked with Fletch. We've discussed the best way to roll with this. They're studying satellite maps so they know the lay of the land. You're gonna need to roll with the punches when you get there. You'll have six men at your back, but your job is Bryn. And only Bryn. Hear me, Fish? Get the hostage out. Leave everything else to the team."

Dane liked that part of the plan. "I can do that."

"Good. Fletch'll contact you the second they land. He'll give you an ETA on when they'll get to you. Your job is going to be to distract Knox as much as possible. Say whatever you need to. Do whatever you need to."

"Got any ideas? The last thing I want is for him to prematurely detonate any fucking fertilizer he's got stored up there," Dane said.

Truck was silent for a moment, then said, "Islamic culture dictates that men are superior to women, and it's given me an idea on how you might get in there and get your Bryn out without starting World War Three or having Knox blow up the fucking mountain."

"Talk to me," Dane ordered.

The two men spent a few minutes discussing Truck's idea and refining it. They went through possible scenarios and the best way to approach the extremely volatile Knox without setting him off.

When they were done, Truck said, "Fish…"

"Yeah?"

"I'll be really pissed off if you get yourself killed. I didn't spend an hour holding your arm together for you to go and keel over in the middle of bum-fuck Idaho."

Dane chuckled, but it wasn't a humorous sound. "I'm not promising anything. Bryn's all that matters."

"Fuck that. Listen to me, Sergeant," Truck ordered, obviously knowing his tone was harsh enough to get Fish's attention once more. "You can't help her if you go in there all pissed off and emotional. Turn that shit off, *now*. Use your head. You're smarter than this, and from what you've told me, Bryn sure as hell is as well. You can't beat Knox if you go in there with guns blazing. That's what he'd be expecting. You need to outsmart him. That's the only way you'll get Bryn and yourself out of this. Lock your emotions down and do what we talked about. Your team will have your back. Got it?"

Dane took a deep breath. Truck was right. As much as it pissed him off, he was right. "This guy isn't going to look favorably on cops coming onto his property. He wants to keep where he is and what he's doing a secret. He might've used his real address on the fucking library card application, but he used a fake name. He's not that smart, but he's intelligent enough to have a plan in place in case someone comes sniffing around…like Bryn did.

He hates all things authority. If the local PD gets anywhere near him, he'll lose his shit."

"Agreed. They'll take positions down from the house. It'll be you and the team. That's it. He won't even know the cops are there until it's too late for him to do anything about it."

"Good."

"I wish like fuck I could be there," Truck said softly.

Dane had some time to think while he'd been waiting for Truck to call him back. There was literally only one thing he could think of that would keep Truck from coming to Idaho with the rest of the team. Only one person.

"You need to make her safe," Dane said firmly. "Bryn will always come first in my life. Always. It's how it should be. Our women should always come first. I understand, Truck. You don't ever need to mention it again."

"Gratitude, brother." Truck's words were hoarse, as if he was holding back extreme emotion.

"I gotta get home and change clothes," Dane told Truck. "You'll call with updates?"

"I'll call."

"Later."

"Later."

Dane clicked off the phone, his mind already in battle mode, considering his options and how he was gonna let things play out at Knox's property. He hadn't lied to Truck. He did need to get to his house. He needed to pick something up, and also, the jeans, button-up shirt, and leather jacket he was currently wearing wasn't going to cut it. Not for what needed to be done.

"Hang on, Smalls. I'm comin' for ya," Dane whispered as he pulled his truck onto Main Street and headed toward his house.

Chapter Twenty-One

B RYN COULDN'T BREAK free of her bonds; she'd tried without success over and over. For the first time in her life, she was speechless. She had no obscure facts in her brain waiting to spill out and had no idea what she could say to convince whoever it was keeping her captive that she was truly an innocent bystander. She'd been pleading with the man and it hadn't done any good. She had no idea how long she'd been there, but it had to have been hours by now.

"Who are you gathering information for?"

"I'm not working for anyone, I swear! I was just lost."

Another bucket of water was flung from somewhere behind the large spotlight, and Bryn sputtered and choked as it hit her in the face once more. She was soaking wet from all of the water that had been thrown on her. It wasn't waterboarding, but at the moment it seemed just as effective. She was ready to say whatever it was the man wanted to hear. Unfortunately, she had no idea what that was. She was cold, shivering in her seat and beginning to think she wasn't going to make it out of wherever she was alive.

"You've said that, but I don't believe you. You work for the library, so you probably looked me up and found out all about my latest project. Do you work for the government? Assholes. The people running this country have no clue. Are you spying for them? Do you work for the FBI? Trying to find out how I'm going to prove how vulnerable everyone in this country is? Rules are made to protect the leaders, not the little people. They don't give a shit about us. When the nuclear bombs start landing, where do you think they'll be? That's right—in their protective bunkers, leaving all of us to fend for ourselves. Well, I'm almost ready to prove it. To show people, at least those around here, how it'll be in the future. Then when…"

He kept talking, but Bryn tuned him out. She'd heard his rants so many times now, she could almost recite them word for word. This guy was obviously an extremist. Someone the preppers online had warned her about. And he had a bunker full of homemade bombs that he was planning on driving into Coeur D'Alene and blowing up. He wanted to prove how easy it was to disrupt society.

She hadn't seen anything other than the six-by-six-foot area around her chair. The spotlights kept her from seeing anything beyond them, and she hadn't seen the man or his wife since she'd woken up. She'd only heard their voices.

Voices that had asked the same questions over and over. She'd tried to talk to them as if they were fellow scientists, then she'd tried once again to pretend she'd just been lost. Then she tried to distract him by asking questions about the end of the world, what it would be like if nuclear bombs were dropped on the area, to try to make him feel like the authority he thought he was...but nothing had worked. The only thing they really wanted her to say was that she was a spy for the government and was on their property to get information to have them arrested, and she wasn't about to say that, as they'd probably kill her the moment the words left her mouth.

Suddenly a soft beeping came from somewhere nearby.

"Fuck! It's the perimeter alarm. I knew she was lying!" the man spat. "We'll just go and see who it is you arranged to meet you out here. Don't go anywhere," he said, then laughed cruelly.

"No, wait!" Bryn said, but it was too late. The couple was gone.

Panicked now, Bryn jerked even harder at her restraints. If Dane had somehow found her, he could be in bigger trouble than she was. He'd probably be armed to the teeth, and though she hated to admit it to herself, with only one working hand, he was at a disadvantage.

When all her struggles did was tire her out, Bryn sagged. If Dane got hurt because of her, she'd never forgive herself.

DANE PARKED HIS truck and tapped on the miniature earpiece in his ear. He received a click in return, letting him know the team was in place and ready to move as soon as he did. It had been way too long since Truck had told him the team was on their way, but he'd managed to keep himself from driving to the address...barely.

Knowing Fletch and the others were now around, and moving in, Dane climbed out, half-expecting to be shot as soon as he stepped out of the vehicle. When nothing happened, he took one step forward, then paused. He would wait for the mysterious Mr. Knox to come to him, rather than the other way around. And Dane had no doubt the man had known the second he'd entered his property. He hadn't seen any alarms or booby traps, but knew instinctively they were there. If this guy was making bombs, he'd be ready for anyone who entered his property, knowingly or not.

Dane clocked the two people immediately, slinking through the trees from the southwest, just as the team had guessed. They might sometimes live in the ram-shackle house next to him, but the bunker was where they most likely spent the majority of their time, and where they were making explosives. And where they were probably holding Bryn.

The two people moved to the other side of the house and appeared twenty seconds later, both armed with a shotgun. "Who the fuck are you?"

Dane held both arms up to show he was unarmed. "Name's Dane Hartwell. I'm looking for my wife."

As he'd hoped, his words made them stop in their tracks. He'd purposely used *Bryn's* last name to lend credence to his story. If Bryn was going to be his wife, then they would have the same last name. She'd most likely told them hers, so using her name would hopeful-ly help prove she really was who she'd said she was.

The plan the team had come up with was risky, but Dane thought it just might work. Based on the infor-mation Tex had relayed, Knox was old school. Had spent time over in Iraq with the Taliban. Lived with them. Believed that women should be seen and not heard. His entire part in the rescue plan hinged on it.

Dane had changed into an old uniform he had from before his injury. It was camouflage, wrinkled, and dirty. He'd packed it away, not wanting to ever see it again, but realized that if he was going to be "one of the guys" to this extremist, he'd have to look the part. He'd strapped an empty holster onto his thigh, leaving his pistol in the truck on purpose, and put on the prosthetic he hardly used around Bryn anymore.

Before today, he hadn't thought much about what the thing looked like, but as he and Truck talked, he knew it was what he needed in this situation. Obviously by his actions at Fletch's wedding reception, he could be just as deadly without his prosthetic, but for this op, he'd wear the arm with the hooks on it. He'd rolled back the sleeve of the uniform to make sure it was easily seen and recognized for what it was.

"Your wife? You misplace her?"

Thankful that his hunch seemed to have been correct, Dane continued in an irritated tone. "Yeah. Bitch is too damn curious for her own good. I've *told* her to mind her own fucking business time and time again. But she's not very obedient. I've obviously got to work on that more."

The man didn't come any closer, but lowered his shotgun until the barrel was pointing toward the ground rather than at him. He also put out his hand and lowered the barrel of the shotgun the woman next to him was holding.

"I'm not saying I know where she is, but sounds to me like you definitely need to discipline her more. Spare the rod, spoil the child and all that."

Dane chuckled. "Sir Thomas Moore once said that

if you let your wife stand on your toe tonight, she'll stand on your face tomorrow."

Dane figured he'd gone too far when the man just looked at him in confusion. He needed to be more direct. Remembering a conversation he and Bryn had had in the past, and how affronted she was by the information she'd researched, he pulled the facts from his head and put a sneer on his face.

"You know what's wrong with this country? There are too many fucking laws that go against a man doing what he's born and obligated to do. How the hell we're supposed to be men, and in charge of our families, when women are going around crying about their rights, I have no idea. It's why I moved us to fucking Idaho. Wanted to teach her how to be a good wife. I can see you're a *real* man, one who knows how to take care of business. Did you know that in India, the government added a clause into their legislation, quiet like, that says any kind of sexual intercourse by a man with his wife, whether she wants it or not, isn't rape? Now *that's* a government I could stand behind. In Lebanon, if a man marries a woman he happened to kidnap, then he can't be prosecuted for it."

Dane held his breath when the man in front of him didn't immediately respond, but was more relieved than he could say when he finally nodded. "How'd you lose the hand?" Knox drawled.

Dane slowly lowered his arms from above his head and crossed them over his chest, making sure the hook was clearly visible. The woman next to Knox slunk off at a head jerk from Knox. He hoped like hell she wasn't circling around to ambush him from behind. Even if she was, however, the team would take care of her.

As if Hollywood could read his mind, he heard, "On her," through the headset in his ear. Dane relaxed a fraction. He could now concentrate fully on Knox and not on watching his back.

"Fucking government, that's how. Joined the Army because I thought I was protecting freedom. Fuckers put a *woman* on my squad. Dumb bitch didn't know what she was doing. Almost got me killed. Panicked the second bullets started flying. Actually screamed and shit, gave away our position and we got a fucking RPG up our ass as a result. We heard the shot and the fucking bitch actually pushed me out of the way in her hurry to get out of the tent." Dane paused dramatically then continued. "Joke was on her, 'cause she ran the wrong way…right into the lot of them. Got what she deserved, dumb fuck."

Dane almost choked saying the words, but if it got him what he wanted—namely Bryn back, safe and sound—he'd say whatever it took. He sent a silent apology to all the women he'd served with. Not only had they been brave and trustworthy, they'd also been his friends.

"So…you got my woman?" Dane asked belligerent- ly. "She's a pain in my ass, but she's a great fuck. A wildcat who's kinky as shit. Likes it up the ass." He shrugged as if it wasn't a big deal. "It's why I've been putting up with her misbehavior. No more though."

"Yeah. I got her."

The relief that Dane felt almost brought him to his knees, but he didn't outwardly show any emotion. "I've told her a thousand times not to leave town, to keep her goddamn nose in her own business. She likes to drive around looking at houses. Fucking stupid when we already *have* a house. I sincerely apologize for her. I know you have the right to discipline her, but I'd like to take care of that myself…if you know what I mean. I've got just the thing in mind too."

"What's that?"

Dane hadn't wanted to make anything up, feeling sorry for Knox's wife, who'd probably have to go through what he was about to say if Knox made it out of this clusterfuck alive, but Bryn was his concern at the moment. "You ever use sensory deprivation to help correct your woman?"

"Nope. Can't say I have."

"It works like a fucking charm. Put 'er in a closet or small room. Tie her hands behind her back and blind- fold her. Then put a pair of earphones over her ears and a gag in her mouth. She can't hear, see, touch anything, or speak. I swear to God, it only takes five minutes before she'll not only agree to do whatever you want, she'll beg for the opportunity."

"Interesting."

Dane hated the look of sick excitement that crossed the other man's face.

"I might be amenable to giving her back. You had her long?"

"Nope. Not long enough to fully train her, obviously, although I'm working on it."

"What's in it for me if I let you have another shot at making her obedient?"

"In return for your…generosity, I've got a bunch of M295 chemical detection and decontamination kits in my truck."

Dane could see the man's eyes light up in interest from where he stood almost twenty feet away. He obviously knew how hard it was to obtain them. The Army didn't allow them to be sold, they were only being used by the military for now.

"How many?"

"A full box."

"How'd you get 'em?"

"I've still got some contacts from my old unit," Dane told the man. "I've got friends who think like us who're in a biological chemical unit. They sent 'em to me, knowing I'm building my own...place...out here in Idaho. When the shit hits the fan, when this fucking country collapses under its own shit because the fucking politicians have no idea how to keep control of its citizens, I wanted to be able to protect myself and my sons."

"Not your daughters?" Knox asked.

"Fuck 'em. Baby factories, the lot of them." Dane tried not to flinch at his own words. Throwing up an apology to the heavens for any future daughter he might have, he held his breath, hoping like hell the bribe would work. If it didn't, he wasn't sure what else he was going to do. He had nothing more up his sleeve.

The door to the large garage opened and Bryn's Corolla was backed out, driven by the woman who had been with Knox.

The prepper looked at Dane, then to the truck, then back to Dane, considering his offer. Finally, he said simply, "Deal. Wait here."

Dane nodded and moved his hand until it was in the front pocket of his pants. He had a pocket knife in it, but hoped he wouldn't have to use it after all. "Obliged."

He hadn't gotten the all clear from the team yet, so he had to keep up with the charade. So far it seemed like it was working, but he needed to get Bryn away from the bunker, and away from the explosives that were surely inside. They couldn't take a chance that the crazy fucker hadn't rigged up a remote-detonation device.

The man disappeared around the corner of the main house again, and Dane kept his eyes away from the direction he knew he was going…to his hidden bunker, and hopefully to get Bryn.

The woman who'd been with him got out of Bryn's car and headed back to the side of the house. She picked up the shotgun the man had left leaning nearby and waited, staring at him blankly, not saying a word.

Dane wanted to say something to her, to tell her to get the hell away from her husband, that her parents were worried about her, but he kept his mouth shut. With his luck, Knox had a microphone hidden somewhere and could listen. He couldn't do anything to jeopardize the mission now. Bryn. She was his only focus.

Ten tense minutes later, Knox made his way back to the house through the field behind the property. He had one hand on Bryn's biceps and was marching her toward him. She was wearing a sack on her head to keep her from seeing where she was going and her hands were cuffed behind her, but she was walking—well, stumbling—and seemed to be all right. Dane had never been so relieved in all his life.

He heard the click in his headset, letting him know that the team was there and in place. The bunker was secure, Knox couldn't run back there and lock himself in. The question of whether or not the man had a remote detonator was still a concern, however.

Letting the other man take the lead, Dane kept quiet.

Bryn was marched up to the house but still out of Dane's reach. "Decon kits first. Then you can have your woman."

Dane nodded, expecting nothing less. He'd gotten the chemical decontamination kits the week before from Truck. They were meant to go to Mr. Jasper for allowing them to tour *his* bunker, but thank God he hadn't gotten around to getting them to the prepper yet. It would've made this entire scene that much more difficult without them. Dane had no qualms whatsoever about giving them to the dangerous man in front of him. None. Even if he thought there'd be no retribution for what the man had done to Bryn, or for being a terrorist to his own people. If it meant Bryn would be safe, he'd hand over a truckload of missiles.

Dane ambled to his truck as if he had all the time in the world and didn't care that his woman was being manhandled. He knew he could take both the man and his wife down easily, but not without the guarantee neither would hurt Bryn before he did. So he played his part, satisfied that the Deltas wouldn't let this home-grown terrorist get away with what he'd done to Bryn, and whatever he was planning on doing to his country-men. He remembered what Truck had said. Bryn was his only objective. He'd let the Deltas handle Knox and the explosives.

Dane opened the back door of his truck and grabbed the large cardboard box with his right hand, balancing the bottom with the hook on his left. He shut the door with his hip and carried the box toward the man.

When he was several steps away, the other man barked, "That's close enough. Put it down."

Dane did as requested, and took several steps back.

The man gestured to his wife, and she came forward and dragged the box back to where her husband was standing. The extremist leaned down and opened it, making sure it really held the decon kits. Pleased at seeing they were just what Dane had said they were, he walked toward Dane with Bryn in tow.

When he was within four feet, he stopped and un-locked the cuffs around Bryn's wrists. Then he shoved her hard. She stumbled, and would've fallen if Dane didn't reach out and catch her. He grasped her biceps the same way the other man had and nodded. "I appre-ciate you looking after my property."

He felt Bryn shiver under his arm. She was soaking wet and trembling, but thankfully kept her mouth shut. *Hold on, sweetheart.*

"You gonna discipline her now?"

Seeing the sick gleam in the other man's eyes that let Dane know he got off on seeing women being hurt, Dane shook his head and said as casually as he could, "Nah. I think I'll save that for when we get home. It's gonna take longer than five minutes for her to learn her lesson, if you know what I mean. Besides, I need her conscious to drive. Looks like you made her docile enough for now. You've obviously got *your* woman well-trained. I can't wait until she," Dane shook Bryn's arm for effect, "learns that her place is to keep her mouth shut and not to think."

"Keep her on her back then knock her up. That'll keep her busy."

"Oh, she's gonna be chained to my bed for the foreseeable future, that's for sure. Thank you again for your...hospitality. You won't be offended, I'm sure, when I tell you that I hope we don't cross paths again."

The other man nodded.

Not prolonging the goodbye, Dane roughly marched Bryn to the driver's side of her car. He wanted nothing more than to get her into his truck and get the hell out of there, but if he truly didn't want to cross paths with Knox again, he couldn't leave her car. Bryn had to drive herself out of there...and Dane hated it with every fiber of his being.

He brought his right hand up and stuck it under the

burlap bag over her head. He grabbed her soaking-wet hair in his fist and pulled the bag off with the hook on his other hand. Putting the cold hook of his prosthetic under her chin, more than aware the man and his wife were still watching him, he leaned into Bryn's face and put on the show he knew Knox was expecting.

"You disobeyed me for the last time, woman. You're lucky I bothered to come and get your ass. I should've just left you here. You cost me a shitload of decon kits. You're gonna pay for that. Get your ass in your car and follow me home. Enjoy driving, because this is the last time you'll get to do it for a long fucking time. I'll beat that curiosity out of you if it's the last thing I do. Got it?"

Bryn looked at him with bloodshot eyes but didn't even hesitate. Her arms came up to rest on his waist and she said in a low, meek voice, "Yes, sir. I'm sorry for all the trouble I caused."

Dane's hand flexed in her hair at her words. She was still shaking and looked scared, but she was keeping it together. She understood exactly what he was doing. That he was acting. That what he really wanted to do was haul her into his arms and never let go. At least he hoped she did.

"I should give you back to your father. He'd be ashamed at how defective you are. But I like a challenge. I think I'll take our friend's advice and keep you on your back for the next month. Maybe I can fuck obedience into you."

Bryn licked her lips, but didn't say a word. Merely nodded.

Deciding he'd done enough playacting, and knowing he needed to get them the hell out of there so the Deltas could do their job, he let go of her and stepped away suddenly. She swayed, and if she fell to the ground it would be a disaster. Dane knew he wouldn't be able to stop himself from grabbing her and holding her against him. Luckily, her hand shot out and caught the open car door, steadying herself and keeping herself upright.

Fuck, she had nerves of steel. He loved her. Every inch of her. Kidnapped, scared out of her skull, soaking wet—he had no idea how *that* had come about, and knew when he found out, he was gonna lose his shit— she was the strongest person he'd ever met. She was one of a kind. He hadn't thought he'd ever find a woman who could put up with him and who understood him...but he had. Bryn was his.

"Stay on my bumper. If you so much as get two feet away, I'll beat you even harder when we get home."

"Yes, sir. I won't let you out of my sight."

Dane nodded and turned away. God. He needed to hold her. He had to play this out. He'd have her in his arms before too long. She was saying all the right things and he couldn't fuck it up now.

Without looking back to make sure she did as she was told, he strode to his truck and hopped in. He lifted his chin to Knox and turned the key in the ignition. He turned around and headed up the long gravel driveway, looking back to make sure Bryn was behind him.

She was so close, he couldn't see her bumper. She was doing just as he'd ordered, sticking close to him. He knew it wasn't because he'd asked her to and more because she was scared, but he was still so very proud of her for not crumbling in the face of real danger.

He also saw three men coming up quickly behind Knox and his wife as they stood there, distracted by the vehicles leaving their property.

Dane realized that he didn't once wish he was there with the Deltas. He was done being a soldier. He had more important things to do...namely, love Bryn Hartwell.

He drove for what seemed like the longest ten minutes of his life until he came upon a police blockade across the road. Knowing the cops had set up the perimeter well away from any fallout that might occur if a bomb was detonated, Dane stopped his truck abruptly in the middle of the dirt road, slammed his foot on the emergency brake, and threw open his door. He was at Bryn's car before he remembered moving, and then she was finally in his arms.

Chapter Twenty-Two

BRYN CLUNG TO Dane as if he was the only thing between her and certain death...and he had been. They both knew it. She wouldn't have been able to escape the bunker where John Smith—or *Joseph Knox*, according to Dane—and his wife had stashed her. She might as well have been held captive in Fort Knox, the famous vault in Kentucky that was used to store a large portion of the gold reserves for the United States.

With every rant and insult thrown her way, Bryn had known she was in big trouble. She couldn't talk her way out, she'd tried, and she'd been so, so stupid, thinking she could just drive onto Knox's property and not suffer any consequences.

Dane had *told* her, but she hadn't listened, had thought she knew more than he did about the survivalist lifestyle because of her research. Bryn knew she sometimes didn't use common sense, and usually it didn't bother her, but the fact that she'd not only put her own life in danger, but had risked Dane's as well, was horrifying.

When Knox had left her the last time, she knew when he came back, he'd probably start torturing her with more and more painful methods. The ice-cold water sucked, but it was nothing compared to what she figured he'd been planning. She'd seen an electrical cord lying nearby. She had no doubt he was going to start electrocuting her if Dane hadn't found her.

But when he'd come back to the bunker, he'd merely shoved a bag over her head and forced her to walk next to him. The first time she'd heard Dane's voice, instead of being relieved, she'd been terrified. Scared she'd somehow get *him* killed right alongside her.

But he'd taken her arm and kept her from sprawling on her face and called her his property, and Bryn knew exactly what was going on. She'd listened to the way Joseph talked to the other woman. Understood that he thought women were beneath him, so the second Dane called her his property, she knew what her role was. Stay quiet and let him lead. Just like she had when they'd gone to visit the other prepper.

The words he'd said to her before they'd left were supposed to sound threatening, but when she'd looked up into his eyes, she'd only seen tenderness for her shining out. She'd agreed to everything he'd said and hadn't felt one second of desire to question him or say anything.

She didn't want to drive, was shaking so hard she

wasn't sure she *could* drive, but she knew as well as Dane that they didn't have a choice, she had to play her part. So she'd taken a deep breath, and followed as close to Dane's truck as she dared.

And now she was in his arms.

Nothing had felt so good in all her life.

Nothing.

Dane went to pull back but she clung harder, not wanting to let him go. There was so much she wanted to say, but she couldn't get any words out. Thankfully he tightened his grip on her instead of making her let go. He'd been bending over, holding her to him, but suddenly he stood fully upright. Because he was so much taller than her, her feet came right off the ground. Bryn didn't say a word, merely clung harder to the man she loved as he carried her to one of the many police cars blocking the road in front of them.

She loved him. Probably since she'd taken care of him when he'd been drunk. But he'd shown her so many times over the last couple months that he liked her for who she was, random fact-spewing and all. He'd come after her when she'd been in trouble. She had no idea how he felt about her, but she wasn't going to let him go without a fight.

Bryn heard Dane talking to someone, but didn't care who it was or what he was saying. She felt him sitting and brought her legs up so she was straddling his waist, sighing in contentment when she could snuggle into him further. His arms tightened around her, keeping her close.

"Thanks. Appreciate it."

Bryn startled when a blanket was wrapped around her back.

"Easy, Smalls. It's just a blanket. You're shivering."

She was. She couldn't stop shaking. "I d-don't know w-why. I'm n-not that c-cold."

"Shock, sweetheart."

"She good?"

Bryn didn't recognize the voice, but felt Dane remove his right hand from her back to hold it out to whomever was speaking.

"She will be. Dane Munroe."

"Jason Briggs, FBI."

"You know what's going on down there?" Dane asked.

"I'm aware," came the response. "Just waiting on the all clear to head down."

The agent lifted a hand to the mic in his ear. After a moment, he nodded and told Dane and Bryn, "Looks like Knox and his wife have been secured."

"According to my sources, this area's a powder keg. I'm not sure the Rathdrum PD should be handling this on their own," Dane said quietly to Briggs.

"I agree. And I'm pretty sure after this, so will the

Rathdrum chief. This area has been on our watch list for a while now."

"I'd say there needs to be less watching and more action," Dane replied impatiently.

Bryn lifted her head for the first time and turned to see the agent Dane had been talking to. "He's got f-fertilizer. Lots of it. He wants to b-bring it down to the city and blow stuff up. I d-don't know what or w-where, but he told me that much when he was t-trying to figure out what I was doing there."

"Damn." The extremely good-looking blond agent looked frustrated at her words. "Appreciate the heads up, ma'am. Glad you're all right, Ms. Hartwell."

"Me too," she responded, and laid her head back on Dane's shoulder, closing her eyes. She was confused about why the agent didn't look more concerned about Knox's plans, but at the moment, didn't care. She'd ask Dane about it later.

"You need to go to the hospital, Smalls?" Dane asked in a gentle voice.

Bryn shook her head.

Dane lifted one of her arms from around his neck and examined her wrist. It was red and chaffed, and would definitely bruise, but the skin wasn't broken.

"I'm okay. I just w-want to go h-home."

Dane put his hand on the back of her head and pulled her into him again, hating having his prosthetic between them, but not wanting to let go of Bryn long enough to remove it.

"Want a ride?" the agent asked.

"If it's not too much trouble," Dane replied.

"It's not. I'll get a couple officers to drop your vehicles off."

"Thank you. Keys are in my ignition, and assuming hers are too."

Bryn nodded against his shoulder, agreeing, but didn't say anything.

"I'll take care of it. Once again, glad you're both all right."

Bryn felt Dane moving under her and refused to let go of him. But he was only shifting until his legs were inside the car. Someone shut the door behind him, enclosing them in the silence and warmth of the police car.

She knew she should probably care that she was sitting in the back of a cop car and getting Dane wet from her clothes in the process, but she couldn't. If it was any other day or time, she'd be exploring and asking a million questions, as it was a new experience, one she hoped she'd never get again, but all she could think of was the danger she'd put Dane in. He'd had to come after her because she hadn't used her brain.

She scoffed under her breath. She might be a genius, but she was so stupid. So, so stupid.

Dane shifted again and pulled his phone out of his pocket. He frowned at it for a moment, then balanced it on the seat next to them and unlocked it. He pushed a few buttons and put it on speaker.

"She good?" the voice on the other end of the phone barked impatiently.

"She's good."

"*You* good?"

"Yeah."

"Thank fuck," Truck breathed out, obviously relieved. "You have any problems?"

"No. Although I have a feeling I'm not going to get that box of M295s back, so I'm gonna need another for Mr. Jasper."

Truck chuckled. "You'll have them in a few days, already got it arranged. I hate to do it, but I gotta go."

"You still workin' on that issue you had?" Dane asked in concern.

"It's turning out to be more stubborn than I thought," Truck said. "But don't worry. I got this."

"Truck?" Bryn interrupted before Dane could hang up.

"That's me."

"Thank you for having Dane's b-back. I'm s-sorry I did something so s-stupid."

"You're welcome. But it wasn't only me. All the guys are there. You really all right?"

"I'm f-fine."

"You gonna go on any more walkabouts anytime soon?"

"No."

"Good girl. You scared your man."

"I scared myself."

"Take care of yourself...and Dane, would ya?"

"I will."

"Dane?"

"Yeah, Truck?"

"Remember what I told you before about women."

"I remember." Dane knew exactly what his friend was talking about. Bryn had told Truck she was fine, but he had a feeling she had a long way to go before she really was.

"Take care of that, okay?"

"I will. Talk to you soon."

"Later."

Dane clicked off the phone and wrapped his arm around Bryn again.

"The guys are all here? Like...Ghost, Hollywood, and everyone?"

"Yup."

"God. I didn't—"

"Don't," Dane warned.

"Don't what?"

"Don't say whatever it was that you were going to

say. It's over. Knox will be going to jail. Nothing's getting blown up, including you. The team has it under control. They'll hand both Knox and his wife over to the FBI and they'll do their investigation."

"Will we see the guys later?"

"No." Dane lifted her chin so she had to look at him. "And they weren't here. As far as you know, we drove out of there and that's that. Got me?"

At the serious look in Dane's eyes, Bryn nodded immediately.

"I know you have a million questions, and later I'll answer what I—"

"No," Bryn interrupted.

"No what?"

"I don't have any questions. For once in my life, I don't want to know. No, it's not even that. I just don't care. All I care about is that I'm safe. And that I didn't get you killed. I'm so glad they were there to have your back, and I don't care why, how, or anything about why they were there. I'm s-sorry, Dane. I didn't come out here to talk to him. I just—"

"Shhhhhh, sweetheart. We can talk later. For now, just let me hold you."

Bryn nodded and relaxed fully into Dane again. She fit against him perfectly, as if she was made just for him. She knew they had a lot to talk about, but all she could do at the moment was breathe him in and thank God he'd come to find her.

Chapter Twenty-Three

THE POLICE OFFICER pulled up to Dane's house and told them, "I'll wait until I know you're safe."

"Thank you," Dane responded. "Bryn, scoot over and let me get out. Then I'll carry you inside."

She stirred at that. The officer hadn't said one word about them sitting together and not wearing their seat belts, not that it would've made her move from her spot. She'd finally stopped shivering, a combination of Dane's body heat and the blanket still wrapped around her back. But she felt weird, still shaky, as if she'd had way too much sugar. The thought went through her that she wanted to go online and try to find out why, but she pushed it away.

"I can walk. I just want to get inside."

Dane didn't respond, but climbed out of the backseat and held out his hand. Bryn grabbed it and let him help her from the car. His left arm immediately wrapped around her waist and Bryn gave him some of her weight as they moved toward his front door.

"I like your arm better."

"What?"

"Your arm. I like it better than this prosthetic. It's...pokey."

Dane didn't say anything, but leaned down and kissed the top of her still-wet head. He unlocked his door and turned and waved at the officer idling in the driveway. Bryn could hear him driving away as Dane shut the door.

"Let's get you in the shower."

Bryn nodded. A shower sounded heavenly right about now.

They walked together down the hall to Dane's bedroom. He guided them straight to the bathroom. He dropped his arm and immediately went to work on the buttons of his green camouflage shirt. Bryn stood there uncertainly as he shrugged out of it and began to unfasten the straps holding the hook prosthetic to his arm.

As much as she wanted to examine it and see how it worked, she hesitated. Finally, when it fell to the ground with a loud clang, she tentatively asked, "Dane? What are you doing?"

"Getting you in the shower."

"I can do it."

He stepped to her then. He put his good hand on the side of her head and leaned into her. "I know, Smalls. I just can't bear to let you out of my sight just

SUSAN STOKER

yet."

"Oh, okay." Goosebumps rippled down her arms at his quiet yet firm tone.

He leaned over to the shower and turned on the water. "Get undressed, sweetheart."

Without thinking any more about it, Bryn did as he ordered. She grabbed her T-shirt at the hem and drew it up and over her head, letting it fall on the floor with a wet splat. She undid her jeans and peeled them down her legs. She turned to glance at Dane, but he was standing with his back to her, his hand under the stream of water, testing the temperature.

In the short time it'd taken her to remove her clothes, he'd shed his pants and boxers. His back and ass rippled with muscles. It was sexy as hell.

Without thought to her modesty, simply wanting to be skin to skin with Dane, Bryn stripped off her bra and panties and stepped toward the shower just as Dane turned to her.

His eyes roamed her body once, as if checking her for injuries, then he held out his hand. Bryn grabbed on and he helped her step into the shower. The hot water almost hurt her chilled skin, but before she could feel uncomfortable, Dane tugged her against his chest and turned so the spray was hitting his back instead of hers.

He held her so closely, Bryn could feel his heart beating against her chest. The *thump-thump-thump* was

320

reassuring and comforting at the same time. She thought she would feel self-conscious about being completely naked with Dane for the first time, but all it felt was right. Their embrace wasn't sexual, it was loving and even a bit desperate.

The tears started before Bryn even knew they were coming. They leaked out of her eyes silently. She'd thought she'd been doing the right thing, but it had almost cost Dane his life. She could handle it if *she'd* been hurt, she was the one who'd made the dumbass decision to be Nancy Drew, but if something had happened to Dane, after all he'd already been though in his life, she never would've forgiven herself.

He drew back and frowned at her tears, but didn't say a word. He simply turned her into the spray and got her hair wet. He then proceeded to shampoo and condition her hair, all without speaking. His hand was gentle and tender as he lathered the soap into her hair, and then as he gently rinsed it. He put a shower pouf into the crook of his elbow and poured a dollop of his masculine soap on it. Then he washed every inch of her body, from her head to her toes.

As the lather washed away, he kissed every bruise she'd gotten that day. Her wrists, ankles, and biceps where Knox had held her so roughly. Through it all, Bryn's tears steadily fell. He let go of her long enough to roughly run the soapy shower pouf over himself and rinse off, but as soon as he was done, he turned back to her.

He shut the water off and reached for a big fluffy towel hanging on a hook next to the shower.

"I can do that," Bryn told him quietly.

"Shhh, I got it."

So she stood in the shower and let the man she loved take care of her. Dane dried her arms, then her torso and back. Then he turned her and ran the towel up and down each leg. Finally, he ran it over her hair, squeezing out as much water as he could before helping her step out into the steamy room.

He quickly ran the now-damp towel over his own body, then threw it over a rack without a second thought. Leaning down and kissing her forehead, he murmured, "I have an extra toothbrush in the drawer. Do your thing and come to bed, Smalls."

She nodded and watched, wide-eyed, as Dane opened the door and quickly shut it behind him, making sure to keep the warm air inside the small room.

Bryn took a deep breath. She couldn't stop crying. She supposed it was adrenaline and relief, but it was beginning to get annoying. She quickly brushed her teeth and used the restroom then looked around for something to put on.

Vetoing the still-wet clothes she'd just taken off, as well as the damp towel, she finally cracked the door open.

Dane was lying on his queen-size bed waiting for her. Seeing her peek out the door, he asked, "What's wrong?"

"Do you have something I can wear?'

Holding out his hand, he shook his head. "No. Come here, sweetheart."

Bryn's eyes got wide, but she slipped out of the bathroom into the bedroom. Dane had turned on a dim light next to his bed that gave the room a soft glow. It was enough to see where she was going, but not bright enough to completely illuminate the room.

Self-conscious at being naked, now that they were out of the shower, Bryn shuffled over to the bed and took Dane's hand. He scooted over and lifted the covers for her. Thankful she'd get to cover up, Bryn climbed in and lay back, sighing in contentment when Dane drew the comforter up and over her quickly chilling body.

He reached out and pulled her arm toward him gently, and Bryn followed his lead, snuggling up against Dane's warm frame. She felt his arm go around her and his large hand rest on her lower back, his fingertips caressing the top of her ass, pushing her hips toward him. His stump brushed her forearm, which had come to rest against his chest. They stayed like that for several minutes, simply breathing each other in.

When she couldn't stand the silence anymore, Bryn

said once again, "I'm sorry, Dane."

"I know you are."

"I only wanted to find out more information about the address. I wasn't planning on talking to anyone."

"I know, Bryn."

She bit her lip, but didn't raise her head. He was being very understanding and it was disconcerting. "Why aren't you yelling at me?"

"Would it do any good?"

"What do you mean?"

"Bryn, you know you made a mistake. Me yelling at you about it and telling you something you already know isn't going to change anything that happened."

"Maybe not. But I think it'd make me feel better."

Dane moved at her words. He brought his stump up to her chin and gently put pressure on it until she was looking into his eyes. "You scared me, Smalls. When I heard your phone message and realized what you'd done, I was upset. We'd talked about how some people in this area are dangerous. And unfortunately for us, this guy was the epitome of dangerous. He was a terrorist, Bryn. He'd spent time training over in Iraq with the Taliban. He hates the United States and would like nothing more than to see it crash and burn."

"I know, I know. I wasn't thinking."

"Actually, you were thinking too much. Bryn, ever since I was wounded, I've felt like I was somehow less of a man. I worried all the time about what other people thought about me. If they thought I was useless with only half an arm, if they were looking at me funny when I was out and about. But you changed all of that. Never, since I was a kid, has anyone taken care of me. I didn't need or want that. But you took one look at me in the grocery store, all jittery and jumpy, and wanted to make my life better...easier. And you acted on that. You didn't let my stupid words chase you off either. I need you, Smalls. I need you in my life, blurting out random facts. I need you to keep me grounded. When you get so into what you're researching you forget all about me, it makes me smile, not piss me off."

"Uh, that's weird, Dane."

"I know. Takes one to know one, sweetheart."

Bryn blinked at that. Then slowly smiled.

"Yeah, I see you're gettin' it. I don't care about your quirks because you don't care about mine. But...as much as I love your brain and how it works...I don't love that it puts you in danger sometimes. Please, *please*, tell me before you go rushing off into the world to find answers. I'll do everything in my power to help you get the information you need...but I'll make sure you're safe while you do it."

"I love you."

The smile that came over Dane's face almost blinded her, but she kept talking. "I mean, I know we haven't been seeing each other very long and I don't want to freak you out. It's just...when I was sitting in that bunker and being treated like a prisoner of war, I was scared I'd never get to see you again, and I was sad that you'd never know. Of course, you might not want to know now, so that was probably presumptuous of me, but there isn't a time—okay, not *much* time—when I'm not thinking about you. Maybe that's because I really am a stalker and not in love, but I'm going with it for now."

"Smalls, I—"

"It's okay if you don't love me back. I mean, I hope you will someday. In two thousand and eleven, there was a study done that found that men tend to say 'I love you' before women. And there was even a survey that calculated men take an average of eighty-eight days to say it, while women usually waited a hundred and thirty-four days. It hasn't been nearly that much time for us, so it figures I've managed to mess this up too, but I couldn't *not* say it anymore. You mean more to me than any degree I've ever earned. Oh, and even more than the time I got to talk to James Watson."

"James Watson? Who's he?" Dane asked, still smiling.

"He's the guy who co-discovered the structure of DNA. He was awarded the Nobel Prize in Physiology or Medicine in nineteen sixty-two. He worked at Harvard for a while and spoke at a conference I attended. I was able to meet him and we spoke for thirteen minutes and twenty-two seconds. It was awesome. But, Dane," Bryn came up on her elbow and brought her hand to his cheek, "I never would've recovered if my stupidity had gotten you hurt or killed. Never."

"I love you too, Bryn."

"You do?"

"Of course. How could I not? And you weren't there, but you should know that the research you did on women's rights in other countries…" Dane's voice trailed off, thinking about the awful things he'd said to Knox.

"Yeah? What, Dane?"

"It totally got us out of there," he said, quickly wanting to move on. "So don't ever stop being you. I love you just the way you are. Okay?"

Bryn plopped back down onto Dane's chest, not hearing the small "oof" he let out when she landed. "I won't. But I'm gonna try to curb the whole not-being-smart-about-running-off-into-the-wilds-of-Idaho thing."

"I'd appreciate that."

After several moments, Bryn bit her lip and asked softly, "You really love me? You're not just saying it because I did or because you feel sorry for me?"

"I definitely love you, Smalls. Every inch of you. From your incredibly intelligent brain that I don't have a prayer of keeping up with to the teeny toes on your adorable feet."

Bryn sighed in contentment and closed her eyes.

"You all right? Really?" Dane asked softly.

"Yeah. My arm is gonna bruise, and my wrists ache from being bound, but it's nothing that a few painkillers won't fix." Bryn thought of something and lifted her head again. "Oh. You wanted to have sex."

Dane chuckled and shook his head. "Not tonight. I'm exhausted, and I'm enjoying holding you in my arms just like this."

"Okay. But…soon?"

"Yeah, sweetheart."

"Good. Do you think it'll be different because we love each other? I mean, I know people have one-night stands all the time, and I know I've never been impressed with the sex I've had so far, but maybe that's because I didn't love the guys I was with. I don't want to build up any crazy expectations, but if what we did before was any indication, I'd have to say that—"

"Shhhhh, Smalls. Go to sleep."

"But—"

Bryn cut herself off when she felt Dane squeeze her butt cheek then press her into him once more. She snuggled in and heard him take a deep breath of her hair.

"I miss the coconut, but I have to tell you, I love

that you smell like my soap. Call me a caveman, but there's something about knowing you were naked in my shower, using my soap, that gets to me. And I have no doubt that being in love will mean that our coming together will be off-the-charts hot. I love you. So much I can't imagine spending even one day apart from you."

Kissing his chest where it lay under her lips, Bryn hugged him to her. "Me either."

"Thank you for letting me handle that today."

"You're welcome." Bryn knew exactly what he meant. If she'd opened her mouth and argued, or in any way tried to "help," they wouldn't have escaped as easily as they had. It was only because she'd trusted Dane to do whatever it took to get them out of there. "I might do stupid things, but when it's important, I know when to keep my mouth shut. Love you."

"Go to sleep."

"Mmmmm."

The last thing Bryn thought about was how thankful she was that she'd gone looking for Dane all those weeks ago. Best. Decision. Ever.

Chapter Twenty-Four

BRYN WOKE UP a few hours later, her mind immediately whirring with all that had happened. She'd wanted to sleep in, but as usual, she was awake four hours after drifting off in Dane's arms.

She carefully picked up her head where it was resting on Dane's chest and saw he was still out. Bryn took the time to examine Dane without his knowledge. The arm that had been resting on her hand on his chest was now over his head and she could clearly see the stump below his elbow.

Running her eyes over it, Bryn tried to imagine what it might feel like to not have half her arm…and of course she failed. Her eyes moved down, over his biceps to this face. He had a scruffy beard growing and Bryn wondered what *that* would feel like against her skin. His lips were slightly open and he was breathing deeply, obviously still asleep.

She shifted and felt his hand fall off her butt onto the mattress beside him. The covers had slipped down sometime in the night and she could see Dane's broad chest under her. She carefully went to her knees, ignoring her own nudity in her eagerness to see all of him.

She'd seen him in the shower and she'd stroked him to an orgasm, but it seemed different this time. He had a few scars on his torso that she hadn't seen before, but all in all, he was perfect. Bryn knew he wouldn't agree, and he'd show her his stump and scars, then probably point out all the other imagined flaws he had...but she knew deep in her heart that he was perfect for *her*.

Her gaze wandered down from his chest to his stomach, then to his penis. It was lying flaccid between his legs and looked so different from the last time she'd seen and touched it. Bryn knew from studies that the average penis length was three and a half inches when not erect, but Dane's looked to be bigger than that. She suddenly wished she had a ruler.

Reaching out, she ran her index finger down the length of him and was surprised at how soft he was. Without the extra blood running through it, it seemed a lot less intimidating...and squishier. Bryn continued to run her finger up and down the length of Dane's cock as her thoughts turned to the blue whale. It had the largest penis of any animal, at eight to ten feet long. It weighed between a hundred and a hundred and fifty pounds and could ejaculate over thirty-five pints of semen. Just once she'd like to see that; it had to be both scary and amazing.

At the same time that Bryn realized the dick under her fingers was no longer flaccid, but quickly growing in size, Dane murmured, "Good morning, sweetheart."

"Did you know there's a penis museum in Iceland?"

He groaned and stretched, opening his body to her as if without thought. "Nope. I had no idea."

"Uh huh. And a man ejaculates an average of seventy-two hundred times in his life, with about two thousand of those being from masturbating. That's a lot of sex. I'm not sure how many of those fifty-two hundred times you've used up, but I can't wait to get started on the remainder."

Bryn shrieked as Dane suddenly sat up and pressed her backwards. He came down on top of her, catching both her wrists in his good hand. She noted that he was careful not to put too much pressure on the bruises that had formed overnight.

"Should I be concerned that you know so much about dicks, Smalls?"

"What? No. It's just that a porn video showed up on my social media timeline. I watched it, and wasn't impressed, but it got me thinking about…stuff. So I did some research."

"What did you find out about pussies?"

"Vaginas?"

He chuckled and brought his other arm down, caressing her lower belly with his stump. "Yeah. What can you tell me about this?" He moved until he was touching her between her legs with his scarred flesh.

Bryn arched up into his touch. "Oh…that feels so good, Dane."

"Facts, Smalls."

"Um…vagina in Latin means 'sheath for a sword.'"

Dane brought his mouth to her neck and nibbled on the sensitive skin there. "Appropriate. What else?"

Bryn shifted in Dane's hold, pressing herself against his stump. It felt so good, but she really, really wanted his *fingers* down there. "Vaginas aren't as interesting as penises."

"I beg to differ. I happen to love yours. Tell me something else you learned."

"Some women can develop an allergy to semen. More specifically, the proteins in it."

"Don't move your hands, Bryn. Keep them above your head. Tell me more."

Bryn signed in relief when Dane let go of her wrists and kissed his way down her chest. He used his hand to plump up one of her breasts, and sucked and nipped at the other. When she didn't say anything, he lifted his head.

"The more facts you give me, the faster I'll move to where you so obviously want me."

Bryn blushed, knowing her hips were undulating

under him, practically begging for him to touch or kiss her there. "Most vaginas look alike. There are over a thousand nicknames for a vagina. Passion flower. Pink pearl. Fish taco. Cod canal. Fuzzy lap flounder. Apple pie."

She heard Dane chuckle but he was moving where she wanted him, so she kept talking. "The average length of an unaroused vagina is between two and a half to three inches. Hair around the vagina only grows for three weeks, while the hair on a person's head can keep growing for seven years. Sharks and vaginas both have a substance called squalene...it's in the shark's liver, and in women it's a natural lubricant. Um...God...Dane...yeah, that feels so good."

Bryn lifted her head and looked down at Dane. He was lying between her spread legs, his stump resting on one thigh, holding her open to him, and his hand spreading open the folds around her clit.

"I know some facts too, Smalls. Wanna hear?"

No. She didn't want to hear. She wanted him to make her feel as good as he'd done before. She wanted his mouth on her clit...but when she didn't respond, he said, "We could get up and watch *Mythbusters* if you wanted to instead."

Bryn heard the laughter in his voice, and wanted to smack him. Instead, she said breathlessly, "Yes. Facts. Go on."

She felt a finger slowly rub over her clitoris in a barely there caress.

"A woman's clit gets an erection when stimulated. It gets engorged with blood when aroused, just like a cock. It's also a lot longer than what can be seen from the outside." Dane leaned down and licked over it once, then said, "And caresses feel a lot better when it's wet. It's a known fact that women's clitoral orgasms are stronger than a man's could ever be, simply because the nerve endings are more concentrated...here...than in a cock."

Dane leaned over, continuing to hold her open, and lapped at her clit. Again and again, he licked her hard nub. Bryn could feel her hips pushing up against Dane's face, but couldn't make herself stop.

"Give me your hand," Dane ordered suddenly, right when Bryn thought she was going to explode. She whimpered but did as he asked, bringing one of her hands from over her head down to him.

"Hold yourself open for me. I've only got one hand and I need it elsewhere. That's it, sweetheart. Help me out. Perfect." His next words were interspersed with his tongue licking hard right over her clit. "Just. Like. That."

Bryn felt Dane's hand brushing against her sensitive folds, then a finger pushed deep into her as his tongue continued its assault on her senses. She bucked once, but Dane's other arm kept her mostly still under him.

"Oh God, Dane."

He didn't respond, but increased the speed of his tongue at the same time that his finger curled upward and brushed against her inner walls. She tightened around his questing digit, wanting more.

He pushed against her G-spot. When she groaned, he lifted his head and murmured, "Yeah. Love to hear you moan for me."

Her other hand came down with no clear thought and grabbed his shoulder, digging her fingernails into him.

"Fuck, you're beautiful, Bryn. You had a G-spot orgasm when I did this before…"

Bryn couldn't talk, she couldn't breathe. She shook her head frantically back and forth, wanting to stop him and order him to keep going at the same time. The last time he'd made her come it had been earth shattering, almost scary.

"Relax and let it happen again. Some women don't like it, but I have a feeling you aren't going to be one of them. You came so hard last time. You're soaked, so beautiful. Come for me, Bryn. Come all over my hand. Let me taste you."

Dane's head dropped and he went back to flicking his tongue over her clit, while at the same time massaging the extremely sensitive spot inside her.

It didn't take long before Bryn knew she was going to come. Her feet shifted and rested on the mattress next to Dane's shoulders and her hips tilted up. He didn't lose his grip on her, and switched from flicking her clit to closing his mouth over it and sucking.

That was all it took, Bryn exploded in an orgasm so hard, she swore she saw stars. Dane's finger inside her kept up its erotic massage for a beat, then he stilled. She twitched and squeezed him as she continued to experience several small orgasms.

"I need to be inside you, Smalls."

"Yes! God, yes, Dane," Bryn choked out.

Before his name had cleared her lips, Dane was moving. Spreading her knees farther apart, he scooted up between her legs and braced himself with his good hand by her shoulder.

"Put me inside you," he ordered. "I can't hold myself up and do it at the same time."

Bryn opened her eyes and looked up into his as her hand shifted to his rock-hard cock. She took hold and tilted her hips, bathing him in her release before pressing the tip to her opening.

They both moaned as he slowly sank inside her hot folds. Bryn's hands moved to his ass and pulled him into her. Dane collapsed on his elbows and groaned, burying his nose in her hair.

Bryn squeezed her inner muscles, loving how full he

made her feel. She wiggled under him and tilted her pelvis, wanting him closer. Dane's left arm came down and pressed against her, holding her to him.

"Fuck, you feel amazing, sweetheart. But before we go any further...I'm not wearing a condom."

"I know. I've got an IUD."

Dane stilled and looked at her with his eyebrows raised in question.

"I have fibroids," she hurried to explain. She didn't want him to think she needed it because she was promiscuous. "Noncancerous tumors. It controls them so they don't cause me any pain."

"But you can still have kids?"

Bryn smiled up at him and nodded. "Yeah. I can still have children. It's removable."

"Thank fuck. I'm clean, sweetheart. I wouldn't put you in danger. I swear."

As an answer, she looked into his eyes and ordered, "Move."

He smiled. "You want me to fuck you, Smalls?"

"Yes."

"Maybe I want to feel you squeeze and caress me some more."

"Dane, please," Bryn whined, grabbing hold of his sides with her hands and digging her nails lightly into the skin there. "I've waited my whole life to fuck the man I love, don't make me wait any longer."

"How can I resist such a pretty plea as that?" Dane asked immediately, and moved his hips back before pressing inside her again.

"More."

"Greedy."

"For you," Bryn agreed.

She kept her eyes open and stared up at Dane as he moved in and out of her slowly. Each glide made her clench against him, wanting to hold him inside her and never let go.

Dane propped himself up on his hand again and looked down to where they were joined. His hips undulated, pressing himself into her, then pulling out slowly. "God, look how wet you are. You're all over my dick, Smalls, it's fucking beautiful. Rub your clit for me. I wish like fuck I could do it myself, but I can't. Not and hold myself up and watch you take me."

Bryn blushed, feeling self-conscious about touching herself in front of him. He caught the blush and leaned down and kissed her hard before pulling back just enough to tell her, "You're gonna have to get used to it. I only have one hand, and it's busy at the moment."

She nodded under him. "Okay."

"Okay," he confirmed, pulling himself up again so he could watch her. "Start slowly, yeah, that's it. Feel good?"

"Uh huh."

"Damn. I can feel how much you like it. Okay, Smalls, this is gonna go fast. I can't hold back. Rub yourself hard. That's it, harder, sweetheart. Make yourself come around my cock, I wanna feel it."

Bryn frantically used her fingers to press against her clit as Dane pounded into her. He wasn't holding back anymore and it felt absolutely fantastic. Bringing her other hand between their bodies, she reached around and pressed against the base of his dick, where he'd told her he was extra sensitive, and the second she did, he groaned, thrust himself inside her and held still. With one last flick of her fingers over her clit, Bryn exploded. It wasn't quite as mind-blowing as the G-spot orgasms Dane had given her, but it was still intense.

She felt the base of his dick twitch under her fingers as his head tilted back. The veins in his neck stood out as he shuddered over her with his own orgasm. He dropped down on top of her, then rolled them until she was on top.

Bryn heard and felt his hot breaths in her ear as he struggled to regain his composure. She wiggled, seating herself on top of him more comfortably, smiling when he stayed inside her even as he softened.

"I love you."

Bryn smiled and snuggled down onto Dane's chest. "I love you too."

"It makes all the difference in the world," Dane said

softly.

Knowing exactly what he was talking about, Bryn agreed. "Love makes orgasms harder and sex so much better. Can we do that again?"

Dane laughed and Bryn felt him slipping out of her.

"No! Don't laugh, you'll...darn. Too late," Bryn grumbled as she felt his cock soften enough that she lost him. She sat up and straddled Dane's stomach while looking down at him. "I'm not going to change."

"Good."

"I mean, I'll always be weird. I can't stop wanting to know stuff, Dane. It's who I am."

"And I *love* who you are, Bryn. As long as you take the time to explain things to me when I don't understand them, and you'll listen when I tell you something is dangerous, I don't give a shit."

"I'll try."

"Good. Then be weird. I love your weird."

She grinned and moved her hips down until they were over his flaccid cock and wiggled, feeling his semen leak out. "If you're gonna come inside me, then it's only fair that you have to deal with the aftermath as much as I do."

"Don't you remember the last time? It doesn't gross me out, in fact, it turns me on. Knowing my come is dripping out of you and how it came to be there in the first place. It's sexy as hell, even if it is messy."

Bryn looked down in disbelief at his rapidly hardening cock, then back up at him. "Cool," she breathed.

Dane pulled Bryn down and captured her lips with his own. He pulled back after an intense kiss and said, "Thank you for not making sex awkward. With only one hand, I can only do so much. You made it fun."

"That's 'cause it *is*. At least with you."

"That it is. Wanna try another position?"

"Yeah," Bryn immediately answered affirmatively.

"Ride me. That'll free my hand up for...other things."

Bryn smiled and lifted up, this time letting Dane notch himself exactly where she wanted him. She sank down over him and sighed in contentment.

Life was good. More than good.

Epilogue

DANE ROLLED OVER in bed and reached for Bryn, not surprised to find himself alone. He glanced at the clock. Five fifty-three. He swung his legs over the side of the mattress and headed into the bathroom.

After taking care of business, he slipped a pair of worn black sweats up his naked legs and went looking for Bryn. Ever since she'd moved in, he'd gone to bed naked, not feeling a shred of self-consciousness. Not with her.

Leaning against the doorjamb, he watched Bryn for several moments. She was sitting on the couch, cross-legged, laptop in her lap, muttering under her breath. Dane had no idea how he'd gotten so lucky, but not a day went by that he didn't thank his lucky stars. They'd lived together for two months, and each day was better than the last.

The sun wouldn't be up for another couple of hours, but they had a busy day in front of them. He waited a beat before shuffling into the room and sitting next to her, putting his arm over her shoulders and pulling her into him and kissing her temple.

"What'cha lookin' at?"

"Did you know that two-point-seven million dogs and cats are killed every year because shelters are too full and there aren't enough adoptive homes?"

"Hmmmm," Dane murmured, and nuzzled her hair off her neck so he could inhale her unique coconut scent. She'd taken to using his soap rather than her own, so now she usually smelled like her beachy shampoo and him. Every time he got close to her, her scent mixed with his made him want to be inside her.

"That's five out of every ten dogs and *seven* out of every ten cats. Not only that, we're paying to put these animals to sleep. One to two *billion* dollars of our taxes goes to pay for the shelters. It's so heartbreaking, Dane."

"What brought this on, Smalls?" Dane asked, massaging the back of Bryn's neck gently.

"I was re-watching season five of *Mythbusters*," Bryn told him sadly, not looking away from the computer screen as she scrolled through a site that featured homeless dogs.

"Can't teach an old dog new tricks?" Dane asked, remembering the episode. They'd watched the shows so many times, and discussed them at length, that he'd mostly memorized which shows were in which season.

"Yeah. I wondered about the dogs, then started thinking about a stray I saw the other day in Rathdrum.

Then I started wondering about what would happen if it got caught, if anyone would adopt it. I started researching, and now I think I want to go and adopt a ton of dogs and cats to make sure they aren't murdered."

Dane smiled at Bryn, loving how enthusiastic and gung-ho she was. She never ceased to amaze him with the goodness of her heart, and how she kept at something until her brain was completely finished gathering enough information to be satisfied she completely understood it.

"We're busy today, sweetheart. But I swear, as soon as we get back from our honeymoon, I'll take you down to either the Rathdrum or Coeur D'Alene shelter and we'll find ourselves some pets. Okay?"

Bryn sniffed, but nodded.

Dane turned her face until she was looking at him instead of the computer screen.

"You been up long?"

"No. Only since four-thirty."

"You nervous about today?"

She looked at him in confusion. "About what?"

"Getting married? Seeing your parents again after so long? Anything?"

She shrugged nonchalantly. "No, not particularly. As long as you love me, nothing else matters."

"I'll love you forever, Bryn."

She beamed at him. "Right." Then she turned back

to the computer, clicking on a new tab to open the local
shelter's adoption page.

Dane smiled and kissed her temple once more and
got up and looked at his watch. They had plenty of time
before they were supposed to be at Smokey's Bar. He
hadn't thought much of Bryn's idea at first. Who got
married in a hole-in-the-wall bar? But the more he
thought about it, the more he liked the idea.

It was where he and Bryn's relationship really started; the day he'd yelled at her in the grocery store didn't
count. They wouldn't have to worry about serving food
or alcohol, since they were having both the wedding and
reception in the bar, and it would certainly be a unique
wedding they'd always remember.

Rosie and Bonnie from the library would be there,
along with a few other employees. Both sets of parents
would also be stopping by, even though Bryn's were
only staying for the civil ceremony itself. They weren't
thrilled about staying in such a small town as Rathdrum,
preferring bigger cities, and didn't really approve of the
wedding being in a bar in the first place.

Truck, Ghost, Beatle, Coach, and Blade would also
be there. Hollywood was staying home to look after his
wife. Kassie had been really ill with morning sickness
recently. And Annie had a school thing that Fletch and
Emily didn't want to miss.

Dane hadn't realized how much he missed hanging

out with his friends until they'd come up and hung out at the impromptu barbeque he'd thrown a few months ago. It was awesome to see all the guys again when they weren't in the middle of an op.

Luckily, there was no chance of Knox taking revenge on either him or Bryn, or otherwise ruining their big day. He'd been thrown in federal prison. Dane didn't know if the man knew for sure it was him who had gotten him arrested, but he had to have a pretty good suspicion.

Right after he and Bryn had turned out of sight of his homestead, Ghost, Beatle, and Coach had swooped in and subdued Knox and his wife. Then the ATF and FBI had come in and searched the property, finding not only illegal guns and ammunition, but enough fertilizer and homemade bombs to blow up every building in Coeur D'Alene.

Knox's wife got a light sentence after the abuse she'd been forced to endure had come to light. But Knox himself would be in jail for what would probably be the rest of his life. He wasn't getting any younger, and the sixty-year sentence meant he'd most likely die in jail.

Dane put the man out of his mind and thought about his almost-wife instead. Life with Bryn was never dull, she constantly kept him on his toes, something Dane had never thought he'd want. But she made every day worth living. She still worked at the library, and he'd bought half of Steve's business, splitting the workload, which give them both more than enough money to live on *and* time to spend with their families.

Dane went and started the water in the shower and looked down at the healed wound on his arm. The stump hardly ever bothered him anymore. The phantom pains had just about disappeared altogether. Kids would sometimes make comments about it, but Bryn would simply explain to them the mechanics of his prosthetic, if he was wearing it, or how he'd been wounded serving his country.

She didn't dwell on it, simply treated him like a man. Her man.

Dane wandered back into the living room and leaned over, taking the laptop out of Bryn's lap and ignoring her "Hey! I was looking at something!"

He picked her up and carried her toward their bathroom. "You can look at it later. I have something you can examine in the shower."

She wound her arms around his neck and smiled. "Eighty-one percent of people who've had shower sex want to have it again."

"Good to know we're in the majority then," Dane told her.

"What position are we trying this time?"

"Well, we've done it sitting, doggy style, Superman, Under Arrest, and the standing splits—which was amazing, but I know you were sore for days afterwards—so I thought today, our wedding day, we could do it our old standby way."

"You just love holding me up."

"I do." Dane grinned at her and pushed his sweats off. He was already hard. It seemed like all it took was one look at Bryn and he was more than ready to take her.

Bryn peeled off his T-shirt she'd thrown on when she'd climbed out of bed earlier that morning. He took her hand and helped her into the shower as he always did. As soon as his feet were stable, he grabbed her and she jumped up, hooking her legs around his waist.

"Thank you for taking my name today, Bryn," Dane told her seriously.

"Bryn Munroe," she mused, rubbing her nose against his. "As much as I appreciate you telling that Knox guy you were Dane Hartwell, I think I prefer your name to mine."

"This'll be the last time we make love as boyfriend and girlfriend," Dane said with a smile, shifting Bryn in his arms until he could reach down and notch himself between her legs. When he was settled, he moved his hand back to her waist to support her and slid home.

Bryn's head fell back and she groaned while squeezing his length with her inner muscles.

"You're so wet, Smalls. Why is that?"

She grinned slyly. "When I got up, you looked really hot. I wanted to do some research, but I kept thinking about you naked in our bed. I know most of the time you wake up horny, and morning sex is your favorite. So I…got ready for you."

"Fuck, you're my perfect match. I love you, soon-to-be Bryn Munroe. I'm keeping you and never gonna give you up. Not ever."

"And I love you, Dane Munroe. Thank you for loving me even though I'm a freak."

"Thank you for not giving up on me when I was an ass."

No more words were spoken as they lost themselves in each other. Even though neither was perfect in the eyes of society, they were perfect for each other.

Thirty-Two Hours Later

"YOU GUYS KNOW why the commander called us in?" Blade asked. "We just got back from Fish's wedding. I could use about twelve hours of nonstop sleep."

"He happy?" Hollywood asked.

"Fuck yeah, he's happy," Beatle confirmed. "Couldn't stop smiling throughout his wedding. Even when Bryn interrupted the officiant to explain where the tradition of rings came from. I think he's found the best way to distract her when she starts going on and on about something."

"What's that?" Fletch asked.

"He kisses her. Shuts her up every time," Beatle said with a smirk.

Everyone chuckled, happy that Fish had finally seemed to find what he needed in order to move on. He'd experienced every Delta Force member's worst nightmare. They were all thrilled he had been able to not only get on with his life, but find a woman who was able to heal his heart at the same time.

Everyone stood and saluted as their commander entered the room. His eyebrows were drawn down in a worried frown, and the tension in the room suddenly became thick. Looked like that twelve-hour nap wasn't going to happen anytime soon.

The commander sat and immediately handed out folders to the men around the table. "Wheels goin' up in two hours," the officer told them. "The daughter of the Danish Ambassador to the United States has been kidnapped. She's a college student and was on a research mission in Costa Rica when she was snatched."

The commander tapped a photograph inside the folder. "This is Astrid Jepsen. Age twenty-two. She, along with two other classmates and her teacher, were taken when they were doing research in the jungle outside a small town called Guacalito. Nearest big city is

SUSAN STOKER

Liberia."

Blade's chair screeched and fell over as he abruptly stood. "What are the names of the other hostages?" he asked urgently.

The commander shuffled through his papers as he searched for the info Blade wanted. "Jaylyn Jones, Kristina Temple, and Casey Shea."

Blade's arm swung before anyone could react. He turned and punched the wall behind him, leaving a fist-sized hole in the drywall. Before he could follow through with a second punch, Truck was there. He grabbed his teammate from behind in a bear hug.

"Let me go!" Blade hissed. "Fuck, Truck, let me go!"

"Not until you fucking relax and tell us what's wrong so we can fix it," Truck told him calmly.

"They've got my sister!" Blade yelled, then sagged in Truck's arms. "Casey Shea is my sister."

"*Fuck*. Talk," the commander bit out.

Instead of Blade explaining, Beatle spoke up. "As he said, Casey Shea, the professor, is his younger sister. They have the same mother but different fathers, that's why their last names are different. She's twenty-seven and has her PhD in entomology. She took a small group of students from the University of Florida graduate program to Costa Rica to study. They've been there, what, a month? Month and a half?" Beatle asked Blade.

He nodded. "Yeah. About that. They had a week

352

and a half more before they were coming home."

"When is the last time you heard from her?" the commander asked, not looking up from the piece of paper he was writing on.

"About six days ago. She called from a pay phone— collect, if you can believe it—to let me know she was good, and all excited about her research and the info they were gathering."

"Did she give you any indication that things were hot down there?" Fletch asked.

"No. None. If she had, I would've gotten her ass home," Blade said firmly.

The commander looked up at the Delta Team sitting around the table...and at Blade and Truck, who were still standing. Truck had let go of his friend and now stood with his hand on his shoulder in support. "The question now becomes, can you all do this mission? Or should I call Trigger and his team? They've covered for you in the past," he glanced at Hollywood, then finished, "when you couldn't make a previous mission."

"We're takin' this," Ghost said firmly.

"I'm not sure—" the commander began.

"No, Sir. All due respect. We got this. Yes, Casey is family, but all that means is we'll be more careful, plan in more detail, and do everything in our power to get all four hostages home, safe and sound. You have our word.

This is our mission. Let us bring Casey and the others home."

The room was dead silent as the commander eyed each and every man around him. Finally, he nodded. "If it were my wife, daughter, or sister down there, you guys are the ones I'd want to go and bring her home. Now, let's plan."

Truck slapped Blade on the back and picked up both his and his friend's chairs from where they'd fallen on the ground.

As the others around them began to talk strategy and logistics, Beatle leaned into Blade and said in a low, earnest tone, "I might not like bugs, but I'll do whatever it takes to get Casey back to you. Lay in an ant mound, eat cockroaches, or make friends with every fucking mosquito I see. You have my word."

Blade's lips tightened, but he nodded stiffly before turning back to the conversation.

Beatle sat back in his chair and took a deep breath. *I don't know you, Casey Shea, but because you obviously mean so much to my brother-in-arms, I'm going to find you and bring you home safe. Mark my words.*

Look for the next book in the *Delta Force Heroes* Series, *Rescuing Casey*.

<u>To sign up for Susan's Newsletter go to:</u>
www.stokeraces.com/contact-1.html

<u>Or text:</u> STOKER to 24587 for text alerts on your
mobile device

Discover other titles by Susan Stoker

<u>Delta Force Heroes</u>

Rescuing Rayne

Assisting Aimee – Loosely related to Delta Force

Rescuing Emily

Rescuing Harley

Marrying Emily

Rescuing Kassie

Rescuing Bryn

Rescuing Casey (Jan 2018)

Rescuing Sadie (April 2018)

Rescuing Wendy (May 2018)

Rescuing Mary (Nov 2018)

<u>Badge of Honor: Texas Heroes</u>

Justice for Mackenzie

Justice for Mickie

Justice for Corrie

Justice for Laine

Shelter for Elizabeth

Justice for Boone

Shelter for Adeline

Shelter for Sophie

Justice for Erin (Nov 2017)

Justice for Milena (Mar 2018)

Shelter for Blythe (July 2018)

Justice for Hope (TBA)

Shelter for Quinn (TBA)
Shelter for Koren (TBA)
Shelter for Penelope (TBA)

SEAL of Protection
Protecting Caroline
Protecting Alabama
Protecting Fiona
Marrying Caroline
Protecting Summer
Protecting Cheyenne
Protecting Jessyka
Protecting Julie
Protecting Melody
Protecting the Future
Protecting Alabama's Kids
Protecting Kiera (novella)
Protecting Dakota

Ace Security
Claiming Grace
Claiming Alexis
Claiming Bailey (Dec 2017)
Claiming Felicity (Mar 2018)

Beyond Reality
Outback Hearts
Flaming Hearts
Frozen Hearts

Connect with Susan Online

Susan's Facebook Profile and Page:
www.facebook.com/authorsstoker
www.facebook.com/authorsusanstoker

Follow Susan on Twitter:
www.twitter.com/Susan_Stoker

Find Susan's Books on Goodreads:
www.goodreads.com/SusanStoker

Email: Susan@StokerAces.com

Website: www.StokerAces.com

To sign up for Susan's Newsletter go to:
www.stokeraces.com/contact-1.html

Or text: STOKER to 24587 for text alerts on your
mobile device

About the Author

New York Times, USA Today, and *Wall Street Journal* Bestselling Author Susan Stoker has a heart as big as the state of Texas, where she lives, but this all-American girl has also spent the last fourteen years living in Missouri, California, Colorado, and Indiana. She's married to a retired Army man who now gets to follow *her* around the country.

She debuted her first series in 2014 and quickly followed that up with the SEAL of Protection Series, which solidified her love of writing and creating stories readers can get lost in.

If you enjoyed this book, or any book, please consider leaving a review. It's appreciated by authors more than you'll know.